# Finding the Past
## Elven Roots Book 1

Jennifer Abrahamsen

Copyright © 2024 Jennifer Abrahamsen
All rights reserved

The characters and events portrayed in this book are fictitious. Any similarity to real persons, living or dead, is coincidental and not intended by the author.

No part of this book may be reproduced, or stored in a retrieval system, or transmitted in any form or by any means, electronic, mechanical, photocopying, recording, or otherwise, without express written permission of the publisher.

ISBN: 979-8-9899852-2-7

Cover Art by Darren C. Leonard

Printed in the United States of America

This book is dedicated to my husband. Every hour I spent working on this book was one less hour I could spend with him; but he still loves me.

# CHAPTER 1

Kindra started and sat straight up in her chair. She peered through bleary eyes and was mortified to discover she had fallen asleep again. She was at the library. It was just another standard Friday night. Kindra peeled her face off the spiral notebook on the desk before her. She knew she would have those telltale sleep lines on her face from the wire of the notebook. She brushed her copper-brown hair out of her eyes and stared at the notes on the top page.

Kindra had sketched a family tree for her mother's family, traced back to ancestors in Guntersblum, Germany. These ancestors were descendants of The "Black" Beckerles from Hessloch. Jacob Beckerle crossed The Rhine River from Biblis, in the early 1700s and settled on the west side of the river in southwestern Germany in the "Black Forest Area." From that time on, the thousands of descendants he produced were called Black Beckerles. Though Kindra knew none of these people personally, she loved researching her family ties to them and the accomplishments of her ancestors. She spent hours at the library, or at home on the Internet, tracing each family line and digging up vital records and historical documents to prove the lineage of each family member. Kindra had even discovered that a local company, Beckerle Tile & Hardwood, was owned and operated by her distant family. She supposed the flooring people had a stronger claim to the Black Beckerles than she did since they still carried the name, but they were the same number of generations removed from old Jacob Beckerle as Kindra and her mother were.

Kindra's mother Gretchen had been born to James Powers and Helen Heimlich in the spring of 1955. It was through her mother that Gretchen carried the Beckerle lineage. Helen was the daughter of George Heimlich and Margaret Hessler. George and Margaret had immigrated to the U.S. with baby Helen, and eight other children in tow back in September of 1923. George had been the son of Margreth Reichert and Johannes Heimlich, and Johannes had been the son of Johannes Senior and Elisabetha Beckerle. The Beckerle name might have been five generations back, but Kindra had every document she needed to prove her relationship to the family.

Kindra always found it ironic that she could tell you every name, birthdate, death date and relationship of all the Black Beckerles, but she could tell you nothing personal. There were no family stories, or a family bible. No one had ever dug up a rich source of information like a diary written by her grandmother describing how a girl, barely out of her teens, had traveled from near the Canadian border to New York City, met a guy and ended up marrying him. Grandma Helen simply lived in Oneida in the 1940 census and was suddenly engaged to be married to James Powers on a marriage license from 1953. It was the mocking aspect of tracing family history. One could learn so much about a person's life through research; even secrets about failed marriages and illegitimate children, but there was no way to fill in the blanks between the official documents. Kindra could spend hours making up stories in her head about why her great-aunt had found herself in a sanitarium by the time she was thirty-two years old. There had been one newspaper article citing a domestic dispute at her aunt's address, but no details about the actual event or any events to follow. Any family member that was alive had taken all the secrets with them when they died. It could be so frustrating!

Kindra had uncovered a buried family secret about her Grandpa James's real father just by using DNA matched for her and her mother on a website. It turns out that the Irish name of Powers wasn't even really hers. James Powers had been fathered by an Italian immigrant and John Powers hadn't married James's mother until James was nearly four years old. Kindra had the facts, but she had no details. Was Mary Powers raped? Was Mary Powers a "lady of the night?" Had Mary been in love with Vito Verde only to find out Vito was a liar who had a wife and six kids living in some tenement building? It was no wonder Kindra came to be sleeping atop her notebook at the public library. There were so many "what ifs" and "whys" to dream about.

Kindra had started her family research ten years ago. She had been sitting in the backroom office with red, puffy eyes. She was cross-legged in front of her filing cabinet, holding the most disturbing vital record she had ever held. In her hands, blurring from the tears in her eyes, was her husband's death certificate. He had been twenty-seven years old. He and Kindra had been married for eight months. The bravery of the first responders on 9/11 had been the reason, after highschool graduation, Tom became a firefighter. He loved what he did, and so had Kindra. Kindra had shown with pride any time someone asked her what Tom did for a living. Her husband saved lives and helped them put the pieces back together during the worst of times. Of course, Kindra had stopped loving her husband's job for a few years after that night in 2010. It had taken a lot of therapy for her to accept that his passion had left her a widow at twenty-five. Kindra hadn't actively started researching her family until about 2014, but she knew it was that sole death certificate in 2010 that had started her fascination with vital records and uncovering evidence of the truth.

"*Truth.*" Kindra laughed to herself. She was in the library; surrounded by the details of her nine times great-grandfather from a tiny town in Germany, but her mother wouldn't even tell Kindra who her own father was. Maybe it wasn't her husband's death certificate itself that inspired her to go down the genealogy rabbit hole after all. She always told people that was what had started her obsession. Kindra lied easily about it, but it was what the certificate had represented that got her started. That certificate held the truth. That was what a vital record was. It was proof. It was proof that someone had died, proof that someone had been married, proof that someone had been born. Kindra had jumped from the death certificate in her hand to thoughts of the other vital records in her filing cabinet. Thinking about her marriage certificate had brought an onslaught of tears. The tears had only ceded when she started thinking about her birth certificate. Actually, she had been thinking about her lack of a birth certificate. What Kindra had in her filing cabinet was a baptismal certificate. Kindra had never seen her birth certificate. Her mother had claimed she lost it. Any time Kindra had needed identification, the baptismal record, along with notes from doctors when she was a child or her driver's licenses when she got older, had always been enough. The next day, to keep her husband's death from feeling real for just a little longer, Kindra visited the vital records office.

Shaking herself from her memories, Kindra scooped up her notes and stuffed everything in her messenger bag. She left the books she had been using on the table so the librarian wouldn't scold her again for shelving the books incorrectly. Kindra carefully tucked her chair in and strode out of the library and into the street.

Kindra took her cell out of her bag as she walked and dialed her mother. The old-fashioned answering machine clicked on after the fourth ring. "You've reached Gretchen. I'm unavailable. Leave your name and number and I'll return your call ASAP."

Kindra took a breath and started speaking, "Hi Mom! I'm headed home from the library. I was just calling to see if we were still on for tomorrow."

Kindra ended her call as she reached her car. Climbing in, she thought about the eight months that she and her mother had not spoken after Kindra finally received a copy of her birth certificate. The certificate had been a disappointment. In the space for her father's name, it had simply had the word "unknown" scrawled in the blank. Kindra had thought she had finally outsmarted her mother. She expected to get the birth certificate in the mail and discover her father's name despite her mother's perpetual refusal to give it up.

Kindra had called her mother, screaming and furious. Her mom had sent Kindra into a tirade when she calmly responded to Kindra's insults and rage by stating and restating the same thing she always said, "Your father is dead, Kindra. He has been gone since before you were ever born. Who he is does not matter. What does matter is that he enabled me to give birth to the wonderful person you are."

Her mother's broken record response infuriated Kindra. It infuriated her every time she heard it, but on that day it had sent Kindra into enough of a rage-fueled spiral that she had refused to speak to her mother for eight months. Kindra knew eight months wasn't really that long when compared to some of the family estrangements of her friends, but it was an eternity for her and her mother. Gretchen called Kindra, or Kindra had called Gretchen once every day since Kindra had left home for college at eighteen. Eight months without speaking might as well have been a lifetime. Conversation between mother and daughter had only recommenced when Gretchen had called Kindra in hysterics, sobbing and screaming at the same time. Kindra had understood the word *"hospital"* and the word *"dead."* That had been all it took to get Kindra diving for her keys and heading out the door.

Staff at the hospital informed Kindra that her mother had sustained severe spinal trauma after a collision involving a Cadillac hitting her mother's Jeep Grand Cherokee. The other vehicle had been a Cadillac Escalade full of teens blasting music and high on a multitude of legal and illegal substances. The Cadillac had hit her mother's Cherokee so hard in the passenger side door that its bumper had crossed through the car and done damage to her mother's spine. All that had happened four days before Kindra arrived at the hospital. The sedatives fed to Kindra's mother kept her incoherent. It wasn't until that day that Gretchen had been lucid enough to ask the staff about Doreen. Doreen, Gretchen's live-in girlfriend, had been riding in the passenger seat of the Cherokee. Gretchen had only two people in her life she could turn to. The Escalade had crushed one of these people to death four days earlier, so Gretchen had called the other.

The next day, Kindra moved into her mother's house and started work overseeing the remodeling needed for her mother, now a paraplegic, to go back home. Kindra had taken personal leave from her job where she worked as a school psychologist and had made taking care of her mother a full-time job instead. After several weeks of sawdust and the steady decline of Kindra's bank balance, Gretchen came home. Kindra stayed at the house and the two women alternated between nights spent sobbing over glasses of Pinot and days huddled over steaming cups of tea ruminating over events, good and bad, in which Doreen had been the focal point.

On one occasion, with lemon-ginger tea steeping between them on the table, Gretchen sighed and pushed a strand of graying, chestnut hair behind her ear. "What are you thinking?"

Gretchen had stared at her daughter for minutes before her mouth had turned up the tiniest bit at the corners. "Kindra, did you know your name means 'greatest champion?' It's an Old Norse name."

Kindra's face had crinkled up in confusion. "Why would you want to call your baby daughter Greatest Champion?"

"I didn't. Your father chose that name. I was unaware of the meaning."

Kindra had become absolutely still. She wasn't sure she was even breathing. It petrified Kindra that the smallest change from her might cause her mother to catch herself and stop speaking.

Her mother had gone on, "The agreement was that if I let him name you, he would disappear. He would return to his life and I would return to mine. I would get to keep the greatest gift…" Gretchen's breath hitched. "…the only gift he had ever given me. It wasn't until Doreen asked me one night where I had come up with your name that I had told anyone about the arrangement. Doreen hadn't even asked about your father. I think she preferred thinking you had been a product of an Immaculate Conception or something. Doreen did still want to know about your name, though. She looked it up right then. She headed straight over to the computer and searched for the meaning on some baby name site. When I heard what your name meant, I was sure your father was not aware that he had been adamant about naming you 'Greatest Champion.' I always assumed it was the name of one of his ex-girlfriends from Norway or something…kinda like a last f-you to me before I walked out the door for good."

Kindra had no choice. She needed to take a breath. It hadn't mattered, though. Gretchen had stopped talking even before Kindra had sucked in the much needed air. A tear had run down Gretchen's face and Kindra had not asked if the tear was for Doreen's loss or if memories of Kindra's father were causing the reaction. In that moment, Kindra hadn't cared. *Those are the only meaningful words Mom has ever spoken about my father and… and… I now know he gave me my name! How could my mother have kept that quiet? My father named me. My name means "Greatest Champion" and is from the Old Norse…wait. Mom said that my father was from Norway.* After so much time, Kindra had new information about her own identity. She had ancestors in Norway.

Kindra blinked her eyes and looked around. She was behind the wheel of her car and still in the library parking lot. This happened to her a lot. Minutes would go buy while she re-lived a memory or invented creative stories for the ancestors she discovered while researching her family. Sometimes, Kindra felt like she spent more time in her own head than in the real world. Having taken every psychology course available, Kindra was an expert at self-diagnosing. Depending on how she was feeling about herself, she would run through diagnosis from depersonalization-derealization disorder to common ADD. Realistically, it was probably ADD, but her other verdicts weren't surprising when one has read as many case studies as Kindra. Kindra turned the ignition, pulled her car out of the parking spot, and headed home.

# CHAPTER 2

The phone was ringing. It's Saturday. It's 8am. If she could get her eyes to open, Kindra was going to answer the phone and give the caller hell! Instead, Kindra opted not to open her eyes and just blindly pushed at the screen on her phone a bit until she was pretty sure she had answered it.

"Who is this?" Kindra's tongue stuck to the roof of her mouth, causing her speech to be garbled.

"Kindra? Kindra it's me. Are you ok? You sound like you're sick. Did those little heathens give you another cold?"

Gretchen loved to refer to Kindra's students as heathens. Kindra didn't mind. She loved her job and truly cared about her students, but listening to her mother refer to them as heathens after a bad day made her feel like she had a partner in crime regarding thoughts she could not share with her colleagues or administrators. They were only thoughts, and they were fleeting. Kindra truly believed that anyone who did not refer to middle school children as heathens from time to time might need a reality check. Kindra was also pretty sure her co-workers agreed with her, but would never publically admit it. *Maybe her co-workers had someone at home who made them feel better on a bad day by calling the kids mean names too?*

Kindra snapped her thoughts back to her mother on the other end of the line. "I'm fine, Mom. I was sleeping. You never told me what time to be at your house today. Am I late?"

"No. You're not late. I'm not even home. I woke up this morning and saw the sunrise. It seemed like a beautiful day, so I went to the park to paint."

The park. It was one of the few minor pleasures her mother permitted herself. Her mother would head to the small area in town with three benches and a statue of George Washington and people watch for hours.

"Listen Mom, this is one of the few days I am available to clean out that back room. Enjoy painting and relax. I will let myself in and get to work on it."

Kindra suspected her mother's real reason for suddenly needing to go paint something was to avoid the memories in the back room. Kindra understood and was letting her mother avoid admitting it. It also meant she could take her time getting out the door.

"That's so much work to take on by yourself! At least give Jessie a call and see if she can help you out. I'll be home later if you still need another set of hands."

That was all the conformation Kindra needed about her mother's reasons for waking up early and heading to the park. Gretchen hadn't even tried to argue with her or reschedule…or offer to come back home early. Suggesting Kindra call Jessie was also an indicator. Jess, as Jessie had been called since she had surpassed the 5th grade, had been Kindra's friend since Jess's family had moved next door to Kindra's childhood home. Little Jessie, with her freckles and round, smiling face, had been easy to like from the start. The blonde girl had been an only child and functioned better around adults than other children, but that was one thing that attracted Kindra to her. Even though Jessie had only been one grade above Kindra, her parents had treated her as if she were in high school. Jessie made her own lunches and walked herself to school. The best part was that her mature aura had worked on Gretchen as well. As long as Kindra was with Jessie, Gretchen felt the girls would be fine, and Kindra found she could do anything she liked. That same privilege had extended through the teenage years as well. If there was a party Kindra wanted to attend, she was granted permission as long as she answered in the affirmative when asked if Jessie was going along.

Jessie was now Jess Bennett. Married to a town cop, and teaching eighth-grade math at the same school where Kindra worked, many of Kindra's heathens were also Jess's heathens. Jess still ran her life like there was a metronome counting out even beats for her. Everything was organized, everything was scheduled, and everything was practical. She and her husband had never had children, and they were the happiest couple Kindra knew. Kindra had worried that her relationship with Jess would change when she and Tom had kids. She supposed that had been such a silly worry and she certainly would never find out if it had been worth thinking about at all. Nearing forty, and not even in the market for someone to share the rest of her life with, Kindra and Jess had stayed close and even allowed Jess's husband, Sean, to tag along on outings most times.

Gretchen pulled Kindra out of her reverie. "Kindra! Come back to me! I'm still on the phone over here!"

"Sorry Mom. I'll give Jess a call. I'm sure she'll head over with me."

"Ok. Good. Let me know if you need anything."

"Ok. Bye mom."

"Bye baby."

*Let her know if she needed anything? I'm not the one hiding out in the park with watercolors to avoid helping in the first place!* Kindra dialed Jess as she forced herself to sit up in bed. She stared at the pile of laundry spilling out of her closet and hoped she had some clean underwear. Jess's phone went to voicemail, so Kindra hung up and sent a quick text asking Jess to meet her over at her mother's house if she was free.

Considering the task for the day, Kindra opted out of a shower and went digging through her underwear drawer. She found a pair she knew she didn't like, but she couldn't remember what was wrong with them. They were clean though, so she slipped them on and dug out a plain blue t-shirt. She opted for the same jeans she wore yesterday, mentally referencing the same reason she had given herself for not taking a shower. She headed down the hall to the kitchen and put coffee on. While it brewed, she played a little Bubble Pop on her phone. When the coffee was ready, she poured a cup and scrolled through her news feed on her laptop as she sipped.

Her phone rang, and Jess started speaking before Kindra could get a word out of her mouth. "I'm sorry I didn't pick up. Butch and I were working on the stay command. He's up to two minutes now, and I didn't want to interrupt his last attempt. I'll see you at your mom's in about forty minutes. I just want to feed Butch and Cassidy before I head out. It'll take me about five minutes to feed them, and then I'll burn about ten more minutes walking them and making sure they do their thing before I jump in the car and head over. It's usually about a half hour drive…"

Kindra loved her friend. Only Jess planned the timing of a trip, as she confirmed that she was about to take that same excursion. "Just get there when you can and don't wear anything nice. We're cleaning out the back room."

Jess took a breath. "Wow! Big doin's! Mom is letting you clean out the memory room! I'm glad you called. You're as bad as she is. If I'm not there, you won't be able to get rid of a thing."

Jess hung up before Kindra complained about the unkind treatment her friend was dishing out. Kindra dumped the remaining coffee from her mug into a travel cup and topped it off from the pot. She slid into the sneakers at the front door and headed out of the house, pulling at her underwear through the seat of her jeans as she went. *So that was why she hadn't liked them!*

Twenty minutes later, Kindra was opening the door to the house she grew up in. It didn't matter how many years went by, she always felt as if she had never left. Things had changed over the years, but none of those changes were evident when walking through the front door. Through that door, was the living room. Though there had been many couches over the years, they had always been in the same place, behind the same coffee table, opposite the same TV stand. The size of the TV had grown over the years, but even the color of the couches had been relatively similar. Aside from Gretchen's one purchase of a floral patterned couch in the early 1990s, the seating had always been a medium tan to dark brown. Kindra was fairly certain the throw rug over the hardwood floor had changed over the years as well, but the light beige was always the same so it was difficult to tell if her mom had purchased a new rug, or just had the old one washed.

Kindra tossed her keys on the table near the entryway and walked to the kitchen. This room screamed of childhood as well. There was a fancy new refrigerator with water and ice dispensers in the door, and her mom had removed one cabinet to add a dishwasher, but the stove was unchanged. It was an offputting, pea-green color, but Gretchen insisted it was better than any stove one could buy today. Kindra could swear there were still bits of fried egg from 1979 in the holes where the burners were. When Kindra had moved back in with her mother after the accident, she had lobbied vehemently for the purchase of a new stove. Eventually, Kindra had waved the white flag, and the stove had remained.

Kindra walked through the door on the far side of the kitchen and into the back room. Well, almost into the back room. There was so much junk packed into that room that it was more like a storage closet than any space you could actually use as a living area. The back room had been where Kindra had slept as a child. Gretchen had taken the primary bedroom and used the other small bedroom next to it as an office and studio. The back room that Kindra had slept in was actually not a room at all when she was little. It was a 3-season porch with no heat. In the winter, if piling on extra blankets had not provided enough warmth, Kindra had simply slept in the living room. For Kindra's fifth birthday, Gretchen had hired a contractor to make the back room into a genuine part of the house. He had insulated the area and added baseboards. The floor was still a little chilly on frosty nights when it was complete, but Gretchen had added a bright pink shag carpet a few months later that took care of that problem. Kindra was never sure if Gretchen had finished the room so her daughter could be comfortable, or simply because she was afraid of what the other moms would think when they discovered her daughter slept in a fancy screened-in porch. That was about the age Kindra's friends had started coming over and each one who came to visit was in awe of the cool porch room Kindra got to call her own. Now that Kindra was thinking about it again, she was leaning toward her mother's fear of the reactions of those little girls' moms when their darlings went home from the Powers' house begging for a porch room like Kindra had.

Kindra forced herself to focus on the room currently before her. She nudged a shoebox out of the entry a bit and exposed a sliver of very faded, pink shag carpet. Kindra stopped herself before she started perseverating on how many generations of dust mites were living in that carpet at this point. Kindra spun back to the kitchen and opened the cabinet next to the pea-green stove. She pulled out the box of garbage bags and went back to the sliver of shag carpet. Kindra sat down in the doorway with her butt on the kitchen floor and her feet and knees crossed over the carpet sliver. She wiggled to get her underwear to behave and then she picked up the shoe box she had toed out of the way a moment ago. She opened it and found handkerchiefs. Not the fancy old-fashioned ones with initials embroidered on them, but the bandanna type. There was an entire box of them, folded into little squares. Kindra was shoving the box into the garbage bag when she paused. *Was there a dark green one in there?* She had the standard red, blue, black and white, but she really liked that nice hunter-green color she had seen bandanas come in. A laugh came from behind her; loud and uninhibited. Jess leaned over Kindra's shoulder and took the box from her. She plopped the entire box into the garbage bag.

"I see I arrived just in time. Were you wondering if you could make a really cool quilt out of those bandannas?"

"No...and how long have you been standing behind me, anyway?"

"Long enough to see you ALMOST have the strength to throw out free craft supplies. I was enjoying the entertainment provided by your struggle, but I saw the question in your eyes and I knew I had to intervene."

Jess allowed no time for Kindra to offer a comeback as she went on, "We need three piles: keep, discard, and donate. If we do this right, the box for the stuff we keep should be miniscule."

Jess turned and trekked out the front door. She was back a moment later with two enormous boxes from the company that delivered dog food, in 50-pound bags, to her home. She dropped the boxes on the floor and squatted down. From the box on her left, she pulled out one small shoebox and smiled. Kindra immediately threw the garbage bag with the box of bandanas at her.

"I get it! The plan is to throw a ton of stuff out and keep next to nothing. You didn't need to bring actual boxes as a visual reference. I am not thirteen, and I can follow directions without having them read out loud and using graphic organizers for reference."

Jess just laughed. "That is where you are blissfully ignorant, my friend. You can read the directions, but you could never follow them. Further testing is required to determine if this is a true disability or just a result of you being a stubborn ass."

"Touché. I am at your mercy, oh organized one." Kindra slid back from the doorway to let her friend gain access to the mess.

Jess began pulling things out of the room like a contestant on that old game show where people ran around the supermarket, throwing everything they could into a shopping cart before time ran out. She was a machine. Grab an item, bring it out to the kitchen, place it on the floor, and go back and grab another item. Kindra looked around at the growing collection in the kitchen. Boxes, bags, blankets, furniture, *wait... was that a doll house?* Kindra sighed and began stuffing the blankets and articles of clothing in garbage bags. It was impossible to throw out any of the boxes without opening them first. Though Kindra had been after her mother for years to throw out everything in the room, she was not naïve enough to think there might actually be nothing of value in the room. The boxes would each need to be checked.

Kindra opened box after box and bag after bag as Jess pulled them from the back room. There were doll clothes, little kid shoes, refrigerator artwork, baby teeth, toys, stuffed animals, and report cards. There was an entire crate of tax returns for the years 1985 to 1998. *Is mom looking to command a one-man protest against the overcrowding situation at the local landfill? Why is all this stuff in this room?* Jess had cleaned out most of the back room and started dragging the garbage bags Kindra had filled out to the curb. She went out the door and dragged the bags down the ramp that spilled out into the driveway and then dragged the bags the rest of the distance to the road. There was no bag without several small holes in it when Jess finished employing the drag-and-drop method. The result was a pile of shiny black with stuffed animal appendages and other less gruesome trash peeking out at the street through little peepholes.

When Jess returned to the kitchen, Kindra was sitting in front of an open box, looking through old photographs. The picture on the top of the pile was of two little girls of about ten years. One was a copper-headed gangly Tom-boy, and the other was a pudgy, freckle-faced blonde. Both girls were on swings and wearing huge smiles. They were not looking at the camera. They were staring at each other. Kindra remembered that day. She had seen Jimmy Newcome cut his finger and press it to a cut on John Snider's knee, then declare to a schoolyard full of children that he and John were now blood brothers. Mrs. Gannon, the lunch monitor, had dragged both boys to the nurse's office. Kindra had spent the entire school day planning how she would convince Jess to be her blood brother. On the walk home, Kindra explained her plan to Jess. Jess was sure to point out that 1) girls can't be brothers. They would have to be sisters. 2) She could see no good reason to get bloody and risk infection when she knew in her heart that she and Kindra were better than blood sisters. They were just sisters. No blood needed. They would always be together. That was Jess. Even at eleven years old, she could avoid pain while simultaneously ensuring her friend knew how much she cared about her.

"We were cute," Jess said to Kindra.

"We're still cute!" Kindra tossed the photos back in the box and tossed the box onto the kitchen table. "Now, help me get the furniture out of this room."

"The furniture too?" Jess asked. "I didn't realize we were literally leaving the room empty!"

Kindra peered over her friend's shoulder at the furniture left in the room. It had once been white. She was staring at a matching bookcase, dresser and writing desk from when this room had been hers. There was also a brass-framed day bed that was something she had begged her mother to get for her through sixth grade. With all her mother's stuff removed from the room, Kindra felt like she was looking at a life-sized time capsule. She looked over at the desk, but her Princess Phone was no longer there. Kindra walked past Jess and into the room. She pulled open the top drawer of the dresser. There was the phone. She smiled. There was nothing else in the drawer. As she pulled open the drawers of the desk, she realized her mom had put nothing in the drawers of her old furniture. Kindra wondered how much more junk could have fit in the back room if Gretchen had thought to fill the drawers of the furniture before piling things on top of the furniture and on the floor. It no longer mattered. It all had to go. Gretchen had finally agreed to let Kindra clean out the room full of memories. A handyman would come in next week and pull up the carpet. He'd put down some vinyl flooring and paint the walls. Kindra and Gretchen would then go shopping for new furniture and turn this room into a guest room and reading nook.

"Yes," Kindra said, "the furniture too. Help me drag it out."

They dragged the mattresses out first. The daybed had the top mattress, and the mattress for the trundle underneath. The brass frame for the top mattress was lighter than it looked, and the girls made quick work of pulling it to the curb as well. Jess made an attempt at the trundle and groaned. She shot a look at Kindra to say there would be no way they were getting it to the curb.

"It's ok. The handy man can move that one. I'll throw him a little extra cash. Let's just pull the dresser out, and I'll pay him to move the other stuff."

Jess and Kindra each took a side of the dresser and they carried it to the doorway. It took some time as they had to put the thing down every five feet and take a rest.

Jess shook her head. "You know, they really don't make solid furniture like this anymore. I should have had you take the drawers out before we moved this thing."

"We're almost there. Let's just get it over with all at once."

It turned out to be easy to slide the dresser down the ramp once they had made it out the front door. Actually, it was very easy. The girls gave it a little shove at the top of the ramp and the dresser slid all the way to the bottom. When the dresser got to the end of the ramp, it hit the ground and the front of the dresser stopped. The back end of the dresser did not stop, however. The back end lifted into the air and tipped the dresser forward so that it pitched all the way off the ramp and onto the ground, where it broke into several pieces.

"Well, it'll be lighter now that we have several pieces to carry," said Kindra.

Jess stared Kindra down and said, "I told you we should have just taken the drawers out in the first place."

"What were we saying about them not being made as solid as they once were?" asked Kindra, ignoring Jess's comment about the drawers.

Jess bent to pick up the back of the dresser. It was much easier to carry now that there were no top, bottom, sides or drawers attached to it. She saw a photo stuck in the spot where two pieces of wood met. She picked up the photo instead of the piece of dresser. The photo showed an absolutely gorgeous man. His red hair hung to his shoulders and his eyes…they were emerald. Jess had never seen a shade of green that color in someone's eyes. Those had to be contact lenses. There was no way any man could have eyes that stunning. He was wearing a T-shirt and jeans. The shirt was tight on top and the jeans hugged his thighs. This man had muscles. Like the girls in the photo from earlier, the man was not looking at the camera. He was looking off to the right as if someone had just called his name. Jess had been around Gretchen long enough to recognize her photographic style. She was pretty sure, like the photo of the girls, Gretchen had taken this photo. Jess flipped the photo over. Scrawled on the back in Gretchen's fancy script was the name Leif Husland.

"Hey, Kindra, check it out."

"What did you find?"

"A photo of a gorgeous man with red hair and a Norwegian name written on the back in your mother's handwriting."

# CHAPTER 3

Kindra grabbed the photo from Jess. Without a doubt, that was her mother's handwriting on the back. There was a date printed on the back of the photo. Thank goodness for old-fashioned photo developing procedures. The rendering date on the photo was 1984. It was likely taken just before Kindra was born. Kindra imagined her mother bringing her brand new baby girl home and decorating a bedroom for her. With her mother's compulsion to save things, she'd probably kept all kinds of odds and ends in the drawers of the furniture. How much space did an infant really need? Why not use a bit for all the things displaced when Gretchen set up the bedroom? As Kindra had grown and needed the drawers for clothing, Gretchen would have moved her own things out. Kindra could picture her mother trying to decide what to do with all the important things that were garbage for anyone else. When her mother grabbed everything out of the top drawer, this picture had tumbled into the void. It fell down behind the drawer and lodged in the dead space between the drawers and the back of the dresser. It would have stayed there forever if the girls had not just smashed the dresser.

Jess yanked Kindra from her vision when she finally spoke again. "Do you think he's your…"

She didn't finish. She didn't have to. Kindra knew. Jess could see it in Kindra's green eyes. A green that was only slightly less stunning than the emerald color of the eyes of the man in the picture. The sun glinted off Kindra's copper hair and Jess let out a whistle.

Kindra ran to her mother's office. She wiggled the mouse of the computer to exit sleep mode and an image of Gretchen and Doreen eating ice cream on the beach popped onto the screen. Jess clicked the image away and entered 1985 as the pin. The women on the screen disappeared, and the desktop took its place. Kindra clicked the icon for the web browser and typed in the name on the back of the photo.

The first results were all from a Norwegian website. She didn't know what "Personsøk: Digitalarkivet meant, but between the Norwegian words were names, Ole Olsen, Magnus Pedersen, and there, in bold letters as a search result, Leif Husland. She clicked the link and a document from Norway materialized. It appeared to be a list of names. Kindra might not read Norwegian, but she had been researching family history long enough to know she was looking at some kind of census. The date at the top of the page was a disappointment. Folketelling 1910 was more than a hundred years ago. The Leif Husland on this document would be dead by now. It could be his father or something though, so Kindra texted herself the web address of Digitalarkivet so she could explore the site at home.

Kindra clicked back to her search results and scrolled down. Someone named Leif Husland had gotten engaged to Tara Hind in Fulton, Illinois, two years ago, but a click on the link showed the beautiful couple in their late twenties at the top of the page. There was an article depicting the arrest of a thirty-seven-year-old Leif Husland in Liberty, NY, back in 2015. That location would have made sense, but that Leif Husland would only be about seven years older than her. She needed a Leif Husland who was closer to sixty-five or seventy, but her initial search revealed no plausible candidates.

Kindra walked slowly back toward the kitchen. Jess looked up from the last garbage bag she was tying off. Those would be the donations.

"Go," said Jess. "I know that look. I'll finish up here and lock up when I leave."

Thank goodness for friends that were like sisters. Jess knew that Kindra could do nothing until she had plopped herself down in front of her own computer and thoroughly researched the new lead. It had happened before. Kindra would lose days of her life following genealogy leads. She'd stay up all night, looking through just one more set of records...and then another.

"I already know the answer, but do you want to just call your mom and ask her about him?"

Kindra scowled at her friend. "You know she'll tell me nothing. If anything, she might make it harder for me to find him."

Jess nodded and went back to work. Kindra sprinted to her car and headed home.

At home, Kindra slid in front of her computer and fired up the web browser. She went to her online genealogy site and opened up the search. Kindra entered Leif's first and last name. She gave a birth year of 1960 plus or minus five years, and a birth location in Norway. The program thought about it for a half a minute but yielded no results. Kindra deleted the birth year. It had been an estimate, anyway. This time, when she clicked the search button, two pages of results appeared. None of the results were from The States and all the results were from before 1950. That was disappointing. Her search program had a database of all public records in the United States. If Leif Husland didn't show up in any of those records, he kept a low profile. At least she hadn't uncovered a death record.

Kindra opened up another tab and went to Digitalarkivet. At the top of the page was an option for choosing a language. She changed the language to English and could now see that she was on the homepage for the Norwegian Digital Archives. There were some records that were searchable and others that were simply scanned, digital images of documents that one could browse. *That is impressive.* Kindra had done a lot of German and Irish research and there was very little in the way of digital records that one could browse. Either the records did not exist, or no one had taken the time to scan and upload them to a website. The Norwegians appeared to be stellar regarding record keeping. It seemed like they recorded everything. Much of the content was from church records that were split up by year and location.

Kindra clicked on the search bar and typed Leif Husland, then clicked the little magnifying glass. She got 10,000 hits. Leif Husland Olsen, Leif Husland, Anders Husland Olsen, Nils Husland Olsen...and each name had a brief description of the accompanying record. Leif Husland Nilsen (b. 1906-01-12, Grimstad), Domicile: Kristiania: Reichweins gate 2, Pos./Status: s ug S. Source: 1910 census for Kristiania.

*Ok*. Kindra scrunched her eyes shut and opened them again. *Some of that made sense and some of it was gibberish. This guy was definitely born on January 12, 1906. Maybe it was my great grandfather?* Kindra clicked back over to her genealogy program and brought up the member message boards. She went to the board for Norway and composed a message asking for help with locating a man named Leif Husland from Norway, who was probably born about 1960 and then leaving for the United States at some point. She posted the message.

Kindra put on a pot of coffee and began searching the web for blogs and sites that might help her read Norwegian church records. Clearly, she was going to need to know a few keywords before digging through even the searchable records would be of much help. She finally found what she was looking for on a site that explained the contents of each Norwegian census and had a key that explained each of the abbreviations used. She committed a few important words to memory: "gift" meant married, "ugift" was unmarried and "kone" was wife. "Datter" and "sønn" were pretty obvious. She found birth, christening, burial, death and a few others to commit to memory as well.

Kindra went back to the tab with her search of Digitalarkivet. Her list had a bunch of people with the last name Husland in the 1920 census for Fjære. She clicked on the first record. At the top of the page, the census district was listed as 003 Moi and the rural residence was listed as 0112 Husland. Kindra clicked the link for 0112 Husland and the page showed everyone who lived at the address. There were several people with the last name Husland. These could all be relatives of Leif Husland. She went to the previous record for 0111 Brattemoen. There were six people living there, and they all had the last name Hansen. She clicked back to the record before that one and found the rural residence to be called 0110 Husland. Interesting… there was a 0112 Husland and the people living there had that last name. At 0110 Husland, the people all had the last name Nilsen. Going back, another record yielded 0109 Husland with some Huslands and two Nilsens living there. She clicked for the previous record again and another residence called Husland popped up. Now Kindra was getting confused. Why were all these properties named with the last name Husland? The more she flipped through records, the more curious Kindra became about that last name. Most of the names in the records ended in "sen" as one would expect from Norway. Husland was not one of those normal names. *Maybe the guy in the picture was royalty and an entire town was named after him or something like that?*

Kindra opened a third tab and performed another quick search. Her search returned a blog post describing Norwegian naming traditions. It began with a description of the patronymic naming system of calling a child after his or her father. Interestingly, the Norwegians seemed to have used this system pretty recently as far as the history of humans was concerned. Fixed surnames, or the practice of using the same last name as your father, instead of taking his first name as your last name and throwing sen or datter on the end, weren't required by law until 1923. That could make finding someone in Norway difficult! Imagine having the name John and a father named Michael. There would be an insurmountable number of records to search for John Michaelsen. It would be even worse than the dreaded genealogical search for someone named Robert Smith.

Kindra scrolled to a section with a heading called "Farm Names" expecting to find out how the names for the unique properties were derived. The section ended up being much more exciting than that. It seems the Norwegians found the patronymic naming system confusing, too. All made sense, in your small town if introducing yourself this way, "Hi. I'm Jill, Tony's daughter." But that didn't work out well once you traveled outside your small little area or had to do official business. The Norwegians would then add a last name to the one they already had. The name Thor Eriksen Lunde, translates as, "My name is Thor. I am the son of Erik, and I live on Lunde Farm." This was excellent. Kindra knew where Leif Husland had lived in Norway!

Since Kindra had accidentally found the 1920 census that included Husland Farm already, she went back to the record and flipped through it page by page, looking at the names. There was no one named Leif, but it was not surprising to Kindra. 1920 was long before her Leif Husland would have been born. She got up and poured herself a cup of coffee. She returned to her seat at her computer and started bringing up all the census records for Husland Farm. These people were all related to, or friends with, Leif's ancestors. If she could start putting together some family trees for the people who lived on the farm, she could trace them down through the generations until she found a child named Leif who was born around 1960. This could take years, but it was doable. She had tackled similar family tree brick walls with less information, but had succeeded with enough time. She could do this too.

In the 1900 census, she found the first available record of a man named Leif that lived on Husland Farm. This person was born in 1887, so she concluded he was three years old at the time of the census. Just a little guy! She followed this family through the years to see if he had any descendants that reused the name. It was a starting place, anyway. Three-year-old Leif Pedersen lived on Husland, farm number 48, property number 1. His parents were Magnus and Amalie Pedersen. Leif lived with his brother Gunnar and his sister Grethe. Both siblings were older than Leif. Kindra started the tree for Leif. She added in the birthdates given on the record. Leif's brother and sister were seventeen and twelve years older than him. *That was un*usual. *Leif must have been a little happy accident.* Leif's mom was listed as born in 1865, so she would have been thirty-two when Leif was born. *That was certainly plausible…but…wait. Something isn't adding up correctly.* According to the record, Amalie Pedersen gave birth to Leif's brother Gunnar when she was fifteen years old. *It wasn't impossible, but even in 1900, that was young to be married and having children. Wasn't it?*

Kindra opened up the 1910 census for the same tract of land. There was Magnus, Amalie and Grethe, but Gunnar and Leif were not listed. Kindra supposed it made sense that Gunnar would be gone. *In 1910, he would have been thirty years old. He had probably married shortly after the 1900 census and was living elsewhere. Leif should be there, though. He would have only been thirteen years old. That was odd.* She tried going backward in time instead. She found the family in the 1891 census. Only Magnus, Amalie and Grethe were listed. Where was Gunnar? He should have been the oldest child and about eleven years old.

Kindra went back out to the main page of Digitalarkivet and clicked the option to browse the church records. She found the church book from Fjære parish from 1881 to 1902. She started at 1894 looking through each record to find Grethe. The male births were on the top half of each page and the female births on the bottom. Kindra flipped page by page until she found Grethe on the fifty-ninth page. She was born on February 22nd of 1875. Her parents were listed as Magnus and Amalie Pederson with the same birth years as they had on the census records. That wasn't so bad. She started searching for Leif in the same digital file.

The Norwegians recorded everything. They were certainly big on their record-keeping. The births of illegitimate children were recorded as well. If a child was born to a servant girl, sometimes the father's legitimate wife was even included as a note in the record. Kindra supposed Norway found it more important to record the truth than to make the official record more savory. Kindra wished her mother subscribed to that same notion. It would make this entire process a lot easier. Kindra had paged through every record from 1896 to 1898 and had not found Leif. She went through 1895…then she went through 1899. There was no birth record for Leif Pederson.

Kindra supposed it could happen. Maybe there had been a lot going on in the Fjære Church and someone had forgotten to record the information. She knew there were tons of errors in the U.S. Census records. Kindra couldn't imagine Norway wouldn't have a few missteps as well. She opened up the file that held the digital images for the years 1867 to 1880. Kindra quickly clicked through the records until she got to 1878 and then slowed down and began reading as she went. She made it to 1879, and then she was at the end of the file. She hadn't found a record for Gunnar. Kindra went back to the other file for the years 1881–1902 and scanned through the first two years. She still did not find a record for Gunnar. It might not be unusual for one child's birth to be missed, but Kindra was sure it would be close to impossible for two out of three children to have missing birth records.

Kindra clicked back over to the tab with the message board, intent on adding a post looking to collaborate with anyone who was already researching family from Husland Farm in Norway. She never got to that post. Someone had already replied to her previous post about Leif Husland. BraatenHunter02 explained some things Kindra had already discovered for herself. Husland was a farm name. Husland is a farm in Fjære. She asked if Kindra knew Leif's family name and then she shared something that had Kindra getting excited. BraatenHunter02 explained that the Norwegians, in their never-ending quest to document family lines, have giant farm books or Bygdeboker. In the books, farm numbers are used to list and describe the properties I the area. A record of who lived at each residence and who those people married was recorded for each property. Often, it also listed where people moved after marrying and which person from which other property they had married. There were photos of the property and, sometimes, photos of the families that lived there. BraatenHunter02 was offering to send scanned images of the pages that pertained to Husland if Kindra would provide an email address. Kindra immediately replied to the post with her email address.

# CHAPTER 4

Kindra woke up the next morning and sprinted to her laptop on the kitchen table. She had an email from Kari Braaten. In the e-mail Kari explained she lived in Bergen and did not have many ties to Fjære but her years of research on her own Norwegian family ad fostered the the habit of collecting Bygdeboker from all over Norway. She had sent a pdf file of the scanned pages she thought Kindra might be interested in looking over. Kindra sent the pdf to her printer and put on the coffee pot. The printer in her bedroom made some noises and Kindra headed down the hall to collect the papers as they spit from the machine. She had to add paper once, but eventually she had about forty pages of genealogical gold.

    Kindra plopped down at the kitchen table with her stack of printed pages and a large cup of coffee as soon as the file had finished printing. She began turning pages and was and balked at the organization of the information. There was some information in the beginning that seemed like background on the farm itself. It was hard to tell with her limited knowledge of Norwegian words, but the similarity of enough of the words to English allowed Kindra to feel safe making the assumption about the connotation of the words. After those introductory paragraphs, each property on the farm was listed by bruk nummer. A quick check of the genealogical Norwegian word list Kindra had found online told her that bruk meant farm or the part of a farm that was usually inhabited by a family. Essentially, she supposed it was like the numbers off of a tax map in the U.S.

About a quarter of the way through the bruk nummer collection, Kindra found Magnus Pedersen's family. Kindra traced back through the list of people who had lived on the property for the years prior. Hans Torsen built the original home in the early 1600s. She followed the names through the years as the property passed to various children until she found Amalie Nilsdatter married to Magnus Pedersen, taking over the property from Amalie's father in 1883 when she and Magnus were married. The only child of the marriage listed in the book was Grethe Pedersen. Even worse than the missing sons was the glaring issue with the dates. Magnus and Amalie were married three years after Gunnar should have been born. The property passed through several more generations and eventually sold to a Leif Knudsen in 1974. At first, Kindra thought she had found her Leif Husland, but this man had married Gerd Eriksen and they had a daughter Kristen who had been born in 1958. The timeline ended with a description Kristen started managing the property in 1998. There was no way the mystery man in the photo had given life to a daughter in 1953, when it looked like he had probably not been born for almost ten more years. There was defiantly some kind of connection on the pages in front of her. Unfortunately, it was not as blatant as Kindra had hoped it would be.

Kindra typed "Leif Knudsen and New York" into her search bar. There was a listing for a certified public accountant by that name. She scribbled the information on a sheet of paper. There was an artist with the correct name announcing an exhibit next week at a small gallery in Westchester. Kindra added the information to her recently created list. She clicked a link for a news article with the heading, "Leif Knudsen Lucky to be Alive." The article, from 2018, described a horrific car accident. Leif Knudsen had been driving while impaired along a twisting road that ran along the Delaware River. He had lost control and driven through the guardrail. His 1970 GTO Judge had fallen hundreds of feet to the river below. Knudsen had been missing for 15 hours when he turned up downriver in New Jersey. He was found by a group of teens who had spent the day rafting the Delaware. It was an absolutely insane story and a miracle he was alive, but the story concluded by stating that

Knudsen had been charged with driving while impaired based on the amount of alcohol that was still contained in his blood.

Kindra had three suspects for the man in the photo, assuming he had stayed in the area. She really wouldn't know where else to look. Even assuming the man's last name was Knudsen was a long-shot, but it was something. Kindra texted Jess. Kindra's phone range seconds later.

"I told you, adults pick up the phone and call. You can't just shoot a text out to me saying you found three possible baby-daddies and you want to know if I want to come along to go spy on them. Of course, I will go. I just wanted it on the record that this invite should have been a phone call."

Kindra swiped away the phone call and used the messaging app to send her friend a text to let her know she would pick her up in an hour. She could hear Jess spewing expletives before she even had a chance to swipe back to the call. Kindra ended the call without saying a word. She took a quick shower and braided back her red-brown hair to create one thick rope that went to the middle of her back. She threw on jeans and a t-shirt and headed out.

Jess was sitting on the tailgate of Sean's pickup when Kindra pulled up. Sean loved that truck. Kindra remembered when he got it. He had left the Ford dealership and driven straight to the school at 3pm. He had grabbed Kindra and Jess and taken them for ice cream. The three of them had sat on the tailgate and stared out at the beautiful landscape. The creamery they were patronizing was located on the end of a winding gravel road. If you drove into the field to park, you could eat your ice cream and stare down at the town. Sean held felt this was the perfect trip on which to take his new F-150. He could try out the four-wheel drive but not have to worry about doing any damage to his immaculate white truck. Kindra had ordered a double-scoop sundae in a cup with Chocolate Cow Tracks ice cream. It had been a challenge to eat it fast enough to avoid the melting of the ice cream by the hot fudge, but also not suffering a brain freeze.

"Earth to Kinda!" Jess yelled while banging on the passenger window. "It's a bit hard to pick someone up when you've got them locked out of the car!"

Kindra quickly hit the button for the door locks and began apologized. "I am so sorry. I was just…"

"You were just lost in a memory somewhere? Envisioning what it will be like when we meet your dad today?"

"Come on, I said I was…wait. Meet my dad? I didn't think we had proven the man in the picture is my father."

Jess smiled with one side of her mouth. "Isn't that what we are thinking? It has to be him."

"Maybe so, but let's not get ahead of ourselves."

"Role reversal! I'm the one getting all dreamy and you're the one chasing facts." Jess said with some awe.

Jess snickered. "Genealogy research makes me all mathy and analytical."

"I knew there was a reason I liked it when you got all invested in chasing dead people."

"The people we are chasing after today are alive, so I thought it might be more up your ally." Kindra was suddenly much more serious as she spoke. "One of the three possible matches to our guy is an artist. He doesn't live locally, but he does have an art show coming to the area. He did live here once though, so he is still a possibility. Unfortunately, he won't be in town until his show opens. Person number two is a CPA. Since it is Sunday, I doubt he will be at the office. I did a search though, and his address is listed. We'll arrive at our first stop in about an hour."

Jess looked at her friend, and not for the first time, she wondered if she might have the finely honed skills of a serial killer. She could stalk the living and the dead with speed and precision. As Kindra put the car in drive and pulled into the street, Jess pulled a stack of math tests out of the bag she carried everywhere. In purple pen, she began marking up the tests as her friend followed the GPS mounted on the dashboard.

"Not a single lost moment, huh?" Kindra asked. "I don't know why you bother writing all those little notes in the margins. It's not like a kid actually reads them. They just look at the score you put on the top of the front page and then toss the test in the trash."

"One or two of them care. They look over the test to see where they made mistakes. If I don't write the notes, then they end up having to come in to office hours anyway for help with finding their mistakes." Jess defended her work.

Kindra knew teaching was time consuming. Many of the people she worked with spent hours a day after the students went home grading papers and planning for the following day. Jess didn't like to stay at work. Instead, she just took her work with her everywhere she went. For her, there was no such thing as free time; there was more time to get work done. If you wanted Jess's full attention, you would need to contact her during the months of July and August. It was one way Kindra knew how much her friend cared about her. She was road-tripping into the unknown and burning precious hours on her behalf.

"When these kids run the world, we are doomed." Jess bemoaned. "How do they not know that a half plus a half can't possibly be two fourths? For that matter, how do they not realize that they just said that a half plus a half is a half? There's just no common sense these days."

"You're sounding more and more like a little old lady every year, Jess." Kindra glanced at the test Jess was currently grading. "Besides, that's an algebra test. Why are you so worried about the kids having issues with fractions?"

Jess glared daggers in Kindra's direction. Apparently, Kindra had stumbled into some kind of math faux pas. She could see the long-winded explanation and lecture building on Jess's features when Kindra stuck out her tongue and announced that she was only kidding. She hadn't been kidding, but she knew it was what her friend needed to hear in order to keep from thinking Kindra was just another one of those adults contributing to the downfall of the current academic system. Instead of the lecture, Jess returned to grading.

Kindra spent the trip relaying everything she had learned about the Norwegian naming system and her possible family connections discovered on Husland farm. Jess nodded and gave a "that's interesting" in several places, but she kept grading. It wasn't until Kindra mentioned the missing birth records that she dropped her purple grading pen and looked up.

"That really seems unusual. The two brothers exist on one census record, but they are not mentioned anywhere in the farm book pages the lady sent you, nor are there any birth records for either child? The sister has a birth record and exists in several census records and in the farm book. Did you try the death records?"

Kindra admitted that she had not gone through the death records. She hadn't felt the need. In her mind, there was already a mystery. *Jess is correct, though. I should have searched for all the available evidence related to Gunnar and Leif Pedersen. Maybe that will be tonight's research.*

The GPS announced a left turn in half a mile. Kindra turned the car onto the indicated road. It was a cul-de-sac. Every house on the street was a towering colonial style mini-mansion. The perfectly landscaped lawns were about half the size of the driveway for each home. There were more ornate shrubs and mulch than there was grass. There were no trees exceeding five feet high. Kindra couldn't understand how people lived like this. Why not just get a townhouse? The people in these homes obviously spent most of their time indoors enjoying the large echoing rooms, looking out the huge decoratively shaped windows, and straight into the decoratively shaped windows of the house next door or across the street.

Kindra pulled the car up to the curb across from the home owned by Leif Knudsen, CPA. It wasn't long before a curly-haired blond boy came out of the house with a small poodle-mix of some kind on a leash. The boy walked down the street to his left. Kindra and Jess watched him go. Kindra jumped out of the car and started after the boy.

Jess watched from the passenger seat, carefully putting away her test papers. Kindra had approached the boy and was gesturing toward the curly-haired mutt. Now Kindra was down on one knee, letting the dog lick her face and the boy was laughing. The boy was probably about ten or eleven. He pointed back toward the house from which he had come and Kindra looked over her shoulder in that direction. She gave the dog one last pat on the head and headed for the boy's house.

Part of Jess knew she should be getting out of the car and going up to the house with her friend. The other part of her was mortified at her friend's audacity. *She was just going to walk right up and ring the bell?* That was exactly what Kindra was doing. A man in his mid-forties answered the door. He and Kindra spoke for a bit, and then the man shut the door and disappeared inside the house. He reemerged and handed something to Kindra. Kindra nodded her head toward the man and turned to walk back to the car as the man, once again, shut the door.

Kindra flipped a business card at Jess as she slid back into the driver's seat and pulled the car away from the curb. She drove down to the cul-de-sac at the end and waved to the boy as she went around the circle and headed back in the direction they had come. Jess looked at the card Kindra had thrown in her lap. There was a fluffy mutt on the front being held by a smiling, yet frumpy, women in her fifties. The name of the business was Goldie's Doodles, and there was a phone number and a web address.

"Would you believe Phoebe was $3000? People pay $3000 for a mutt! Why don't they just go to the shelter and pay a $200 adoption fee for the tons of mutts already there? What a racket! Anyway, it's not him. I introduced myself as Kindra Powers, and he didn't even bat an eye."

As Kindra pulled out of the development and onto the main road, she brought up the next destination on her GPS. "Shall we take the Palisades or the Thruway?" she asked Jess.

"Palisades. There's no toll." Jess replied without hesitation. "Where are we going, anyway?"

"The Catskills" was the only reply Kindra offered.

Kindra wound the car up the tree-lined parkway, passing a makeshift memorial every mile or so. The road could be dangerous. It was built as a scenic route for people headed upstate for weekend getaways and sightseeing. Over the years, the endless construction on the Thruway caused the Parkway to be overtaken by commuters. The posted speed limit was about thirty miles per hour less than the average car was currently traveling as Jess kept to the right lane. Cars entering the parkway from the right had only a short entrance ramp before finding themselves thrown into bustling traffic.

"I'm not sure this was worth saving the couple of dollars for the toll." Kindra said as she glanced down at her whitened knuckles and trying to relax her grip on the steering wheel.

Jess looked up from the papers she was once again grading as soon as the car was in motion. She glanced around at the cars flying by on the left and the ones pushing in from the right. The GPS noted that there were only two more miles until they would exit left. "So, what's the next guy's story?"

Kindra explained the newspaper article about Leif Knudsen surviving an accident where his car had gone off a cliff and into the Delaware River. By the time she got to the laughable part about the miracle man being charged with a DWI in the end, she was guiding the car up and over a mountain and deeper into Orange County. Before heading down the other side, the women experienced a beautiful view of the town below. Kindra pulled into the little pull-off used for stopping to take photos and turned off the car. Jess took one look at the hot dog truck Kindra was eyeing and rolled her eyes.

"None for me, thanks. I'll eat at some point, but you could not pay me to eat anything for sale off that truck."

Kindra came back from the truck minutes later with a hot dog covered in sour kraut, relish, mustard and ketchup. No wonder the woman did not mind eating off the truck; with all those condiments, it wasn't like you could actually taste what you were eating. Kindra shoved a soft pretzel at her friend. Jess smiled. No salt. That's what friends were for. Jess thanked Kindra and began peeling pretzel bits off and stuffing them in her mouth. Ok, the truck couldn't be as bad as she had thought. They had soft pretzels.

Kindra finished her hotdog in a few bites and tossed the paper wrapper into the back seat. She cleaned the backseat out every now and again, but currently there was enough trash on the floor of the back seat of the little Honda Civic to reach the actual seat itself. With the number of candy bar wrappers and coffee cups, it was a wonder there weren't ants or roaches colonizing Kindra's entire car. Kindra guided the car back onto the road and the women were on their way again. Now on a highway, the shopping centers and towns zipped by. In twenty minutes, they were near Wurtsboro and the GPS was sending them off the highway. The little contraption was showing its worth, as it had Kindra navigating right turns and left turns, pointing the car farther from civilization. It finally announced the women's arrival at the destination they had desired.

Kindra stopped the car. *There was nothing here. Wait. On the right.* There was a gravel road so narrow. Kindra was not even sure her car would fit down the skinny strip. Kindra parked the car near the start of the road. She looked at Jess. "Wanna go for a walk?"

It wasn't a long walk. The gravel road turned out to be a driveway. Kindra and Jess had only walked a few tenths of a mile when, following a bend in the driveway, a clearing materialized ahead. Kindra stepped off the gravel and into the trees. Jess followed Kindra, but not without giving her a disapproving look.

"What are you doing, Kindra? Are you planning on creeping through the woods and spying on this guy?"

"Well, yes. I don't have a reason to be randomly walking through the woods, in the middle of nowhere, and knocking on doors. I think the only option we have is to attempt getting a look at who lives here."

"If we just go knock on the door, the worst that happens is we're asked to leave. If we get caught snooping through the woods, we risk getting charged with trespassing, or maybe even shot, in this area. I'm pretty sure the people who live in this part of New York aren't the type to disapprove of firearms."

"You're probably right. We better be sure we are extra quiet."

Jess followed Kindra through the woods as quietly as she could. She was careful not to step on any sticks or walk through any dry leaves. Kindra was a natural at this kind of thing. There had been a time in Girl Scout camp that Kindra moved quietly through the camp one evening and stole all the girls' flashlights. When it had become full dark, not a single girl would leave the campfire out of fear of what they could not see. When it had been Kindra's turn to tell a ghost story, it had started with a camping trip in which all the flashlights had gone missing and ended with the campers going missing and some hikers finding only a pile of flashlights a few weeks later. Jess had to work hard to control her laughter when Kindra had pretended to uncover the pile of the other scouts' flashlights near the outskirts of camp about an hour after her story. She was pretty sure several girls had dropped out of the Scouts after that trip.

Standing in the cover of the trees a moment later, Jess was proud of the silence she managed as she got to this spot. The birds were still chirping, so even the animals had not been disturbed by the women's approach. Jess thought she could hear voices coming from the cabin at the center of the clearing.

Kindra whispered, "He's playing video games."

"What? How on earth do you know that?"

"I can hear it. First there was a bunch of fighting sounds, and then I heard a demon-like voice say, 'Finish him!' I know you know the game, Jess. We played it through most of our childhood."

Jess did know the game. They had even made a movie out of it. What she didn't know was how Kindra could hear all that. Jess definitely heard sounds and voices, but she didn't even know it was a video game, let alone the exact game that was being played. She heard the sound that came from the cabin next though.

"Fuck!" shouted a man's voice from the cabin.

There was then a crash, and the door swung open. A man about the same age as the women stumbled out onto the little front porch. The man had red hair that fell a bit past his shoulders. He pushed it out of his face where it had caught in his stubble, like the short hairs had been Velcro. The man was tall, but slumped as he walked. It was as if he were too tired to bother holding himself up straight. The stance made his belly stick out, and with his shoulders also pushing forward, he looked a bit like the letter S.

The man was very unstable as he walked toward the railing. Jess found herself holding her breath, waiting to see if he would fall down the steps. The red-head made it to the railing and placed a bottle down on it. Jess was too far to see what was on the label, but she was pretty sure it was some kind of liquor. The man pushed his hair back again and reached down to unzip his pants. He then began peeing off the porch.

Disgusted, Kindra's heart sank. *This guy is too young to be the man from the photo. If it iss the guy's son or something, he won't even be capable of coherent conversation in his current state.* Kindra was just about to motion to 'Jess that it was time to go when the man on the porch stiffened. He turned toward the woods, where the women were standing out of sight. Kindra looked at Jess, eyes huge. No words were needed. Both women spun and took off through the woods.

As they broke from the trees and into the driveway, they heard the man yelling. "Kindra! I know that was you! I knew you would come! Kindra!"

The women reached the end of the driveway and turned for the car. Kindra stopped short and Jess tripped over her and went sprawling, face first, to the ground. Kindra's mouth fell open and Jess lifted her head from the ground. The red-haired man was leaning against the trunk of the car. "I suppose you have questions."

Jess got to her knees and touched her chin. Her hand came away bloody. The man's hair was greasy. His bare feet were filthy. He looked as if bathing had not been a priority for some time. Of all the things that should have worried her right now, the biggest worry was Kindra. She was not moving. She had gone so still that Jess was not sure she hadn't frozen in place. She was also very pale.

"Shall we go back to the cabin? I'd like to at least put a shirt on. I wasn't expecting company," said the man from Kindra's photograph.

Jess could see it now that they were close to him. His hair was longer, and he was dirtier, but this was the same man. The problem was, he was not old enough. He was far younger than the senior citizen he should have been. Assuming the booze hadn't aged him even more; this man looked just shy of forty.

Kindra started back toward efficacy. "I can smell who you are. You smell like…you smell like I am a part of you."

"Yeah," Leif said. "We had better head up to the cabin. I'm going to start walking. I think you should join me." The man started walking. He wasn't stumbling anymore. He actually walked so gracefully, he appeared to be gliding as he moved.

Jess turned to Kindra. She put her hands on her friend's shoulders. "We can just leave if you want to."

"You have blood on your chin." Kindra reached out to flick away some of the drying blood from her friend's face.

"Let's put you in the car." Jess guided Kindra to the passenger side and opened the door for her. She ran around to the driver's side and slid in behind the wheel. "Keys." She said and held her hand out.

Kindra handed over the keys and Jess stuck them in the ignition, but did not start the car. Jess looked at Kindra and waited for her friend to decide. *Are we going to stay, or are we going to run?*

"He's my father." Kindra said. She was shaking her head back and forth as if denying it would make everything go away. "How is it possible? He's barely older than us. How can I just…know? How does he simply feel like my father?"

Jess looked at her friend. "If you want the answers to those questions, we will most likely need to go up to the cabin. If you would rather leave, we can take our chances interrogating your mother and hope she has some of the answers you're looking for."

Kindra continued to stare out the windshield. Jess could tell she was concentrating on breathing. The women sat there for several minutes before Kindra picked up her phone and sent a quick text.

"I told mom we are here and headed up to the cabin. Let's get moving before I change my mind."

Jess reflected on the rational thought process that had led Kindra to send the text to her mother before heading up to the cabin. Her friend might look like she was in shock, but clearly her synapses were still firing away. If anything happened up at the cabin, at least someone would know the women had been there. Jess turned the car on and pointed it up the narrow driveway. She slowly bumped the Civic up the path to the cabin. She parked the car in front of the porch that Leif had recently relieved himself from and cut the ignition.

Kindra swallowed. She sat up a little straighter. She took a few more deep breaths and put on her game face. Kindra wanted answers, and this was how she was going to get them. She exited the car and headed toward the cabin. She heard the car door as she hit the first stair of the porch so she knew Jess had followed her. There was nothing on the little porch. No chair, no welcome mat, not even a bag of garbage or bin for recycling. Then again, Leif did not look like the recycling type. She stood in front of the door, bracing for what she would find on the other side.

Kindra turned the handle, and the two women stepped into a normal living room. There was a couch and a coffee table. There was a TV stand and an empty spot to hold the gaming console that was now on the floor. It explained the crash they had heard, but otherwise, the room was relatively neat. Leif came down the hallway in jeans. He was still not wearing a shirt and his feet were bare. His hair was wet, providing evidence that he must have taken a quick shower before the women had mustered the nerve to head back up to the cabin.

Leif was in much better shape than he had seemed when the girls had seen him stumbling around on the porch. He appeared to be a different person. It was also possible that he was the same person, but had managed to go to sleep and sober up, then take a shower and get ready for the day. What should have taken over twenty-four hours had occurred in about fourteen minutes. He sat down on the couch and motioned for the women to find a place to sit as well. Jess took a seat in a rocking chair, but Kindra remained standing by the window.

Leif started speaking even though Kindra had not sat down. "I am much older than I look. I know that is the part of this whole thing that is causing you so much confusion. I suppose my body is the equivalent of a person who is about forty years old. It is unbelievable, but I'll get to my age a little later if you'll let me put it off for a bit. It has been thirty-five years since you came into this world, and I know nothing about you."

Jess felt a bit like an intruder at this point. It felt like this should be a private conversation between father and daughter, but she could not move. Firstly, she had wondered about Kindra's father almost as long as Kindra had and secondly, this man could still be a murderer. Just because he had invited them into his quaint little cabin and was admitting to being Kindra's father did not mean he wasn't the greasy drunk they had seen less thirty minutes ago and did not mean he wasn't planning on raping and murdering the women.

Kindra looked straight into Leif's eyes and asked, "Why didn't my mother want me to know who you are?"

"I'm not a good person, Kindra. I am selfish and have never been responsible to anyone or for anything. I don't like my life and I spend as much time escaping it as possible."

"What, was she afraid that you would neglect me or kill yourself or something?"

"I would have neglected you for sure. She needn't have worried about the killing myself part though. It would be the perfect solution if it were possible, but it's not. I think she just wanted to keep you away from the cloud that follows me. Even when things are going well, I find a way to make sure they don't continue to do so. I don't really fit in this world, but I have no desire to find where I fit within the world I was meant for."

Jess had to roll the answer over in her mind several times before she concluded that it really hadn't been much of an answer at all. Were they just here so this guy could spin some kind of quasi-philosophical explanation for why he had been a dead-beat dad?

Kindra hadn't seemed to notice Leif's non-answer. "I think you should start at the beginning. When and where were you born? How did you meet my mother? Why do you live in the woods? Why didn't you find me?"

"That feels like a little more to answer than simply starting at the beginning will address. Why don't you sit down? This really is not a short story and there are no simple answers. I will do the best I can, but you are going to be here for a while."

Jess nodded to her friend and motioned for her to have a seat. She could see the conflict in Kindra's eyes and didn't want her friend to regret getting this far and not allowing herself to hear the story that drove her here. Kindra walked slowly to the couch and sat as far from Leif as she could; closest to the rocking chair that held Jess. Kindra was sitting with her back straight, slightly angled toward Leif. She nodded her head for him to begin.

# CHAPTER 5

Jess had been correct about Leif spinning a lot of bullshit. Eventually, Kindra had relaxed and started jotting some notes down in a notebook she had pulled from her bag. There really hadn't been much to write down though. There were very few facts in Leif's story and most of the bits of information that might be considered facts did not really seem all that reliable. Leif had spent more time complaining about his circumstances than he had explaining them. Many of these circumstances, Jess felt, Leif had created on his own and could blame no one but himself.

"I think my favorite part was when he explained that he would be a better person and more a part of society if it weren't for New York State taking away his license." said Jess. "If you can't figure out how to not drive your car when you're drinking, then you probably shouldn't get to have a license, right?"

"I don't know. There is something that feels wrong about how DMV can just permanently take away your ability to get from place to place. It makes sense if you get three DWIs over a few years, but Leif said it was a lifetime thing. If you got a DWI at age 21, then another at 41 and a third at age 65, you lose your license for the rest of your life. To top it off, it's a fairly new DMV rule, so it didn't even exist when you were doing all that stupid stuff in your twenties and no one was even cracking down on DWIs."

The fact that Kindra was even somewhat defending Leif's life-choices was a bit disturbing. He was obviously a selfish addict that felt as if the world was against him, but even more concerning was that she wasn't willing to talk about the rest of the things Leif had said. Jess had tried talking about fairies, elves and magic, and Kindra had pretended not to hear her. She had started off with an attempt at a conversation about the possibility of eternal beings and different realms, but had received no response from Kindra. The only conversation-starter that had worked dealt with the injustices of the government not recognizing one's ability to change. Jess supposed it was Kindra's career choice that made her feel the need to defend the mentally ill, but Jess was a math teacher. She was trying to wrap her head around the supernatural, but she was hard-wired for evidence and things that were black and white.

The women were nearly back to Jess's house when Kindra finally said, "I'm not ignoring the fantastic details of Leif's story. I just need to go home and unpack it a little at a time. It is obvious to me that the man we just met is ill. There are signs of depression, addiction, and bi-polar disorder, among other things. He clearly lives in his own world and much of what he described is purely from his own imagination. I'm going to have to sit down and sort through what is real and what he made up before I have a talk with my mother."

At the mention of her mother, Kindra turned her phone back on. She had turned it off immediately following the text she had sent to Gretchen. The phone immediately began pinging with messages. Jess pulled the Honda up in front of her own house and cut the ignition. She handed the keys to Kindra. Once she had asked her friend if she was okay to drive for the eighth time, she strode up her driveway trying to think of which parts of the day's events to share with Sean.

Kindra ignored the messages she knew were stacked up on her phone and climbed back into the driver's seat of her car. She rolled out and headed home, thinking about Light Elves. Leif had called them Ljósálfar, but had explained that the word translated as light elves. He had rambled on about light elves, control by Vanir Gods, and war with Dwarves and other Dark Elves. It had all sounded like some children's tale manufactured for the sole purpose of explaining Kindra's existence, with the bonus of avoiding one shred of truth. *"Had Leif really thought she believed all of that nonsense?"*

Then again, what could explain the reality but a fairytale? Her father was almost 125 years old and was in better shape than her, without a shred of gray in his red hair. He had been wasted one moment, then seemingly teleported to her car, showing no signs of having had a single drink. He had known it was her standing on the edge of the clearing without having ever met her. Kindra had smelled their relationship once she had been close to him. *Maybe it wasn't Leif who had lost his mind. Maybe the stress of dealing with all the kids' problems at school had caused her to snap. Maybe she was the one who was crazy?"*

Kindra groaned audibly as she pulled into her driveway next to a familiar van. Her mother was here at her house. She fortified herself and stepped out of the car. She counted every tedious step as she headed to face her mother. This would not be a fun conversation. She opened the door, prepared for the wall of anger that would undoubtedly hit her. Surprisingly, the door opened to silence. *Nothing?* Kindra dropped her bag on the entry table and walked to the kitchen. Her mother was at the table with a cup of tea in front of her.

Gretchen looked up at Kindra with resignation in her eyes. "I think you should take a trip to Norway."

Kindra was speechless. She had been so ready for a fight that she hadn't considered what she and her mother might actually speak about. Kindra didn't respond to her mother as she walked to the electric teakettle. She clicked it on and it clicked back off before Kindra had even readied her tea bag in a cup. The water was still hot. She threw a bit of milk and some sugar into a mug on top of her tea bag and added the hot water. Slowly, Kindra walked to the table and pulled out a chair. She sat down across from her mother, but kept her eyes on her steaming mug.

"I didn't want you to find him, but now that you have…" her mother gave a little shrug. "The best thing for you to do is to go to Husland Farm. The house is still there. Your sister looks after it."

"Of course I have a sister. Why on Earth would I have felt this whole situation was weird enough without one?"

"Actually..." Gretchen paused a little too long to keep Jess from getting nervous. "You have a few sisters and a few brothers. There may be some I don't even know about but..."

Kindra held up a hand. "I can't hear this right now. I have lived 35 years as the only child of a single mother whose father died before she was born. I can't just suddenly sit and listen to all of this because your dirty secret is now out and you want to fully unburden yourself."

Gretchen stopped talking. She looked horrified, and Kindra softened a bit. She tried to see it from her mother's side. There had been years of lies and hiding the truth. Her daughter accidentally uncovered part of the lie and instead of holding firm; Gretchen had chosen to go full speed ahead with the truth. She felt badly about the lie and was trying to make up for it by uncovering everything that was still hidden.

"I'm sorry, mom. I do want to know everything. I just feel like I can't hear it all at once. I'm still spinning from my conversation with Leif today and now you're piling on even more information."

Gretchen spoke softly, "Can I answer any questions? Big or small, I'm ready when you are."

Kindra thought about it. "Ok. Let's start small. Are you my real mother?"

Her mom's eyes flashed with pain and then smoldered a little. Gretchen took a deep breath and said, "I supposed I deserved that sting. You must feel like nothing in your life is a truth. I am your real mother. Your birthday is your real birthday and Leif is your real father."

That hadn't been so bad. Kindra asked the next question, "Why did you leave Leif and keep him out of our life?"

One side of Gretchen's mouth turned up in what was almost a smile. "You did meet him, right? You saw him? I mean, really saw him? Did you get to see him before he knew who you were?"

Kindra could see where this was going. Before Leif had realized it was Kindra out in his woods, he had been a slovenly drunkard. He had been dirty and unapproachable. Even after Leif's miraculous transformation, he had shown some pretty undesirable qualities. He had a tendency to blame others and had made it a point to mention that things were out of his control when giving a reason for his poor choices. That had been while he was trying to make a good impression. Kindra suspected his personality tended more toward that of the man they had seen peeing off of his porch.

"Ok. Point taken.", said Kindra with a small smile of her own. "Then tell me what attracted you to him in the first place."

"That's easy" started Gretchen. "He's gorgeous, for starters. When I first met him, he was dressed to impress and the smoothest talker you've ever met. I had gone to see a friend play in her band at The Newt Café and he knew one of the other band members. We sat and listened to music all evening. We danced a little, and

I felt as if nothing mattered in the world except me.

"After that night, he started going to each gig the band played and we would spend the night together, forgetting our lives and just enjoying each other's company. Over time, we started to meet up outside of the evenings when the band was playing. We went to see other bands, and we traveled on little overnights to the beach and up to Lake George. I was in love and enjoying the time of my life.

"Things were perfect for the five months I had known Leif, when he changed. It was almost overnight. He didn't want to go out anymore. He spent all his time in front of the television or playing video games. There were few moments where he wasn't drunk or asleep and the fun had dried up. At that point, I was already pregnant with you, but I hadn't told Leif yet. I distanced myself. It started to feel like I was being sucked into a void of negativity every time I was with him."

Kindra cocked an eyebrow. "If you were no longer seeing him, and he didn't know about me, how did he end up naming me and promising to stay away?"

"When I was about four months pregnant, he called me up one morning, all bright and cheery. It was as if the last two months had never happened. As if he hadn't just spent weeks wallowing in his own filth in front of the television. We went to a local carnival and had a great time. He was the guy I had met at The Newt Café again. We were having such a delightful time. I told him about you. He was angrier than I had ever seen any person before.

He was angry that I hadn't told him, angry I was pregnant, angry I hadn't been there for him when he needed me. If there was any tiny thing that he hadn't liked in the last few months, he was suddenly angry about it and seemed to feel all of it was my fault. That was the last time I saw Leif. Our arrangement, and my promise to name you Kindra, was all through phone calls. I absolutely refused to have a man like that in our life."

"I think you made a very hard choice. It's obvious Leif struggles with depression and probably some other…"

"That's the thing!" Gretchen interrupted. "He is a goddamn elf! Elves have miraculous healing powers. At any time, he can fix anything that is wrong with himself. He can even keep himself from getting drunk if he wants to drink all night. He actually makes a conscious choice to get the way he does."

Kindra tried to ignore the elf part of the whole outburst, but focussed on the idea that being depressed and drowning himself in alcohol was an actual choice for Leif. It helped explain how the stumbling man from the porch could seem fine a minute later as he met them at the car. The idea that anyone would simply choose to waste life away as he did was crushing. It pushed against everything Kindra knew about alcoholism, addiction, and depression.

Kindra took a deep breath and prepared herself for the next question. *"Was she really about to ask this?"*

"So, he told you about being an elf…and…and you just believed him?"

Gretchen puffed out a laugh. "I had no choice but to believe him. There were things he did that were impossible to explain. I already told you he could drink all night and never get drunk, but there were other things, too. He always knew when I was around; even if there was no way he could have seen or heard me. He told me once that he could smell my presence. He would be in the kitchen near the stove one moment, and the next moment he would be running the shower for me as I headed for the bathroom. Leif did that a lot when no one else was around. He'd be one place, and then he'd be somewhere else; with no time in between.

"Then there was the whole animal thing. It was like he could speak to them and understand them in return. I laughed it off when he told me he really could talk to animals, but there really was no other explanation. Leif could make birds sit on his wrist and eat out of his hand. He had deer walk right up to me so I could feed them. He even got a bear to stop eating out of my garbage cans."

"Did it occur to you that he had just trained the animals over time with food?" Kindra asked. "Maybe he just had a lot of time on his hands and a little patience?"

"Time!" Gretchen exclaimed. "That's the one that sealed the deal for me. He told me how old he was… I mean how old he really was, not what it said on his driver's license. To get me to believe that one, he took me to Norway to see his childhood home. It's the reason I think you need to go there."

Gretchen spun Jess's laptop around. It already had the airline website pulled up. She placed her credit card down next to the computer. "I'm the reason you're here struggling with this. I'll be the one trying to help you understand. I suggest you take a bit of time off work. The kids will be fine, but I'm not so sure you will be if you try to avoid confronting this. I know Jess would never take time off, and the school might be a bit suspicious if you're both missing anyway, so I will go with you if you need me to go. I should mention though that Leif's family does not particularly like me, so you might have a better experience on your own."

Kindra was not sure if this was just another of Gretchen's excuses to avoid an unpleasant activity, or if Leif's family truly hated her. It didn't matter. Kindra was about to go to Norway. She liked to think of herself as a bit of a free-spirit, but this was a bit more than she had ever taken on for herself. None-the-less, she would go alone. She typed in her personal information and used her mom's credit card to book a flight to Oslo.

# CHAPTER 6

Kindra went into school the next day to set up her files to aid her colleagues in finding any information they needed while she was in Norway. Noone at school knew why she was actually going to be out and due to the HIPPA law; no one would even have the nerve to ask. Kindra was fine with everyone assuming she was having some kind of operation on her bowels or something just as embarrassing. She did, of course, tell Jess.

Jess had taken it better than expected. Kindra had been greeted by an email this morning with a list of all the things that could go wrong. It ranged from her plane crashing into the ocean to Leif's sister taking her hostage or murdering her. Jess must have felt a little guilty because a second email contained a link to an online Norwegian language course. It was only free for the first few lessons, but considering Kindra was leaving tomorrow morning, it would be about all she would need.

Jess spent period one doing the first introductory lessons. She learned to say hello and use the words for boy, girl, woman and man. She learned to say she was from the United States and that she had a cat and a dog. Since she had neither a cat nor a dog, Kindra was not sure that the last part would be all that helpful. She had finished up lesson 1 and was getting ready to go to her period two meeting. She made a mental wish that lesson 2 would provide some useful phrases such as, 'Where is the bathroom?' as she headed out of her office.

Her workday was a boring one. She alternated between Norwegian language learning, attending meetings, and conducting fifteen minute sessions with her students. By the end of the day she had learned the important phrase, 'Hvor er toalettet?' and had reassured herself that none of her students were in crisis and that each could handle Kindra going away for several days. She left the files of her frequent flyers on the desk so one of the many counselors in the office could grab them in an emergency and exited her office. As Kindra headed for her car, she shot a text off to Jess that said 'Tussen takk' for the language learning link and that she was heading out for the day.

Kindra's phone rang as she was getting in the car. "I assume what you sent means thank you, so I am calling to say 'you're welcome'. Be safe and be sure to take pictures. If you meet any hot gentlemen, be sure to share those pictures first!"

"There will be no hot gentlemen. I'm staying with my half-sister. My mom made all the arrangements."

"Half-sister? Kindra! You're not an only child anymore!"

"Yeah.", Kindra said. "Good old Leif married a woman named Grethe back in Norway. They had a daughter, Kristen, in 1958. She now takes care of the property. I get to stay with her on the farm where Leif grew up, disappeared, and came back to as an adult."

"Sounds like you two will have tons to talk about," Jess said in a chiding tone. "Seriously though, have some fun and give this woman a break. She didn't ask to be Leif's daughter. If he was anywhere near as bad as he seems he can be now, then she probably doesn't think of him so fondly, either."

"You're right. I'm just not thrilled about any of this. I'm going to be living with a stranger who has complete knowledge of the father I never knew I had. I don't know which part is worse! I hate that I have to stay with a stranger, but it's so much more unbearable because of her connection to the biggest mystery in my entire life."

Jess started, "I suppose he is a little less of a myst…"

Kindra cut her friend off. "I kinda wish he had stayed a mystery. That man is not a good one! My mother filled me in a bit more on his lovely personality. He definitely suffers from depression, but it seems like he can choose not to at any time and doesn't! He gets drunk, drives, and crashes cars. When he is feeling depressed, he basically tries to take the whole world down with him, or at least make those around him miserable."

"True.", said Jess. "But, as I was saying, you love a mystery. If Leif had been dead and you had learned he was your father, you would have been interested in all the little details about him. You'd have been clipping out the news articles and going on and on about the terrible things he had done, but at the same time those things would not have upset you. He would be dead and all those things would be just facts. Now, you actually have a living person to deal with, and it almost seems as if you have no interest in finding out everything there is to know about him! How many times have you shared stories, good or bad, about your ancestors and then wished they were still alive so you could talk to them and learn more? You finally got your wish."

"Maybe I only wished for it because I knew it was impossible?" Kindra mused. "I really don't think I wanted to speak to them. I just wanted a way to find more details; preferably in a way that didn't involve actually having to talk to anyone."

Jess pointed out the obvious. "Well, you have no choice. Suck it up and go meet your sister."

At this point in the conversation, Kindra was already nearing her house. She signed off of the call with Jess as she pulled into her driveway. She went inside and plopped down at the kitchen table with a notepad. It seemed appropriate that she should at least put all the facts about her father on paper so she'd be able to fill in the blanks easily when she inevitably spoke to Kristen.

Kindra started writing. She had actually collected quite a bit more information about Leif than she had first thought. The problem with the information was that she did not really know how to use it. In traditional genealogical research, knowing a person's age on the 1900 census would give you ranges for birth years and death years. Since Kindra was dealing with a man who seemed to age five times slower than a normal person, Leif's birth year having been listed as 1897 was actually useless.

*"Maybe it wasn't useless?"* Kindra started pondering the pattern in her own head. A birthdate of 1897 would mean that a normal human child would have been 3 years old. This meant Leif must have looked to be

about three in 1900. Kindra was born in 1985 and the picture of Leif that her mother had stashed in the dresser showed a man of about thirty. Her mother had been 30 when Kindra was born, so Leif had probably declared himself to be around 30 when they met. *"Interesting...that means Leif only ages about three years for every ten human years."* Leif had been around for about ten years in 1900, so his real birth year was about 1890. One mystery solved, of many.

Using her discovery, Kindra started mapping out Leif's travels. After the 1900 Norway census, Kindra found Leif Pedersen, age 6, living in Manhattan in 1910. Also, Gunnar Pedersen, age 25, listed as Leif's father. Kindra would have never made this connection. Both the ages and the relationship are wrong. Kindra supposed this was a sound strategy for hiding the fact that one didn't age correctly. Stay somewhere for a few years, then go far away and become someone else, living as a different family unit entirely. That led to more questions. *"Are Gunner and Leif, brothers, or father and son? Are they related at all?"*

Kindra found Leif with Gunnar in Norway ten years after they were in Manhattan, then found Leif alone in Middletown, New York, in 1930. She knew he was living as Leif Knudsen in 1974 when he and his wife Gerd took over Husland farm with Kristen. Kristen had been born in 1958. How had Leif hidden his slow progression in years from that family? Maybe he hadn't hidden it. Maybe the family had all left the place they were before Husland to protect Leif's secret? Something had then made Leif leave his daughter behind in Norway and return to the United States for Kindra to be conceived in 1985.

Gretchen had known about Leif's true heritage. Kindra supposed it was very possible that Gerd and Kristen had been aware as well. Maybe Leif had started exhibiting some of his less desirable behaviors when they returned to Husland, and Gerd had been more than happy to ship him off to America alone. When Leif had returned and met Kindra's mother, he had been using the name Leif Husland. It showed he still had good memories of the place. He had still been Leif Husland when he was arrested and caused that newspaper article to be published out of Liberty, New York.

Kindra hadn't thought much about it when she had found the article because she hadn't thought it was about the correct man, but now she wondered why he had been arrested. She put down her pencil and headed to bed. It was already 9pm. *How had time just slipped away like that…again?* As Kindra brushed her teeth, she decided the arrest had probably been another DWI. It fit the image that Kindra had formed about her newly discovered father. He had complained about how DMV was able to permanently revoke his license after three DWIs, so she was fairly confident she had the reasoning correct. Three years later, when he had driven off the cliff and into the Delaware River, he had been using the name Leif Knudsen. *Did that mean he had three DWIs as Leif Husland, so he had changed his name to start the process again? Was that even possible? Also, he is an elf with the power to heal his body. Why the hell hadn't he just cleared his system of alcohol before they tested him? More self-inflicted pain…*

Kindra crawled into bed and set her alarm for 3am. She still used an old-fashioned digital alarm clock radio. Of course, the antenna in the thing could never pick up any music stations without having static, but the alarm sounded like it was announcing an air raid, so it was perfect for her. It would go off tomorrow morning and she would only need to get dressed and grab her bags. The car service was would pick her up at 4 o'clock to take her to the airport. She'd even be able to slip in a quick cup of coffee.

Dreams plagued Kindra as she slept.. There were beings hovering around from place to place. They all had pointy ears and carried bows and arrows. The beings glowed and were all stunningly beautiful. Kindra wasn't part of the life her dream beings were living, but watched as if it were a television show. The television screen dream darkened, and the elves became scared. Kindra felt their fear as if she were one of them. There was no indication of what the threat was, but it was something bad. She woke with a start and checked the clock. It was only midnight.

Kindra chuckled to herself. *I have spent way too much time in Tolkien's world.* She dropped back to sleep thinking about how Leif, though good looking, was far from the beautiful elves in her dream. The elves returned to her dreams and this time, all was peaceful. There was no darkness, no threat from the unknown.

# CHAPTER 7

Kindra stood on a small stone stoop, taking in the property of Husland Farm. She could tell the house itself had been updated, but it looked as if the original foundation was still intact and holding the structure up. Kindra had expected acres of rolling fields, but that did not describe the property at all. This house was built directly into the rock face of the hill behind it. There was a boulder behind the house that was so large you could jump into the second-floor window if you could manage to climb the boulder itself.

*What the hell did they farm on Husland Farm?* The next house was practically on top of this one and the backyard was all rock. It looked like the final glacier of the ice age had crept right up to within thirty feet of the back of the house and suddenly halted. There were no fields, no cows, no plowing, no farm at all.

Before Kindra had a chance to further contemplate how much of a "*non-farm*" Husland really was, the door in front of her opened and her attention was on a beautiful blond woman. The woman was wearing a huge open smile that made her eyes crinkle up at the corners. The woman looked to be somewhere between Kindra's age and her mother's age; maybe close to fifty.

Kindra gave a shy smile in return and introduced herself. The woman's smile seemed to get even wider. "I am Kristen." said the woman. "I believe I am your half-sister. Velkommen! Come on in!"

"Oh, my!" Kindra was caught off-guard. "You seem so young! I didn't think it was you! I am so sorry."

"Not to worry, Kindra! It is simply one of the perks of being Leif's daughter. We may not age as slowly as he does, but you, too, will find that you age much more gracefully than most of your friends."

"Well, I suppose that is a plus," said Kindra, as she stepped into the house.

The home was adorable. There was a lot of exposed wood, which gave it a cabin-like feel. There were built-in bookshelves and a built-in reading nook under one of the front windows. From the front door, Kindra could see into the kitchen area where a wood table folded down from the wall. A long bench was built-in to the wall on one side and two wooden chairs on the other side of the table. There were handmade elements adorning most of the home's surfaces. Embroidered doilies and knit throw blankets covered tables, couches, and chairs. Kindra felt like she had just walked into an entry for 'the coziest house' competition.

Kristen pointed down a hallway. "Head down toward the end. Your room is the last on the right. You can drop your stuff in there. The bathroom is the door just before yours if you would like to freshen up. When you're ready, come on back to the kitchen and tell me about your trip here."

Kindra turned left and headed down the hall. She passed the bathroom and noted that it had a pedestal sink and a claw-foot tub. It was made to look antiquated, but the fixtures were actually quite new and probably expensive. She continued to the next door. She put her bag down and took a breath. This would be her room for at least the next seven days.

The door swung open to another welcoming space. There was a little wooden writing desk and a single bed with a wooden frame. On the bed was a red and white quilt with a Norwegian Star at the center. A four drawer wooden dresser stood on the other side of the bed, next to a single window. The curtains on the window were the same red as that on the quilt, and Kindra noted their stellar quality as she pushed them open to look outside. She took in the tiny bit of grass and then rock, leading almost straight up. Kindra looked to the right and could see that the back of the house was, indeed, built right up to the rock-face. She had seen windows in the kitchen, so it wasn't that part of the house against the wall, but there was another room or something because from here she could clearly see the house stretching right up to the rock face and attaching to it.

Kindra left her bags on the bed and started back toward the kitchen. She stopped in the bathroom on the way down the hall and washed her face and hands. She smelled all the little soaps in the dish and admired the embroidered hand-towel she used to dry her hands. Entering the kitchen, Kindra found Kristen already had coffee on the table, along with a small pitcher of milk and a bowl of sugar.

"I wasn't sure how you take your coffee." Kristen wrinkled her nose as she spoke.

"How did you know I needed coffee?" laughed Kindra.

"You're my sister. I took a guess. I run on the stuff, so I assumed you must at least like it, if not need it." Kristen smiled warmly as she said it.

Kindra had been extremely nervous about meeting this older half-sister she was now looking at. She wished she had known how warm and welcoming Kristen would be. It would have saved Kindra from the knots in her stomach over coming here if she had known this lovely woman was the person awaiting Kindra's arrival.

"So," Kristen started as Kindra added milk and sugar to her mug. "How was your journey?"

Kindra told Kristen about her uneventful flight and about trying to understand the Norwegian people who were speaking on the train from the airport. She even conceded that she had tried to speak Norwegian to the cab driver who had brought her here from the train station before he kindly explained that almost all people in Norway can speak English. The women agreed that the driver had probably appreciated her attempt, at least. Kindra finished relaying the details of her trip, then asked, "so what did they farm on Husland Farm?"

Kristen laughed. It was a boisterous laugh that exploded from her chest. "Many years ago, before I was born, this whole town was a working farm. It wasn't a town then. It was just Husland. There were many houses, though less than there are now, and the farm workers lived with their families here at Husland. The farming and livestock area was actually far down the hill, where the newer houses are now. They tried to keep the original homes on land that did not lend itself to farming.

"Even when papa lived here, there really wasn't much farming happening. Some people had their own small plots, but there was no longer a central farm. People sold things at the market where the shops are or worked at the docks or on the ships."

Kindra understood that Kristen was referring to the first time Leif had lived on the farm with the Pedersen family. "Are we related to the Pedersens?"

"I'm sure we are related to some Pedersens somewhere, but if you mean the family that took care of Papa when he was young, no. We are not related to them. Erik and Amalie took care of Uncle Gunnar and Papa from the time they were quite young until they each left the farm to strike out on their own. If you are wondering, we are related to Gunnar. He is Papa's full brother."

Kindra was having a hard time reconciling the man she had seen in the woods with Kristen's "Papa." She just couldn't imagine anyone using a term of endearment like that to describe the Leif she had met. "What about Grethe?" asked Kindra.

"Grethe was the Pedersen's only child. She is not related to us by blood, but don't ever say that in front of Papa or Uncle Gunnar! To them, she was a sister and, to be honest, I suspect she may even have been Gunnar's first crush, of sorts. She was about twelve years more mature than Papa, so he was partially raised by her. She taught him many of the ways of this world and he always speaks of her with such love."

Kindra drew up at the last few words. "You say Leif always speaks of Grethe with love. Do you still speak to our dad?"

"I do…though not as often as I once did. He became pretty distant after mom died in 1980, and then he became almost unbearable to speak with when he lost you."

The information hit Kindra like a slap to the face. It had not occurred to her that the circumstances of her birth had caused some of Leif's downward spiral. It did make some sense, though. Her mother had been flippant when she had told her the deal she had struck with Leif. It didn't seem like a big deal to Kindra that Leif would have no contact with her because Kindra hadn't known Leif. Leif had been asked to give up all contact; any chance he had to know his daughter. It could not have been as easy as Gretchen had made it sound. It was now evident to Kindra that there had been a substantial amount of regret for Leif, after striking the deal with Gretchen.

Kristen was staring at Kindra. She must have asked her a question. "I'm sorry. I was just thinking."

"I can see that," said Kristen. "You get that from your father. Anyway, I asked if you had any other questions about the family tree."

*"Any other questions?"* Kindra had many! Some of which she knew she would have answers that were difficult for Kindra to comprehend. She still had no idea how the Elven ancestry part worked beyond her father and her Uncle Gunnar. Maybe sticking to this world was safer for the moment.

"Do we have any other brothers or sisters…here on Earth, I mean."

"Earth!" Kristen laughed. If you mean those who are alive, they are all here on earth. Some are simply in a different realm."

*So much for sticking to this world…* Kindra digested that vast chunk of information. *One Earth, many realms, they are all on Earth… Ok, maybe it was more than one piece of information.*

Kindra clarified, "Do we have any other brothers or sisters in this realm?"

"Quite a few," said Kristen. "I don't really keep tabs on all of them. I do follow the ones with a little magic in their blood, though. Those that have a bit more magic are usually of interest to Leif and he makes sure to be in touch with them. Some of them eventually go to live in Alfheim, especially those with a substantial amount of natural ability. If you'd like a list of some of those in this realm, I can give you that, but I don't suggest you go visit. Most of them have never met Leif. For those that are near-mortal, Leif is the consummate absentee father."

Kindra took a few breaths and a sip of her coffee before summarizing, "So we have many brothers and sisters in this realm, and I assume they span several generations, but most of them have never met Leif."

"Some have met him. The issue really was the speed, or lack of speed, with which Papa ages. If he did not trust the mother enough to confide in her about his heritage, then Papa was sure to be gone from the woman's life, and therefore the child's life, before anything seemed amiss."

"So our father travels back and forth between the U.S. and Norway, changing his name and leaving a trail of unwed mothers?" Some anger started to creep into Kindra's voice. "He does nothing to help with all these babies he makes?"

"For those with gifts, he is always sure to provide and eventually seek his children out when it becomes time for them to understand their own powers. For those with little or no magic, Papa is more subtle. He does his best to ensure the mother or child experience some kind of windfall when it is needed. He never allows them to suffer."

Kindra's eyes flashed with anger. "I'm not sure which is worse! Taking just enough care of your spawn to ensure he or she doesn't die, or doting on him or her until that the child can be brought into the fold and shipped off to Elfhome as prized creations."

"Alfheim." said Kristen.

"What?" Kindra snapped.

"Alfheim. It's the realm of the Elves. You called it Elfhome. It does show me you understand the meaning behind the name of the realm, though."

"We're discussing our father's misogynistic and abhorrent behavior and your concern is that I mispronounced the name of the realm to which he ships off his children?" seethed Kindra.

"Well, no. I just ignored the other parts because he didn't actually ship them anywhere. They ask to go. With regard to the ones that stay here, do you really think they would be better off with Leif in their lives? This way, the moms find new men and create stable families. I love Papa, but you've met him. He is not the most stable father-figure I've known."

Kindra sipped her coffee and rolled the information over in her mind. She supposed living with Leif, the depressed alcoholic, would be more of a punishment than him disappearing. After all, that was why her own mother had struck a deal with Leif to keep him out of their life.

Kindra looked up from her coffee to see Kristen waiting for her to digest her own thoughts. "Why would they want to go to Alfheim? Why would someone want to leave behind everything they know and everyone they love to go to a whole different realm?"

"I don't know." Kristen looked slightly sad. "I've never been to Alfheim. Other than looking younger than I actually am, I didn't get any of the good elf stuff. Papa trusted my mama though, and he told her everything. When we moved here, he had already told me this place would be left to my care. It is part of the reason I never married. There are secrets here, and they are mine to watch over. I never found a man I felt I could trust with those secrets."

"The guardian of secrets, huh? I feel as if you've already told me quite a few of them. Are you sure you are doing your job?" Kindra gave Kristen half of a smile.

"You are family. Papa trusted your mother, and I'm not telling you anything that your mother doesn't already know. I have a feeling she felt you would take it all a bit better hearing it from me."

Kindra sat up straight. "You are quite right on that count! I'm not screaming at you. I think I'm handling this quite well. I have a propensity to yell before thinking when it comes to my mother. Barely knowing you, it kinda forces me to try to think a bit before I react."

"Enough secrets for one night," Kristen decided. "You can explore the property tomorrow and come up with more questions. You had a long trip. Go get some rest."

# CHAPTER 8

Kindra awoke the next morning, ready to explore the property. Kristen wasn't letting her out of the house without breakfast, though. On the table, in the kitchen, was a pot of coffee, hard-boiled eggs in little holders, and something that looked like tortillas for burritos wrapped in paper towels. Kristen forked one of the wrap things onto a plate for Kindra. The look on Kindra's face must have prodded an explanation from Kristen.

"It's Lefsa. You can top it however you want. There's sour cream, sugar, lingonberries, and butter. Would you like a dollop of cream?"

Kindra dropped a pad of butter onto the Lefsa and then sprinkled some sugar on it. She watched Kristen top hers with berries and cream, and then roll it up and start eating it. Kindra rolled hers up and took a bite. These were not burritos. They were sweeter and had more flavor. She tried the next one with berries and cream. It was a very different taste, but equally good. She started on the egg in the holder and discovered it wasn't exactly hard-boiled. It was softer on the inside than she expected, but she found she liked it this way.

Kindra and Kristen ate in silence and sipped coffee. It only took about twenty minutes for the two women to finish up almost all the food Kristen had prepared. Kindra helped Kristen clear the table, and she washed dishes while Kristen dried them and put them away. It felt as if this had been the routine for years and it was pleasant. Kindra couldn't help thinking that having a sister was proving to be a pleasant experience.

Once the women finished clearing breakfast, Kindra headed out to explore the property. She went out the front door and headed to the right. It didn't take long to work her way around to the little back yard. Kindra identified her own window, followed by the smaller bathroom window. The large kitchen window came next as she traveled along the side of the house. There was a small window, even smaller than the bathroom window beyond the large kitchen window. Kindra had not seen a door from the kitchen to go anywhere else in the house. There hadn't been any unidentified doors anywhere in the house. She could see there was another room, next to the kitchen that was built directly into the rock face behind the house. Kindra was not about to try to climb the rock face and go over that part of the house, so she headed back the way she came.

When Kindra got to the front yard and passed the front door, she admired Kristen's little garden. It was mostly rock, with some pretty flowers speckled throughout. There were little lawn gnome-like statues peeking out from behind some rocks and plants. It looked like a whole little Wonderland created just for the statues. She supposed it was similar to the Fairy Gardens some of her friends had created when they had all been in their twenties and had thought they should consider becoming Wiccan. Though she knew some of her friends had kept fairy lights as part of their outdoor décor, they had all grown out of the impulse to join the Witch craze.

Kindra continued to the end of the front lawn and turned left to find barn doors that took up most of that side of the house. Though the structure's design made it look as if it were still part of the house, this was more of a garage or some kind of carriage house. There was no way to get around to the back side of the house from here, as the right door's hinges were almost right up against the rock face. Kindra pulled the left door, and it swung open easily. It was dim inside, but Kindra quickly assessed that this was, indeed, a garage/storage-shed/basement type of area.

Wishing she had investigated the possibility of Norway having poisonous spider species, Kindra stepped inside the area. Near the doors, she found yard equipment, a metal toolbox, a ladder and snow shovels. This gave off a district garage feel. As she pushed a little deeper, she found boxes and giant plastic containers that made the place look more like an attic or basement. Kindra knew she had been invited to poke around, but she wasn't sure this extended to opening storage boxes that undoubtedly would contain some personal things. She wasn't sure whose personal items she might find, but if they were stored here in boxes, the contents weren't meant for public consumption.

Kindra looked at a stack of boxes in front of her. The stack was three boxes high and she could see there was writing on the side of each box. A label on the top box read, '*Jul*' and she could see a bit of greenery and a red and white blanket poking out through one hole in the intended to be used as handles. The next box in the tower read, '*Kristen through 1968*'. Kindra figured that was probably a bunch of photo albums and other memories from Kristen's childhood. The box closest to the floor had '*Leif*' written on the side. There was no other description.

Kindra decided she's rather poke through the box than be polite. Here was her chance to learn more about her father through the items he deemed important enough to store. This was familiar ground for Kindra. Poking through boxes, reading old letters, and looking through old photo albums was a common occurrence for Kindra, as she learned about deceased family members. She shifted her body to begin freeing up the bottom box when she heard music.

It was faint. "*Was Kristen playing music in the kitchen?*" The music wasn't coming from the back wall, though. It was coming from Kindra's right side. She abandoned the box she had been trying to free and headed in that direction. The music was louder. It was a gentle melody that sounded as if it were being played on some kind of woodwind instrument. The sound made her think of spring and the feeling of being content. Kindra took a diagonal path toward the little window in the back right corner. As she drew closer, she could see three quarters of the structure's right-side wall was comprised by rock face. As Kindra neared the area where the rock face met the wooden wall and the little window, she realized the music was coming from her right side.

Kindra turned and headed back toward the garage doors, but stayed close to the rock face. The music was perfectly clear now. She looked around for some kind of music box or something that might have been disturbed to have started making music. Kindra moved some boxes around but couldn't find the source of the melody. She threw aside a moving blanket that had been sitting on top of a pile of plastic crates and started at the sight of a sword.

The sword was large and looked heavy. Its blade was stuck in a holder that was attached to a leather belt. The handle of the sword was rounded and there were definitely some pretty rocks, possibly real gemstones, embedded in the part that would stick out over one's hand for protection. Kindra now found herself wishing she knew more about swords. It didn't really look like the ones in the pirate movies. It was more like the swords from movies set in Medieval Times, but this one was really fancy. Even all dusty and dull, Kindra could tell this sword was meant to sparkle and catch the eye of those who walked by its barer.

Kindra reached out to pick the sword up as carefully as possible. Care probably wasn't necessary. The sword had to weigh twenty pounds. *How the heck do people use these things?* The thing that shocked Kindra more than anything, though, was the realization that the music was coming from the sword. It had gotten louder when she picked the sword up. Was it her imagination, or did the music pickup in tempo a bit as well? Kindra put her ear to the sword. It was definitely making the noise.

Kindra dropped the ancient-looking sword straight to the filthy floor of the garage when a voice came from behind her. "It's singing to you, isn't it?"

Kindra whirled around to face the direction of the soft, male voice. There was no one there. The voice spoke again. "Over here!"

Kindra looked up and slightly to the left. Waving at her, with his legs hanging off the side of a stack of storage boxes, was an animate version of one of the lawn gnomes from Kristen's garden. It was an old man with a long beard. Dressed as a farmer, his clothing was a little dated. Kindra supposed the clothes were about as old as him. Though Kindra was surprised to run into any man in this outbuilding, this man made her jaw drop. He was only about a foot tall.

"I asked you a question." The lawn gnome said. "Is it singing to you?"

Kindra couldn't speak. She had heard the question, and she knew the answer. She didn't particularly like the answer, but she knew it. Still, she could not form words to answer.

"Maybe we need to start a little slower. You seem pretty new to all of this. My name is Nils. I live here on the property and I help where I can. You might say I watch over the family. I've been doing so for quite some time. Kristen told me to expect a visitor and that you would be a daughter of Leif."

Kindra was thinking it was a good sign that this little gnome of a man at least knew Kristen's name, and he hadn't just wandered over to the property. Of course, he could be lying about everything else, but at least he was familiar with the house's occupant. She swallowed once, and then swallowed again. "Hi." She croaked. "I followed the sound of the music."

"So! It was singing to you! It's a beautiful song, isn't it? It's been a very long time since I've heard the sword's song. I was pretty sure it was a display for you, but I had to check to be sure you could actually hear it." Nils was rambling on as if all was normal.

Kindra's head was still too light. Singing swords, talking lawn ornaments...wait...living lawn ornaments! Living lawn ornaments who help out on the farm and live on the property. She was digesting it all. Kindra didn't quite believe it, but she was taking it in. There was definitely a very tiny, old man talking to her, and she definitely had heard music. Those were things she knew to be true. The music had stopped when she dropped the sword, but it started back up again softly.

"Go ahead," Nils urged. "A sword like that wasn't meant to be left on the floor."

Kindra bent to pick the sword up. As she touched it, the music quickened again. She had expected the sword to be cold, but the metal was actually quite warm, a bit like it was a living thing. As Kindra turned the sword over in her hands, the music slowed and eventually stopped. The metal glowed slightly through the dust, and then dimmed.

"I think I broke it." Kindra said.

"No. You can't just break a sword like that!" exclaimed Nils. "It's simply done greeting you. Its name is Forsvarer, and it has been in your family for millennia."

"The sword has a name?" Kindra said incredulously.

"All great swords have names." replied Nils.

"If this sword has been in my family so long, why is it sitting here in the garage?"

"It was waiting for you," said Nils, as if the answer to that question should be obvious.

It wasn't the answer Kindra was expecting, and it wasn't quite what she had meant by the question. Kindra slowly put Forsvarer back down and began backing away from Nils. She gave him a wave and turned for the double doors. She picked her way to the exit, slammed the door shut behind her, and quickly headed back to the house.

# CHAPTER 9

Kristen eyed Kindra as she entered the kitchen. The girl was as white as plaster. It made her copper hair look redder than it actually was.

"I take it you met Nils?" she said to Kindra.

Kindra dropped her body into the chair across from Kristen. "Yes. You have no idea how happy it makes me to know you are aware of his existence. That being said, I am still incredibly uncomfortable with the whole thing."

"Nils is harmless! Well, as long as you don't get on his bad side. Nissen have been known to play a prank or two on those who treat them unfairly."

"Nissen?" asked Kindra.

"Nissen are little troll-like people who live in the barns and outbuildings on peoples' farms. They look after the place, do some of the yard work, and feed the animals. Nils has been with our family for generations."

"He did mention something to that effect," sighed Kindra. "I suppose I'm going to need to stop being so shocked by this magical stuff. I have a dad who can teleport, and a whole family with abnormally long lives. There is a living lawn decoration in the garage and a singing sword to go with him."

"Forsvarer sang for you?" Kristen asked excitedly. "He's beautiful, isn't he? He won't sing for me no matter how many times Nils and I have tried to get him to do it. I can't believe I missed it."

Kindra was not sure what was more surprising; Kristen knowing about the sword, or that she seemed so happy the thing had played music. She knew Kristen had knowledge of a wealth of family secrets, but she had expected the unbelievable events of the last hour to illicit a reaction other than the glee she saw on her sister's face. Kristen was now tugging at Kindra's arm, attempting to pull her from the chair.

"There's something we need to know," was all Kristen would offer.

Kindra was not ready to try her legs, let alone return to the garage. She hadn't even moved on from Nissen watching over barns and singing swords with names, and Kristen was dragging her toward something else. Even as a child, Kindra had not easily swallowed myths and magical legends. She had let herself dream they might be real, but her heart was always grounded by the belief that all those stories had been created to explain the unexplainable. Kindra had never actually thought the unexplainable existed; she just figured no known phenomena was a cause for something, and everyone would laugh about how silly the legend was once the events could be explained logically.

Kindra wished that even that small part of her childhood-self had not desired any of those things in the stories to be true. She felt as if those childhood fantasies had made it possible for dreams to be real and therefore it was her own fault she was, in this moment, trying to grapple with fairytales meeting reality. Here it was, though, and her sister was tugging insistently, as if she was also embracing her inner child.

Kindra finally stood and allowed Kristen to tug her out the door and around to the side of the house. Kristen held her hand, tugging the entire distance as if they were two girls trying to catch the ice cream truck before it pulled away from the curb. Kristen flung open the door to the garage and called for Nils. The two women wove through the stacks of boxes back to the sword's resting place and found Nils still sitting on his stack of boxes.

"I figured you would return shortly." said Nils. "You were so pale when you left, I knew Kristen would have you back here in just a bit of time."

Kristen spoke breathlessly to Nils, "We need to have her try the door!"

"She didn't give me a chance," Nils moaned. "She was backpedaling out of here so fast, I couldn't even explain the significance of Forsvarer singing. I figured she would have tons of questions, but she just ran away! We're going to need to work on that."

Kristen went to the wall of the garage, about three feet to the right of the little window Kindra had seen from the backyard
. She beckoned Kindra over to her. Kindra picked her way to stand before the blank wall at Kristen's side. Nils hopped off his stack of boxes and scuttled over to stand behind the two women. Kristen took Kristen's hand and placed it on the wall at a height just above Kindra's left shoulder.

The wall was quite cold. This was the part of the wall that was created from the rock face behind the house. It had a bit of moisture to it, but it had no moss or algae growing on it. Kindra drew in a breath and waited for the wall to glow or to sing like the sword had. Nothing happened. Kindra turned to Kristen with a raised eyebrow. *And?*

"Just wait a moment," Kindra said in a tone that suggested she was a tad frustrated. "I've heard it can take a few –"

The wall moved. It was just a slight shift and may have even been Kindra's imagination. It moved again. This time a rough, rectangular portion of the wall had broken away and slid about a half inch away from Kindra. It was just enough for Kindra's hand to lose contact with the rock's surface.

"Go ahead," Nils said. "Push it open."

Kindra used both hands and leaned into the newly formed door. She easily slid the giant door-shaped boulder about a foot farther into the rock wall. If she pushed any farther, she would have to stand inside the wall itself to maintain contact with the rock. She pulled her hands back and looked at Kristen.

Kristen stared back at Kindra, open-mouthed. "I've only heard that this could happen. I've never actually seen the door open. I knew the door was here, but since Forsvarer has never even made a peep around me, I also knew I could not open it. Don't get me wrong, I have looked for the door, and I've tried to make it work. It has never even cracked."

Kristen took a step toward the door and made to push the slab a little farther back so the women could gain entrance. Kristen jumped back as if bitten by a snake. She whipped her head in Nils's direction. The little man only chuckled.

Nils looked sorrowfully at Kristen. "Though you are a daughter of Leif, the world beyond that doorway is not meant for you. Your place will always be here."

Kristen's blue eyes flashed ice at Nils but calmed as quickly as they had flared. "I guess I always knew that. No matter how many times we spoke of the adventures we would have together once we found the door, I think I always knew I wouldn't be able to use it. I couldn't help myself just now. I had to try."

Kindra was backing away from the door as this conversation was happening. Her sister and Nils were absolutely insane. Kristen seemed disappointed that she couldn't step into a dark, damp, unknown place. There was magic involved, and these two were not even afraid. Magic meant the rules had changed. Dealing with the dark didn't mean there might be spiders and bats anymore. If swords could sing and there were secret doors guarded by little mythical men, then there could be anything in that dark passageway.

Kristen caught her trying to leave. "Aren't you even curios what it is?"

"I have no interest in walking into a dark tunnel to be murdered by vampires or something. I came here to find out about my birth father, not to go spelunking. Looking through some photo albums and hearing some good stories were what I envisioned, not marching straight toward my death," said Kindra.

Kristen chuckled. "You want to see the ultimate family tree? That door is a passage to your father's realm; the realm of the elves. You have a substantial amount of family there. I'd say you would enjoy several generations of your family tree if you crossed here and now. The only time Papa even visits here is to send his truly gifted children to Alfheim. I've never even been allowed to watch. I am simply a guardian."

Kristen had a point. There were so many nights she had sat in front of her computer screen, wishing she could time travel to speak to her ancestors. She had wished to hear her great grandmother tell the story of her great grandfather courting her. Life had been so hard during the times of prior generations. Kindra had wanted to hear the survival stories from the family members themselves. On paper, her mother's family had seemed so strong. They had come through epidemics, food shortages, wars, sea voyages, and financial crashes. The stories were all lost now. Kindra had amassed documents depicting many of the events and how her family had been involved in or had been effected by, but could not even imagine the stories of how it had felt to them as the events unfolded..

"So, I take it you're going?" Kristen's voice broke through Kindra's thoughts.

Kindra had been so lost in her regrets for having no way to speak to her mother's ancestors that she had not realized she had started back toward the door in the rock wall. Kindra's hands were on the stone and she was about to push the rest of the way through.

"Wait!" Kristen spun around and pulled Forsvarer from its place among the crates and boxes. She pushed it into Kindra's hands. "You better take this; just as a precaution."

"None of Leif's other children took the sword when they went through the door. If they had, the sword wouldn't still be here."

"Well," said Kristen. "They went through to Alfheim, with Leif as a guide. They had him to explain things and protect them. Leif could make introductions on the other side. You are going alone. The sword will tell people where you came from. The sword is known in Alfheim. Also, if you encounter trouble, you can always try slicing at it with the sword!."

Kindra strapped the sword's belts around her waist. It took some time for her to figure out that it was basically two belts that formed an "x" below her navel. One belt was low on her left hip, but sat up on her waist when it got to her right side. The other belt crossed the first from low on her right hip to the right side of her waist. Where the two belts crossed on her left, they pinned a scabbard in place. The whole contraption was made of tooled leather, depicting symbols and rudimentary drawings of birds and flowers. The leatherwork was beautiful and fit to carry Forsvarer.

"See you soon," Kindra said to Kristen and Nils.

Kristen and Nils smiled and waved. The excitement was still sparkling in their eyes.

"I can't wait to hear all about it!" Kristen called to Kindra as she watched her sister push the stone open another six inches and disappear into the darkness beyond.

It was quiet for a few seconds, and then there were some muttered curses from Kindra. Kindra came stomping back into the garage with a scowl on her face. "Do either of you happen to have a flashlight?"

Kristen quickly picked up a torch that was hanging by the door. She grabbed a box of matches off the top of a nearby crate and handed them to Kindra. "Papa takes this. I'm guessing there are more of them along the passage. You can use this one to light the others."

Kindra took the torch and lit it with a match. She put the small box of matches in the back pocket of her jeans. She leaned into the dark tunnel and held the torch high. It threw about a ten-foot circle of light around her. It was nice to see around her, but there was a definite downside as well. The torch light made the area beyond seem even darker and Kindra could see nothing outside of her circle of light. Still, the things close to her didn't seem as creepy as she expected. Though the tunnel smelled damp, the rock that created the tunnel was dry to the touch. It was chilly in the tunnel, but not unbearable.

Kindra walked slowly in order to see what her circle of light permitted. If she walked too quickly, she was afraid she would stumble upon something without being able to prepare for it. The light from the doorway she had entered had just about disappeared behind her when she came to a torch hanging on the wall. She lit it with her own. As soon as she was sure the second torch had caught, the door behind her slid back into place. She was now alone in the passageway.

Kindra moved on, deeper into the tunnel. There were no creepy crawly things, which was a pleasant surprise. The tops of her ears started to itch slightly, and she brushed at them, thinking something was crawling on her, but she could see nothing else alive in the cave. The light from the torch behind her had only cast a small circle and was beginning to fade away when she saw light coming from in front of her. It was bright, like sunlight, but still seemed far off. Kindra headed for the light. She couldn't help wondering if she was now that silly moth headed toward its death and her stomach became queasy. Actually, she was somewhat light-headed as well. Kindra supposed the air was thinner than it had been outside of the tunnel.

As the light grew brighter, fresh air from the mouth of the tunnel caressed Kindra's face. When she reached the tunnel exit, she saw there was a place to hang her torch. She placed the torch in the holder and pulled the box of matches from her pocket. She placed them on the floor of the cave beneath the torch so they would stay safe and be waiting for her when she came back into the cave to head back to Husland.

Kindra went to the mouth of the tunnel and stepped out. She was standing on a ledge, several hundred feet up. This end of the tunnel was also in a flat rock-face, but it was not at ground level. Kindra reached for her phone to take a picture. Her phone! She had left it on Kristen's kitchen table. There would be no pictures on this trip. There would also be no texts or calls to her mother or Jess. Hopefully, Kristen would keep the phone charged and answer any calls if she was gone for more than a few hours. She really didn't need any search parties from The States being sent to Norway.

Kindra stood on the little cliff, in her jeans, t-shirt and tennis shoes, with a sword strapped to her waist and felt ridiculous. The mouth of the tunnel she had just vacated was behind her. She was high above a forested area, and the lands looked beautiful. She couldn't tell if there was any life below her, but if she found anyone, she was pretty sure they would get a laugh from her outfit.

# CHAPTER 10

Kindra located a staircase to her right. She supposed it was a staircase. There were many rocks jutting out of the cliff and they seemed to meander back and forth across the cliff face in a stairway like fashion. If she wasn't planning on sitting on the cliff and admiring the view all day, then this would need to be a staircase. She stepped down onto the first ledge and then made her way to the next. As long as she didn't look down, it was fairly easy. She made her way from ledge to ledge and was feeling at home, making the small leaps that were slowly bringing her down to ground level.

She stopped with about thirty feet to go. The stone steps were a bit more spread out here. Kindra took a moment to survey the area below her. She was in a forest of pine trees. Needles and pinecones covered the earth below. She saw no people, but there was life everywhere. There were deer, rabbits, and birds singing. It was cool and peaceful in this place. Even if Kindra had no idea where to go once she was on the ground, she felt like it would be a pleasant walk to wherever she went.

Kindra lined up for her next leap. The stone cracked beneath her back foot. Kindra moved her front foot to catch her balance, and the stone cracked even more. She was falling! She couldn't breathe. Her stomach was in her throat as she fell backward and watched the ledge on which she had been standing grow farther away. She was going to land on her back. She was going to die or never walk again.

Kindra opened her eyes. It was getting dark. She was lying on her back in the grass. The cliff face with the little stone ledges was off to her right. Birds chirped, and the sounds of the forest were all around her. She could hear a stream trickling somewhere in the distance. She was alive. Kindra was working hard to think through her pounding head. She was afraid to move. If she were alive, then she had to have broken many bones, including her back or neck.

There were footsteps behind Kindra. She was unable to see the owner due to her position on the forest floor. A man leaned over her. Well, not a man exactly. He had ears that rose to a graceful point and his canine teeth extended a bit more than was natural for a human. He was beautiful, though. Long, straight, blonde hair was loosely braided and left wisps framing his face. His hair was so blonde it was nearly white. He had a powerful jaw and high cheekbones that gave him the look of a younger person than he probably was. Kindra was about to fall in love with his radiant, almost glowing, face when he spoke.

The speech was not in a language she understood. It wasn't English; it wasn't Norwegian, and it was not directed at her. Three other males crowded into her view. They were now standing around her. All of them were beautiful in their own way, but the one to her right had a familiar feel to him. He had the darkest hair of all of them. Similar to Kindra's hair, it was brown and red to give the illusion of a copper color. Kindra was trying to place the familiarity when the first male she had seen drew a sword and placed it at her throat.

"Who are you and why have you walked through the gate into our realm?" asked the male with her life at the end of his sword.

Kindra didn't know if she could speak. She felt her eyes open wide and attention bouncing from face to beautiful face above her. She refocused on the one with the sword and croaked, "My name is Kindra Powers." None of the males showed any recognition when they heard the name.

"Whose bastard are you, halfling?" demanded the male on her left. He had a terrible scar from his right eye-brow to his left cheek that crossed the bridge of his nose. It looked as if the wound that had caused it should have killed him, but somehow it took very little from his otherwise perfect face.

Kindra wanted to answer them. She wanted to explain herself so she would not be killed for trespassing or some other written or unwritten law she had undoubtedly broken, but she couldn't speak. Scarface sounded so angry, and *'halfling'* was definitely an insult. *Was she a halfling? She supposed she was, by definition. She was half human and half elf. That would make her a Halfling.*

The familiar male on her right saved her from her own thoughts and probably saved her from having her throat cut over her inability to reply to the question. "She is another bastard of Leif's" he said. He kicked at the hilt of the sword pinned beneath Kindra's back. "She carries Forsvarer. She has come through the gate at Husland."

The male at her head removed his sword from her neck slowly. He came around to her left side. Scar face moved toward her feet to allow him space. Kneeling down beside her, and beginning to check Kindra's body for injuries, he spoke to her. "I am Krish." He gestured to Scarface and went on, "The angry one over here is Joral. Since Gunnar has already discovered the answer to Joral's question, I suspect Joral no longer feels the need to harm you."

"Gunnar!" It came out as more of a burst of surprise than Kindra would have liked. "My Uncle Gunnar?"

Gunnar scrunched up his face in what may have been disgust. "Yes. I suppose I am technically your uncle, though I have not considered Leif a brother for a long time. If not for the sword, you would not be identifiable as kin. You did not arrive with Leif and I have never heard him speak your name. I must hear how you have found yourself here, alone and in possession of our family sword."

"Later. We'll have time for stories later. Darkness is upon us and we will have bigger problems than a lost girl if we do not return to the castle soon." Krish looked to the male at Kindra's feet. "Help her up Bane. Let's be on our way."

Bane squatted and placed one arm under Kindra's neck and another under her knees. He pushed up with his legs and was standing with her in his arms as if she was weightless and the act had taken no effort at all. The man was massive. That may have been why he had lifted her with ease. The arms under her body were solid, and each had a circumference similar to that of her waist. Though the other three males in the group were powerfully built warriors, and Kindra's knowledge of Elves was limited, she could still tell Bane's excessive size and strength were unusual.

Bane lowered Kindra's feet to the floor and steadied her while she took in the feeling of wholeness. She had been afraid to move. She had thought she was paralyzed, her limbs bent and broken, but none of that was true. Kindra was fine. She was sore, but otherwise uninjured.

Krish must have seen the wonder on Kindra's face. He smiled at her and asked, "Did you not feel the change as you walked through the tunnel? The tickle in your ears? The ache in your teeth and body?"

Kindra had felt it. She had not known what it was at the time. Krish saw that on her face as well and he went on, "Your body has shifted to its Fae form now that you have left your world. Your world suppresses all things magical. It is a blessing to those trying to hide, but it is also a curse that allows evil to hide among humans without being noticed. You will still recognize yourself in a mirror but, while you are here in Alfheim, you will find your body and senses are...enhanced."

*Enhanced. What the heck did that mean?* Kindra understood it to mean she was either harder to break or faster to heal, but she suspected that was not the whole of it. As they started off away from the cliff face, she understood even more. She was light on her feet. Her steps were more intuitive. She did not find herself thinking about avoiding rocks and roots in the ground. It was different to the point where she sometimes found herself stumbling because her body wanted to step one way, but her mind wanted her to go a different direction. At least that explained how her enhanced body had accidentally fallen to what should have been her death.

"Stop thinking so much." growled Joral. "You're making a quick ten miles feel like ten times the distance!"

Kindra paled a bit. Ten miles was long enough to have them walking until dawn. It would take hours of trudging the uneven ground of the forest to reach their destination. She certainly didn't want to think about that. Instead, Kindra took in the forest. There were little eyes everywhere. Though the party walked only by moonlight, Kindra found she could see quite well. There were creatures she recognized, like raccoons and opossum, and some she didn't. Most were happy to go about their business without acknowledging the elves walking through the forest. Frogs peeped around them and moths flew by Kindra's head. Those little eyes were watching them from everywhere.

"Uncle Gunnar, what are the little things watching us from the trees and bushes?"

"Stop calling me that and calm your nerves. It's just the little folk and you have little to worry about. They seem to have taken an interest, but it is the good kind. It is fortuitous but lucky. We shall know when danger is near with so many little folk about us."

Now Kindra really wanted to see one. *Could she go over to a bush and call one out like a stray cat? Were they little old people like Nissen, or maybe they didn't look like people at all?* Kindra began weaving brief visions in her mind of the little folk with their little families in little houses with even littler pets. She was pretty sure she was getting none of the correct imagery when lights started appearing between the trees ahead.

"Welcome to Aergroth," said Krish as they broke through the trees and into a clearing. The group crossed the field of grass and stepped onto a wooden bridge that spanned a canyon about forty feet wide. As Kindra marveled that they had trekked ten miles and she had not even started sweating, let alone needed to stop to rest, she looked over the side of the bridge. She could hear the water running below, but could see nothing but darkness. It must have been a long distance to the bottom.

On the other side of the bridge, iron gates swung open at their approach and they trooped into a city bustling with activity. Kindra did not know what time it was, but it was several hours after dark and this place was still very much awake. There were vendors peddling on cobblestone streets, outside of shops of all varieties. Everything was lit by glowing balls mounted atop wooden posts. The light was greener than the streetlights in her realm, but the purpose was the same. Kindra was led down street after street, all lined with buildings of one to three stories and all lit by glowing light from fireplaces or greenish orbs like those in the streets.

The next turn had Kindra's mouth dropping open. Before her stood an actual castle. It was made of wood and stone and had spires like those in fairytales. There was a stone wall that ran from either side of an iron gate. These gates were already open, but they were flanked by two guards in uniforms of green and silver. Each guard stood impossibly still, with one hand on the hilt of his sword. Kindra might have thought the guards were statues, or at least frozen by magic if the one on the left hadn't dipped his head slightly in greeting to the males who paraded her through the gate.

Kindra fully expected to be marched into a throne room and made to kneel before a king or something, but it became evident that it would not play out that way at all. Bane and Joral peeled off in a different direction as the group entered the castle through the main archway at the end of the path from the gate. Kindra, Krish, and Gunnar went to the right and down a narrow staircase. The stairway spilled into a narrow passageway with other flights of stairs and passageways leading off in a multitude of directions. An elderly female in a plain tunic passed them as she headed in the other direction. She was carrying a woven basket of linens.

At the end of the hall, Krish pushed open a heavy wooden door and warmth met Kindra's face. The three walked into a bright kitchen with a large open fire in the center. Krish motioned for Kindra to go sit at a rectangular wooden table with benches attached on either side. She and Gunnar sat down and Krish went to speak to an older male, standing at a counter peeling potatoes. The male dropped his current task and set off on a new one.

Krish came to sit at the table. "Einar will bring us some coffee and something to eat. He has been the kitchen master here at Millspare for over sixty years and I think you'll find his brand of magic very tasty. Also, he is one of the few people in this world that I trust without reservation."

In no time, Einar had coffee poured in mugs. He placed a pitcher of milk and a sugar bowl on the table. Carefully, Einar laid small spoons beside each mug and a plate with a fork folded in a green cloth napkin edged with silver piping. Einar dropped a bowl full of something that smelled and looked like some kind of chili in front of each of them, placing a larger spoon at the side of each bowl. Lastly, he brought over a wooden board with breads and cheeses and a platter of small cakes and cookies. Einar then disappeared from the kitchen, as if he had never been in the room.

Gunnar turned his eyes to Kindra. He did not look at her with kindness, though his eyes were not cruel either. "It is time, daughter of Leif, for you to tell your story."

# CHAPTER 11

It took longer for Kindra to tell her story than it should have. The food Einar had provided was astonishingly good. The chili had actually been more of a stew, but made with ground quail meat. Kindra was grateful she had not been informed of that prior to tasting it because she may have balked at tasting the concoction and missed out on the amazing flavor. Kindra relayed her story, beginning with her discovery about whom her father was and the revelation of the promise her mother had made him keep.

To their credit, the males at the table stayed quiet and rarely interrupted the tale Kindra unfurled. At one point, between bites of bread seasoned with garlic and rosemary, Krish stopped Kindra to ask her impression of Leif. He was curious to know how he was surviving in her realm and if he seemed inclined to return. Kindra had shaken her head, explaining that he was little more than a drunk and appeared to be angry at the world. Gunnar stared at the wall during that explanation. With sadness in his eyes, he had only nodded his head slowly, as if things had been that way for a long time, and he was not surprised to hear that didn't seem to be changing.

Gunnar made her slow down and tell the part of her story where she came to discover Forsvarer in great detail. He was wide-eyed when she described the music that came from the sword. He was shaking his head in amazement. "Our family sword has not called to anyone in hundreds of years. Many of us have wielded it and it has served us well, but it has not been since before the time of King Andril that it has chosen its bearer."

"Nils told me it was rare for the sword to sing to anyone, but he didn't tell me it meant the sword chose me for anything."

"King Andril was chosen by the people and the sword to lead the country of Lillerem to victory over the Svartålfar." said Krish. "After the war was won, Lillerem enjoyed peace for thousands of years under Andril's rule and then that of his son Blaith"

"What happened? Are you no longer at peace?" Kindra questioned.

"We are at relative peace right now," Gunnar answered. "Blaith's eldest son was weak. When he took the throne, Lillerem fell into a slow decline. Minor transgressions went unpunished and grew into larger transgressions until those transgressions became more like treason. Lords in some parts of of the country declared themselves King of their own land and seceded from the country of Lillerem. There are now five separate kingdoms in the area that were once all part of the same country. Lillerem is the largest, but there has been unrest between all five Kingdoms, that grows with every year that passes."

"Somehow," Kindra said. "I knew this was all a land of fairytales, but I wasn't really expecting wars and rival kingdoms."

"There is nowhere in the Universe like the stories in your fairytales," said Gunnar quietly. "You probably expected that elves live in trees and go around planting shrubs and talking to flowers. There are no fairies flying around and sprinkling magic dust on young girls to make sure they get a chance to go to the ball and meet a prince. Evil is real, though. There is at least one wicked sorceress and several cruel kings. There are creatures of the darkness that make the monsters in your fairytales look like common house cats. The myths are based on reality, but much has changed in the interpretations over the millennia"

Kindra sat silently and finished her quail chili. She was coming to the realization that much of what she thought she had known about the world she was now in was just an outline. Her knowledge base was full of lies and half-truths. The rules she thought she would be playing by may or may not exist. She would have been better off coming here with no preconceived notions at all. The things she thought she knew could very well get her killed.

"Come now," said Krish. "Let's find you a room and let you clean up and rest. Tomorrow we must take you before Viktor. He is a mayor of sorts in this city. He and his wife Ruth rule over the people of Aergroth."

Gunnar wished Kindra a good night and left for his own duties. Krish took Kindra back into the servants' passageway and flagged down the elderly woman who had been carrying the laundry basket earlier. The woman looked Kindra over with distaste. Kindra was not sure if it was she herself that had the woman scrunching her face up like that, or if it was the state of her hair and clothing. She suspected she smelled even worse than she looked.

Mildred, as the woman was called, took Kindra up one of the staircases near the middle of the hall. Kindra had no idea how this female, or anyone for that matter, could know where one would arrive using each stairway and passage. The stairs Mildred took with Kindra let them out in an ornate hall with a plush green carpet running its length. There were sconces outside each of the wooden doors along the hall, and in each was a faintly glowing green orb. Mildred opened the first door on the right and Kindra fell right back into one of her fairytales. The room was decorated with pink and lavender pastels with white accents. It looked like the room should belong to a young girl, dreaming of becoming a fairy princess. The wood floor had a white oval carpet covering most of it. It stopped about a foot shy of a stone fireplace sitting just to the left of the door from which they had entered. The fire was burning and welcoming.

There was a large bed with four posts to the right. Atop the four posts was a lacy white canopy that came down all around the sides of the mattress to the floor. Through the sheer canopy, Kindra could see a lavender blanket with embroidered pink and white flowers. There were enough pillows on the bed, all pink and lavender, to rest eight heads, though the bed could probably only fit three people comfortably.

Kindra crossed the room to the large double window. She turned the metal latch and pushed the frames out like shutters to let in the crisp night air. Kindra moved right and went to a large armoire. She pulled open the two doors at the same time. On the left were drawers and on the right was a rod for hanging articles of clothing. The entire freestanding closet was full of women's clothes. Mildred came to Kindra's side and pulled open one of the drawers. She withdrew a white nightgown trimmed in the same pastel pink as the room and spread it on the bed.

Mildred gestured toward the door standing on the wall opposite the bed. "I've drawn you a bath. Go drop yourself in the tub and I'll be in soon to scrub that filth from your hair."

Kindra crossed the room and opened the door to a small bathing chamber. There was a free-standing tub near a small window of stained glass. She dipped her hand in the water and found it to be hot. Kindra saw no faucet, but there were several buckets at the foot of the tub. *"Well, if there is no running water, I better hop in before the water gets cold."* Was her only thought as she dropped her clothes to the floor and climbed into the tub.

Mildred had not been exaggerating when she had said she would be in soon. Kindra had just lowered herself into the tub and started looking around the chamber when Mildred strode in with a basket of soaps, tonics and powders. The basket made the room immediately smell of lavender. Mildred set the basket down on the floor and took a seat on a stool behind Kindra. She then set to work scrubbing Kindra's hair, then her back.

"Dip under to rinse and be sure to scrub the rest of your parts. The water is probably getting a chill already. I'll leave a cloth for drying and some scents to apply if you wish. Your night gown is already on the bed, as you know. Shut the wash door behind you when you enter the bedchamber. I'll send the young maids in to scrub the tub clean. Get some rest." Mildred called the last part as she scooted out a door that did not lead back through Kindra's bedroom. *This place is a maze.*

Kindra mused as she scrubbed her legs, feet, arms, and hands. Those were the parts that seemed to have the most dirt caked on them. She finished bathing and stood up in the tub, wrapping the huge towel Mildred had left around her body. She made sure to shut the door behind her as she entered the bedroom, and it was only seconds before she heard the bustling of the cleaning crew in the bathroom behind her. *"Better than any hotel service I've ever experienced."* Kindra thought.

Kindra put on the nightgown and wrapped the towel around her hair; twisting it up over her head and tucking it in like a turban. She climbed into the fluffy bed and proceeded to push all but two of the pillows to the far side. She closed her eyes and had the faintest thought that she should be nervous about meeting Viktor and Ruth in the morning before she fell asleep.

Kindra was awake again in seconds. Well, it was several hours, but it felt like mere seconds to her. Mildred was bustling about the room, pulling clothing from the giant armoire. She tossed a green gown with gold lace trim at the neckline onto the bed. She then opened a drawer and pulled out a pair of velvet slippers in the exact same shade of green. Golden flowers were embroidered over the toes.

"Am I going to meet the mayor or am I going to the prom?" Kindra quipped.

Mildred didn't even glance at Kindra when she replied, "I have no idea what these things are you are speaking of, but I gather the meaning. You will dress in court attire to meet the Lord and Lady of the house."

*"Lord and Lady? This is not a house, it's a freakin' castle! How am I even going to get into that dress? It is beautiful, though."* Kindra's mind was firing in all directions. The nerves were definitely here now. She was starting to feel nauseous. Kindra went to stand up and her head spun. She sat back down on the bed.

"Goodness girl!" Mildred exclaimed. "You look like you've lost all your blood! This is no time to fret so much. You'll go down to breakfast and my husband will make sure you are well fed and prepared for your visit. It is only a dress and Viktor and Ruth are kind people. There is no need to worry."

Kindra took a few deep breaths. She understood why she was panicking. She had taken in a lot of unbelievable information in the last twenty-four hours. She had then turned into an elf with healing powers. Kindra was in a parallel world with magic. There were kings, and courts, and evil monsters. She had to give herself a bit of a break. It was a lot to absorb. After a few more deep breaths, Kindra stood. She was ready to face the day.

That was true until Mildred ripped Kindra's nightgown off over her head and she had to spin around to hide her womanhood from the old female. It was only embarrassing for a few seconds, though. Mildred had Kindra lifting her hands up and had slipped the dress over Kindra's head, pulling it down over her body before a minute had passed.

As Mildred laced the back of the dress, she said, "I have been dressing young ladies of the court for longer than you have been drawing breath. Trust me, girl, there is nothing you have that I have not seen."

Feeling a bit foolish, Kindra slipped her feet into the velvet slippers. Mildred guided her over to the dressing table and sat her down in front of the mirror. Kindra watched the reflection of Mildred twisting and pulling her hair. She made several braids and then swooped them up and pinned them to Kindra's head. The braids met at the top of her head, where Mildred wrapped them around each other in a bun-like creation, leaving one long, thicker braid coming out from the center and down to Kindra's shoulders. The hair style allowed her ears to show. Kindra could see that her ears now held the slightest point at the ends.

"That looks amazing!" Kindra said through grinning teeth. "I wish I could style hair like this!"

"You have beautiful hair, girl. It is one thing you have going for you. The many colors in your hair will show because of the braids and the long waves will ensure the hair stays put. You can't do this with limp straight hair. You need the hair to be a little wild from the start to get it good and tamed in this way."

Kindra saw the twinkle in Mildred's eyes. The old female had enjoyed this part. Kindra supposed Mildred would have made an excellent hair stylist in her world. She could play with hair all day and spread gossip in her very own shop. Kindra pictured Mildred, with a lot more years to practice than any human, being booked all day, each day. Women and girls would brag that they had hair styled by Mildred. Brides would be complimented more for the stunning up-dos Mildred could create than the pricey dresses they wore for the big day.

It was a sweet picture until Mildred's curt voice reminded Kindra that Mildred did not have the personality for such a job. "Come on, girl.

You absolutely cannot be late and you'll want to eat before you head to breakfast with the Lord and Lady."

"Wait." Kindra was confused. "Why would I need to eat before I go to eat?"

"The formal breakfast is more of a brunch and it spans about two hours. There are many courses and they are each quite small. If you do not wish to starve before you receive one of the larger courses, or worse, gobble your food like a starving hound, you will have a light breakfast before attending the formal meal."

The formal meal sounded pretty complicated, but Kindra supposed eating before going to that meal did make good sense. She allowed herself to be whisked down to the kitchen where Einar was just laying out a cup of coffee, a bowl, and a spoon. Mildred gave Einar a peck on the cheek and patted his shoulder. She then hurried off.

"Wait…" A smile slowly crept across Kindra's face. Are you and Mildred…"

"Married for over 200 years." The old man chirped with a smile on his own on his face.

Kindra nodded. That was a long time to love a person. More than that, how could they not get bored with one another's company? She and Tom hadn't even been married long enough for Kindra to get her last name changed on any official document other than her Social Security Card. It was the primary reason she still used her maiden name for most occasions. At school, she would always be Ms. Powers, so she hadn't gotten around to changing her name with DMV or the Department of Education for her School Psychologist License. In the short time she and Tom had lived together, Kindra had already had the feeling of being bored a few times. They had easily settled into the routines of life, and Kindra had wondered if it would be enough for her. The hope had been that starting a family would break up the monotony for them and make things more exciting. They had never found out if it would work. Kindra would do anything to have a second chance at her monotonous life with Tom. The first one had just been far too short.

Einar had provided plain oatmeal. He put a bowl of brown sugar next to her to add as she wished. Kindra had never been a fan of oatmeal, but she supposed it would be perfect for filling her stomach.

Einar stood hovering behind her, as if waiting for approval regarding the meal. He was not a tall male, and he was a bit more plump than the other elves Kindra had seen so far. He had a bit of a roll to his walk and his face was always a little red. It may have been from the heat of the kitchen, or it may have been from carrying around a bit of extra weight. Kindra wasn't sure she could bring herself to compliment the male on a bowl of oatmeal. There really wasn't much to it.

Finally Kindra relented, "It's good" she said. "It reminds me of home."

"Oh no, Princess, I was not looking for approval. I was merely waiting for you to have a few bites before hoping to ask you a few questions about your world."

"Princess? I am no princess. I know the dress makes me look like royalty, but I assure you, I am just a normal woman. Why don't you sit? Answering questions is a good way to thank you for the food you've been giving me."

"I beg your pardon, princess, but I fear Krish and Gunnar may have left out some important information about your lineage. You are, indeed, royalty."

"Ok Einar, you've got my attention. Sit down and we can answer each other's questions."

Einar sat across from Kindra with a small mug of coffee. He took a seat, swallowed, and then asked a question he had probably been holding in since she arrived. "I saw by the sword you carried that you are descended from King Andril. Since Krish and Gunnar had no knowledge of you prior to last night, I knew you had been hidden in the human realm. There is only one elf who remains in the human realm of breeding age, so I have deduced that you are a daughter of Leif. Mildred and I raised Leif from an infant to the time he and his brother were hidden in the realm of the mortals. It was very long ago, but we still think of him. I was hoping you might tell me something about him. Gunnar insists all is well and tells me Leif prefers mortals to his Elven brethren. How is Leif really fairing? Why has he never returned?"

"I don't know much I'm afraid, and what I do know does not seem to paint a very happy picture. I suspect Gunnar has been protecting you from the truth. I was told by a sister of mine that Leif was once happy in the world of mortals, so Gunnar may have simply omitted the most recent parts of the story."

"Please tell me the truth. I may be an old male, but I can bear the weight of it," implored Einar.

Kindra took a breath, and then told Einar all she knew about Leif's current location, the trouble he had found for himself, and how he allowed himself to remain sick when he could easily heal himself. "I suspect he is punishing himself for things he perceives as wrongs he has done to others."

Einar bowed his head. "I suspected as much. Even as a young one, Leif reminded me of his kind-hearted uncle. He and his uncle both loved fiercely, but this made it impossible for them to lead. Their forgiving nature extended to everyone but themselves. It was as if Leif were created from the same mold as King Blaith's son, King Lars.

"I'm sure Gunnar told you that Lars's reign was the downfall of our peaceful kingdom. Understand that this was not intentional on the part of Lars. Lars was just never able to manifest even an inkling of stern leadership. The people loved him for his compassion, but it did not take long for many to take advantage of the kindness and empathy of which Lars was made. Maybe Leif knew he was cut from that same cloth. Maybe that is why he stayed far from Alfheim, even after he was of age and was called to return."

"It sounds reasonable and does fit with what I saw of him. You say Lars was Leif's uncle. Who was Leif's father?" Kindra asked.

"King Blaith had two sons and a daughter. You already know of Lars. Ulford was the younger son. He was cruel. We often said it would have been better for Blaith to have had one son with the compassion of Lars and the strength of Ulford. That would have created the perfect heir to the throne. Instead, Blaith ended up with one son who was loving and far too kind to be a good ruler, and another son who took pleasure in hurting animals as a child and grew to take pleasure in hurting people as an adult.

"Ulford was the first to take control of his own kingdom and succeed from Lillerem. He has declared himself king of the second largest region in Alfheim. He calls his Kingdom Dredfall and rules over it mercilessly. Those who oppose his rule are enslaved, as well as any who cannot provide for themselves while still helping to provide to the King and the Kingdom."

"I can see why Leif might have some mental issues. He has the heart of his uncle but was raised by a cruel monster!"

"Oh no, child! I didn't mean to mislead you. Ulford is not Leif's father. I simply began the story by telling of Blaith's three children. Leif is the child of Blaith's daughter, Ekkelle. Ekkelle is the beautiful, and eldest, child of Blaith. She would have been the best choice for an heir to Blaith's throne had she not been female. Ekkelle fell in love with a farmer named Knut and left royalty behind. She never would have been accepted as a ruler anyway, since Lillerem has always had a king, never a queen. Knut and Ekkelle raised animals and farmed Knut's lands for several centuries before Ulford's men killed them both and razed the farm. The eldest children of that marriage were the ones who ushered as many of the younger children as they could to the human realm, and to the hidden safety it offered."

"I'm not sure which is worse for one's mental well-being. He didn't have a cold-hearted father, but instead, had parents who were murdered by a cold-hearted uncle. Great uncle Ulford sounds like he has an inferiority complex and felt the need to rid himself of any competition," Kindra offered her psychological diagnosis.

"You are correct, child. Ulford killed many of your aunts and uncles on the day your grandparents were murdered and has killed several more since that day. He desires to remove the entire family line from existence. Lars never married. He and his mate were both male. They adopted a son, Erik. Erik currently sits on the throne of Lillerem and is just passive enough for Ulford to allow him to remain there. You met his eldest son, Krish, last night."

"So, both Gunnar and Krish are princes and Krish is heir to Lillerem's throne?"

"Actually, all four males who found you in the woods are princes. Joral is the son of Ulford. Joral left his father's kingdom to serve under Viktor and Ruth. It was his own father who gave Joral the scar on his face. Bane is a bit of an experiment. He too is a reject offspring of Ulford's. Bane was the result of Ulford raping one of his own half-troll slave women. I doubt Ulford even knows Bane is related to him. Since the last King of Lillerem in its entirety was Blaith, all of his descendants are considered to be princes and princesses."

# CHAPTER 12

Kindra stood before the ornate double doors of the dining hall with the four princes, contemplating her family tree. Uncle Gunnar stood to her left and her second cousin, Krish, was beside him. On her right were half-brothers, cousins once removed from herself, Joral and Bane. If Kindra, with her background in Genealogy, was having this difficult of a time connecting the family dots, she couldn't imagine others would be able to figure out the family relations easily. Kindra did know, with certainty, that all five of them were royalty and all five of them were related to the King of Lillerem and the King of Dredfall in one way or another.

"Before you take me in there," Kindra started. "Are we related to Viktor and Ruth in any way?"

"I see you are catching on cousin," said Krish. "You must have spoken with Einar or Mildred. Ruth is sister to Leif and Gunnar. She is the eldest surviving child of Ekkelle and Knut."

"So, do I call her Aunt Ruth?" asked Kindra.

"No. It is best you simply call her Lady Ruth, like everyone else in the castle. She will know who you are because we have already informed her. There is no need for the rest of the court to know that more of Ekkelle's family has arrived at Millspare." said Gunnar.

"Is that why you don't want me calling you Uncle Gunnar?"

"Partly. The other reason is because I do not like it." Gunnar pushed open the doors to the dining hall, effectively ending the conversation.

The brightly lit room was enormous. Kindra could see the elegantly dressed couple at the far end of the table that were undoubtedly the Lord and Lady of the house. Along each side of the table were about twenty other lords and ladies of the court. Two seats on the right side of the table and three seats on the left side of the table nearest to Viktor and were vacant. Bane and Joral moved off to the right, so Kindra followed Gunnar and Krish to the left. Krish held out the chair next to Viktor for Kindra to take and gently guided it under her as she did.

There was no time for uncomfortable silence when Ruth immediately leaned over her husband to place her hand over the back of Kindra's wrist. "Welcome to Millspare Kindra! We're so very happy to have you as our honored guest."

"Thank you, Lady Ruth. It is very nice to be here. Your home is beautiful." Kindra wasn't sure what she meant by the word home. She could have meant Millspare, she may have meant Aergroth, or even Lillerem. Kindra supposed she was probably referencing all of Alfheim, though she had only seen about ten miles of it.

Viktor smiled at his wife, then at Kindra. "We do try. I hope you have found all that you need and desire to be available to you."

"I have! Thank you. It was incredible that the clothing in my room all seems to fit me perfectly." Kindra gestured toward the gown in which Mildred had dressed her.

"It's magic." Viktor said and winked. The man reminded her of the uncle all the kids loved. He would be the man that slipped dollar bills into your hand when he wished you Merry Christmas at the family party.

Though there were countless others at the long table, no one addressed Kindra or the four princes. They politely continued the conversations they had been engaged in before the arrival of the party of five. Kindra had never seen such impeccable manners. While Gunnar filled his sister- and brother-in-law in on the activity the four princes had seen on patrol the prior day, Kindra stole glances at the others around the table.

Viktor had dark hair. It was brown, but so close to black that Kindra decided it was easier to think of it as such. His eyes were violet. It was a color one would not see in her human realm, and it was beautiful. He had laugh lines around his eyes and mouth, suggesting his good nature was a constant, even when he was not meeting a newly found niece. He was well-muscled and Kindra suspected it was a good thing he had a pleasant personality or he would have no trouble using his strength for less than good actions.

Ruth was absolutely stunning. When Kindra had been told she was nice, she had immediately pictured a plump woman with rosy cheeks and bright eyes. The only part of her vision that had been correct was the sparkle in Ruth's ice-blue eyes. Ruth was very fair. Her hair was so blonde it looked white. Her fingers were long and delicate. Though Ruth was seated, Kindra imagined she must be fairly tall, and she was anything but plump.

The people sitting on the far side of the table from Kindra reminded her of well-dressed high school students. They may have had the best manors of any beings Kindra had ever seen, but the more she watched them, the more she could see the façade. The females were cliquish. Some women seemed to ignore others while trying to gain the favor of additional females. The males were boastful. Their conversations revolved around land holdings and winning the attention of females. It was actually quite comical. With the little Kindra knew of the important issues brewing between Lillerem and the surrounding territories, she felt as if these people placed themselves above those issues. It was like they were sitting and discussing important concepts like the weather while the rest of the world was concerned with petty things like war. It all seemed very backward. If these were the people with power and money, shouldn't they be the ones discussing the future of Lillerem? Maybe it was simply not polite conversation.

Kindra became aware of the lord sitting next to Bane. He was staring at her. He must have decided to speak to her and was now awaiting an answer. Kindra hadn't been paying attention. Some things did not change, no matter which realm one was in. Kindra was about to ask the male to repeat his question when the entire room shook as if there were an earthquake.

Mildred burst through the servants' door, off to Kindra's left. She looked into

Krish's eyes. "You must get the family out. Aergroth is under attack."

Mildred thrust Forsvarer into Kindra's hands and pulled her up out of her chair. "Stick close to Krish and Gunnar, girl. They will keep you safe."

The guests at the table had been silent as Mildred spoke. There was now a rush for the wooden doors where Kindra had entered only minutes before. Bane and Joral followed Mildred to the servants' door. They led the way, with Viktor and Ruth behind them. Gunnar grabbed Kindra's hand and tugged her along with Krish bringing up the rear. They went down the stairs into the servant passage. The group veered off to the right and down another flight of stairs. They took another short passage and pushed through a door at the end.

There were horses in stalls. The group had come out of the passage and into the stables. "Can you ride?" asked Krish of Kindra.

"I can, but it's been about ten years since I've been on a horse."

"Let's hope you get the feel back quickly. We're going to need to move fast."

Krish boosted Kindra up onto a beautiful brown mare. Kindra spread her skirts around the sides and back of the horse. Kindra had certainly never ridden a horse in a dress before, and it may have actually been closer to twenty years since she had been on one of the animals. She adjusted her sword so that it fell behind her right thigh, against the flank of the horse. She gripped the reigns Western Style and prepared for the inevitable bouncing and jostling, but then she decided to switch her style to English. Though she was not familiar with the type of saddle used by these horses, she assumed English riding would be closer to what a horse would expect in a land of kings and courts. This also had the added benefit of freeing up her hand to hold down her skirt or to grab her sword if she needed it…not that she actually knew the proper way to use that, either.

The seven horses thundered from the stables and across a short field. There was no bridge or canyon to cross here at the rear of the castle. It was just a quick dip into the forest after passing through another iron gate embedded within the stone walls. Mildred had not mounted a horse and had been left behind. Kindra imagined Mildred would never have left her husband, but she did briefly wonder how she might be able to change her dress without Mildred's help. The horses were fast. Kindra was glad her horse was content to run with the rest of the pack. Between the branches whipping her in the face and there being no discernable road or trail to follow anyway, Kindra had her eyes closed more often than she had them open

It didn't seem like anyone was following them, but her champions were not taking any chances. They rode at the same breakneck pace as they had from the start, for miles. Bane led the pack, cutting a path through shrubs and picking the routes up hills and over streams. He finally slowed the group to a leisurely trot when the horses started frothing from their mouths. Kindra wasn't sure if Bane felt bad for the horses, or if he was concerned the pace might kill their transportation, but the horses appreciated the change of pace. They stopped at the next stream and dismounted to let the horses drink and rest.

Kindra's dismount was more like a graceful slide that turned into a plop when she discovered she hadn't been as close to the ground as she expected. When her feet did hit the ground, her knees buckled and Kindra fell backward onto her rear. She just sat on the ground and watched as Viktor, already on the ground, held a hand out to Ruth and helped her gently to the ground.

Ruth turned her sparkling eyes down to Kindra. "You had only to wait a moment, and our gallant warriors would have kept you out of the dirt."

Kindra could see how hard Ruth was working to keep herself from laughing. "I'm glad you have kept your sense of humor as we flee for our lives."

Viktor helped Kindra to her feet. "My wife is an accomplished with a sword and upon a horse, but I have found that donning a beautiful gown renders her absolutely useless."

"In your wife's defense," Kindra was whined a bit, "these dresses are beautiful, but they do restrict one's movements quite a bit."

"You know," Ruth began, "You could also use your magic to take yourself down from your horse."

"I don't have any magic." Kindra reminded Ruth. "I am but a lowly human."

Ruth looked at her husband with the eye twinkle that was becoming more annoying than stunning. Ruth turned back to Kindra and looked at her with no twinkle. Her eyes were icy and cold. Kindra had no idea the woman could have possessed such an expression.

"A half-ling daughter of Leif, to whom the family sword has sung, thinks she possesses no magic? Ruth gestured toward Kindra's pointed ears. You are certainly no human, and I'm willing to bet you possess more magic than any of us standing here now. Leif has power so strong that he is even able to wield it in the human realm, and the sword has never chosen to sing to him. He kept you so secret that none of us even knew of your existence until you fell from a cliff in our front yard. It took your body less than an hour to heal itself from injuries that would have killed a lesser Fae and you believe you have no magic?"

As Ruth spoke, her words went from being about Kindra to being directed at Kindra. Kindra could not help but feel as if she were under attack. The sweet and beautiful Lady of Aergroth; Kindra's Aunt Ruth, now looked as if she may slice Kindra's throat here in the woods next to this passively trickling stream. Gunnar came to Kindra's rescue by calmly walking between the two females. He placed his hand on Ruth's shoulder and bent to say something to her that only she could hear.

Ruth's eyes quieted. The rage that had been there a moment before was gone. Ruth's head bowed slightly and when she looked up again, her eyes were apologetic. She quietly turned away from Kindra and went to her husband. Viktor's violet eyes apologized to Kindra as he turned to guide his wife toward a large boulder to sit her down. Ruth was crying.

"What the hell was that all about?" Kindra demanded of Gunnar.

"There is a good possibility that you may need a bit more information about your background and our position here in Lillerem. Please don't hold anything against Ruth. Many of us have a great deal of hope for what your arrival here means to our realm. We all just thought we'd have a bit more time to prime you for the tasks ahead."

"The tasks ahead?" Kindra was incredulous. I came here to learn about my Elven family and lineage. I'm trying to complete my family tree. I was convinced to come here because of a genealogy hobby and a desire to discover where I come from. There was no mention of magic, war or tasks to be completed!"

It was Kindra's turn to be angry. She had been scared as they fled the castle, through the trees. She had felt as if she'd accidentally stepped into someone else's problems. She had been willing to outrun them for now, holding onto the knowledge that she could wait until they stopped and then ask to be taken back to the gate so she could go back home. The expectation from these extended family members that she might stay and that she may play a role in dealing with the unrest in this country was sending her into a near rage.

Kindra had been backing away from Gunnar as she seethed. She had backed herself right up to the edge of the stream. She felt the heel of her left foot come down on open air and she knew she was about to tumble onto her rear again, and this time she would be wet. Gunnar lunged to try to catch her, but he was too far from her to be in time to prevent the fall. Kindra accepted her fate and stepped back to tumble into the water, but she did not fall.

Instead, Kindra found herself gliding over the water to the far side of the stream. She hovered on the opposite bank for a second and looked at Gunnar. In an eye blink, she was back on the other side of the stream and standing before Gunnar. A slow smile took over Gunnar's face. He slowly shook his head from side-to-side.

"No worries, Ruth!" he called to the woman on the rock. "We were wrong. She definitely doesn't have any magic."

He turned away from Kindra and went to help the other three princes set up camp. Kindra slowly walked over to Ruth and sat beside her on the rock. Ruth didn't say anything. The performance Kindra had just given had been enough for Kindra to prove Ruth's point. Ruth had been correct, and Kindra was now forced to admit she did, indeed, have magic.

# CHAPTER 13

After they had all eaten a dinner of dried meats and bread, Gunnar handed Forsvarer to Kindra and beckoned her into a small clearing. Kindra knew where this was going. She had been carrying the sword for about twenty-four hours now and had no clue how to use it. Actually, she still felt silly with it strapped to her body; as if she were on her way to a Halloween party.

Gunnar drew his own sword and held it before his body with two hands. Kindra lifted her sword and placed her feet in the same position as Gunnar's. Well, Kindra had thought she had mimicked Gunnar's stance, but he immediately dropped his own sword and went over to her and repositioned her feet. He raised her arms up about two inches and turned her upper torso to face slightly to her right side.

"Drop your sword and take two steps to your right."

Kindra did as she was instructed. She let the heavy sword fall to her side and stepped twice to her right.

"Now," continued Gunnar. "Take up your stance again."

Kindra positioned her feet again and raised her sword in two hands. As an after-thought, she twisted a bit to the right. Gunnar repositioned her hands, having to raise them up again, and kicked her feet together a bit.

"Not terrible." Gunnar said. "Do it again."

They spent an hour like this. Kindra breaking her stance and taking a few steps, then repositioning herself. Gunnar spent less time readjusting her at each attempt until she was finding her stance flawlessly. It was very difficult for her to raise the sword as high as he liked, and she sometimes forgot to twist her body so she would be ready to strike. She repeated the exercise hundreds of times. When Gunnar finally allowed her to stop and told her to get some sleep, Kindra was exhausted. Who would have known that simply striking a pose could be so draining? She curled up on the pile of blankets that now made up her bed and tucked Forsvarer beside her.

Kindra had only been sleeping for an hour or two when Gunnar shook her awake. The forest was absolutely silent. She heard no threat and could not imagine why she was not still sleeping. It then occurred to her that the silence probably was the threat. It was unnatural for there to be no noises in the woods. She sat quietly, listening for any sound. It was not her hearing that alerted her to the problem, though; it was her new Elven strength sense of smell.

She picked up on the smell of decay. It wasn't overpowering, but it was relatively close. The scent wasn't the same as a rotting animal, not that death aroma that is unmistakable. It was more like the smell of mushrooms as you slice them. It was a damp kind of smell that had not been in the air when she went to sleep, and it was getting stronger. There was slow movement off to her left, and she turned her head to see what had caused it. She saw nothing.

The same movement flashed to her right. This time, when she swung her head in that direction, she caught a stocky, humanoid form dipping behind the trees. Kindra's eyes widened. She felt a scream coming and commanded herself to remain silent. Kindra was beginning to shake. She took a few deep breaths and began inching her right hand to her sword. Kindra simultaneously picked up the sword and got to her feet. She assumed the fighting position she had been practicing a few hours prior; raising her hands an extra inch or two at the last moment.

Something big burst from the trees and headed straight for her. Gunnar jumped in front of her and sliced his sword swiftly through the air through the creature's chest. The sword glided as if it were slicing through air and the creature disintegrated before Gunnar had even finished his swipe.

Gunnar turned toward her and poked his sword over her right shoulder. She swiveled her head in time to see a second creature disappear, turning into a dark mist. Kindra looked to the far side of their camp in time to see Krish swipe through one of the creatures and Bane through another. The creatures did not actually die; they just disappeared when someone sent a sword through their dark bodies. The scent of rot grew stronger with every creature that was ended.

Only a few minutes had passed. The princes, Kindra, Viktor and Ruth, all stood as statues throughout the camp, waiting for the next attack. Kindra heard a cricket. A frog then took started peeping near the stream. Slowly, all the night sounds of the forest returned and Kindra relaxed her fighting stance.

Gunnar cut off the questions about to spill from Kindra's mouth. "Well, your highness, your fighting stance is impeccable. With any luck, the next time we are attacked, you might deign to actually help fight off the assailants."

"You didn't teach me anything else! I took up my stance. I wasn't going to go chasing after those creatures when I've never even swung a sword! What were those things, anyway?"

"Relax Kindra. I merely found it amusing that everyone around you fought for their lives and yours, while you became a statue. If anything, I've learned that you are a good student and you train easily. I also learned not to expect you to take things into your own hands though and that I should probably dedicate some time to showing you at least some basic sword play as soon as possible if I expect you to be able to defend yourself or be helpful in a scrap."

"I'm glad you find my inability to defend myself entertaining and educational. I'll ask again, what were those things?" Kindra said in a far from amused tone.

Krish came to stand beside Gunnar. "I am unsure what they were. They are nothing like the evils I have seen here or in my travels. I only know they had malicious intent by their smell."

Gunnar added, "I have never seen them either. I saw the moment when you picked up on the scent, Kindra. That is part of your training as well. All of your senses are heightened by your Fae blood here in Alfheim and you should trust those senses at all times."

Joral climbed onto a large rock near the stream and sat atop it. The moonlight lit up the scar across his face. "I will remain on watch. You all get some sleep."

No one argued. Kindra felt like the males should have been a bit more like in the movies, and each offered to *'take the first watch'* so the others could sleep. She had to remind herself, crazy as the situation was, this was not a movie. It made good sense to take Joral up on his offer and then make an offer yourself the next time the opportunity arose. As Kindra tried to go back to sleep, she realized how silly those movies really were. At the first sign of danger, the men started politely arguing over who wasn't going to sleep The following nights, there always seemed to be a schedule of watches, though the viewer never actually saw the scene where the schedule had been created. For once, Kindra's over-active mind played in her favor. It was much easier to drift back to sleep thinking about ridiculous movies than it would have been if she were thinking about the attack.

In the morning, Kindra startled awake. She knew she had been dreaming, and it had been horrible, but already the subject of the dream had faded. Even the fear and dread that had lingered through her waking was dissipating quickly in the bright sunlight that greeted her. The princes were already awake, but Viktor and Ruth lay sleeping.

Gunnar gave her some bread to put in her stomach. When she had finished, he gestured for her to grab her sword. She did so and followed him to the clearing. She took up her stance and immediately let the sword fall. Her shoulders had screamed at her as soon as she had lifted her arms. Gunnar just laughed and waited. She struggled back into her fighting stance. Just when she was about to break her stance and pull back into it, Gunnar held up a hand.

"Not like last night," he said. "Hold your stance and watch me. When I am done, repeat the movements."

Gunnar demonstrated several steps and swoops with his sword and then turned to watch Kindra complete the same steps. She did the best she could and finished her movement back in her stance. Gunnar repeated the movements again and turned to her once more to watch. He repeated the steps until she was doing them correctly without his demonstration. He did not allow Kindra to stop, though.

"You will do this several times a day for at least a half-hour. You will build muscle memory as well as strength in those same muscles to make swinging your sword easier. You will be sore. Without having trained since you were a child, this is the best I can do to get you in fighting condition."

Kindra repeated the motions again. "How much fighting are you expecting me to do? I've never fought a single person in my life."

"I won't be asking you to fight, but I fear it may be required for your survival. It is much better for you to have some knowledge and training and then hope you never need to use any of it."

Kindra thought she saw resignation in Gunnar's eyes. She suddenly felt as if she were a disappointment. It was very possible that these people had thought her entrance to the realm, with Forsvarer strapped to her back, had been their salvation. Kindra was far from a warrior princess.

The troop mounted their horses shortly after Kindra finished her morning training session. They crossed the stream and continued in the direction they had been going the evening before. Kindra was unsure where they were headed and found she did not really care. She had lost her sense of adventure when she gained the heaviness in her muscles and her mind. The sword training and realization that this was all indeed real, and her life really was something she could lose, had worn her out.

As her mare blindly followed Gunnar's mount, Kindra let her mind wander. Those little eyes were peering at them as they blazed a trail through the trees. What did these people expect of her? Was she supposed to lead her Elven brethren into the Kingdom of Dredfall and depose King Ulford by will and a few swoops of her sword? This was ridiculous, and Kindra was far from her comfort zone. She thought of the colorful Mood Meter graphic hanging in her office at school. Right now, she placed herself in the blue zone of the chart. She felt disheartened and drained. She was far from her typical upbeat and enthusiastic yellow zone.

Kindra wondered if her leave replacement used the graphic as often as she had. If one asked a middle school student how they felt, it always resulted in a response akin to "fine." Having asked them to read the descriptive feelings on the chart and place themselves in a particular color zone had always been very helpful to Kindra. She found she quickly had a good understanding of how any child coming into her office felt at that moment.

Missing her comfortable office back home was put on hold when Gunnar's horse reared up and Kindra's mare almost ran right into him. Swords were drawn. The party charged from both sides. Kindra drew her own sword as a male came up beside her horse on foot. She swiped down at him with Forsvarer. She sliced his shoulder, and he dropped the sword in his hand, but she had almost cut her own horse's hind leg in the process.

Kindra didn't get a chance to be more aware of her horse's proximity to her sword the next time, as a second attacker jumped from a horse of his own onto Kindra's horse. He scrambled into the saddle behind Kindra, but Kindra slipped down the other side of her horse and onto the ground. This time, she found herself landing gently as she allowed some of her magic to come to the surface. The male followed her to the ground and lunged for Kindra. She raised her sword, wishing he'd slow down so she could get a good swing at him. He did slow down. It was as if he were moving through water, and it gave her plenty of time to adjust her feet and swing her sword at him. Forsvarer connected with the man's neck and blood sprayed. His fall to the ground was not slow. He fell immediately and with finality.

Kindra looked up to see her group staring at her. Only Krish and Bane had dismounted. Everyone else had fought from horseback. All had blood on their swords and Joral had blood leaking from a wound on his forearm. None of them spoke. What were they waiting for?

Kindra looked at the male on the ground in front of her. "Oh God. Oh, no. Oh God."

Kindra turned her back on the others and wretched. She had killed that person. She had cut his life short. He may have had children, a wife, even a dog who loved him. Tears started to come as she heaved.

"When you are done mourning the man who tried to end you, we should really be on our way," said Joral with pain on his face. He was holding his bleeding arm.

Bane went to wrap the arm in a piece of linen, tightly to stifle the bleeding. "Give her a second. You know how the first one feels...even when he deserves it."

Gunnar's face was less harsh than the other two princes had been when he spoke. "I'm sorry there is no way to train for that and I hope the feeling you have now returns each time you are forced to kill. That feeling is a reminder that you are a good person. Be aware, though, that you will probably have to kill again. Do not expect mercy from any threat you face here. Those that wish you harm and do not kill you right away will do such awful things to you that you will wish they had killed you quickly. It is best that you take the upper hand and put them down before you find out what the intent behind the attack actually is. You reacted well. I'm a little impressed."

Kindra supposed the alternative to killing the man was not a possibility. If she had allowed him to mount her horse behind her, he could have taken the reins and ridden off with her. She did not know where he would have taken her or what he would have done with her, but she was sure it would have made her wish he had simply killed her. Since she had no desire to die, the only other option had been to kill him instead.

The logic was there. Kindra would need a little time to get her stomach to cooperate with the truth. As she remounted her horse, giving herself a little magical boost into the saddle, she kept reminding herself it was better to kill him than let him kill her. She continued to repeat this to herself as the horses began moving up the trail again. No one spoke. Kindra continued to repeat her mental mantra. The sounds of the forest started to creep back into her senses. She slowly let go of the gruesome act she had just perpetrated on an unknown male and let the woodland sounds soothe her. Surprisingly, it only took minutes for her to let it go and return to watching the eyes of the little people follow her and the others as they rode.

# CHAPTER 14

Kindra was pretty sure she was seeing things when her horse broke through the trees. They were all on top of a hill, looking down into a valley. She was almost certain that was Millspare, far below. She had been on horseback for more than a day and had somehow been steered around in a circle and pointed right back to her place of origin. All the time she had thought they had been riding away from danger and to a place of safety, they had only been avoiding the immediate danger. It was quite possible they had never even left Aergroth.

"This is the grand plan?" Kindra scoffed. "The castle is attacked so you put the Lord and Lady on horses and go ride around for a little while until the threat is gone?"

"Don't be silly." Bane answered. "The attack was one of many. Dredfall sends a handful of troops to test our defenses a few times a month. Each time, we make sure to change our defensive plan so they do not get enough information to plan a formal attack."

"Next time, could we use the plan where we hide in the closet instead of the one that causes me to remain in my filthy clothes and relieve myself in the bushes?" Kindra tried to hold anger on her face as she said it, but she ended up cracking a small smile.

"Have no fear Princess." Joral rolled his eyes. "You can pack a bag and have it ready to go at a moment's notice for next time."

"It's not a laughing matter!" Viktor was angry. "They're attacking more and more often. How long will it be until they bring the entire army?"

Ruth gave a sad smile to her husband. She then kicked her horse and headed off toward the castle. Kindra followed her and the males brought up the rear. It took about an hour to get back to Millspare. It felt good to ride with the wind in her hair and no branches to avoid.

Einar greeted them at the stable. He immediately gave a report. The male noted the number dead as three and the wounded at fifteen. Einar couldn't be sure, but he thought they had wounded many from Dredfall. For certain, there had been one Dredfall soldier killed.

Kindra smiled at the old man. "I thought you were the cook!"

"I have been the cook for the last sixty years or so. Before that time, I was a general who could also cook." Einar winked at Kindra.

"Well, General Einar, I am going to take a bath. Where is your lovely wife?"

"I'll get one of the other ladies to help you. Like me, my mate is not the warrior she once was. She is among the injured."

Kindra whirled toward Einar. "What? Why did you not say something? Where is she?"

"All is fine, child of Leif. I am grateful for your concern and will pass the sentiment on to my mate. She has been seen by the healers and will be back on her feet in no time. The healers have instructed her to rest for several days and I am requiring her to follow those orders. I'll send a servant up to your room to help with your bath."

"There is no need for that, Einar." Ruth came to stand beside Kindra. "I'll take Kindra to her room and tend to her myself. We have some matters to discuss."

Ruth headed through the door and down the passage, leaving Kindra to follow. She had to hurry to keep up, especially because she still had no idea how to use the servants' passages to find her room. Ruth took Kindra up a stairway and opened a door into the hall holding the entrance to Kindra's room. It did not appear that any of Dredfall's men had been in this hallway. They reached Kindra's door. Ruth held her left hand before her and the door swung open on its own. Kindra followed Ruth through the doorway as if the magic were normal. She was getting the hang of this place.

As Ruth unlaced the back of Kindra's dress, she started speaking. "You are my niece, and a descendant of Andril and Blaith. As you know, this makes you a princess. Your grandmother Ekkelle held the most power of Blaithe's three children. Through thought alone, she could bend the world, and the people in it, to her will. Had she taken the throne after Blaithe, she would have been the most powerful ruler Lillerem had ever seen. As a female, Ekkelle was never even considered as a ruler. Knowing this, she chose to marry a farmer and live a simple life.

"I can only imagine how she must have entertained her many children through the years. I remember her making objects float around my head to pacify me as I fell asleep in my cradle. Elven women do not come into season monthly as humans do. Most do not even bleed yearly. My mother managed to have over twenty children. By the time I was born, most of my elder siblings had families of their own and I never even met them. Leif and Gunnar and I are the youngest of her children. Though there are many years between each of our ages, we are similar in age when seen by human eyes. We were very close growing up."

A servant girl crept into the bathing chamber with buckets of hot water and Ruth stopped speaking. A second girl followed with two more buckets. The young girls filled the tub and filed back out of the chamber. Kindra dropped her dress to the floor and headed for the steaming tub. Ruth had volunteered to tend to Kindra's needs, but it was clear that Ruth was serving as a companion more than an attendant. Kindra had just seated herself n in the bath and Ruth began speaking again.

"I had only recently married Viktor and moved here to Aergroth when my parents' farm was attacked. Everyone there was killed. It was almost thirty years before Gunnar returned from your realm, and I found out he and Leif had survived. Of all my mother's children, I had the least magic. Ulford knew this. I feel as if he let me continue to live my insignificant life here with Viktor because he felt no threat from me. Ulford hunted down all my other siblings and killed them and any offspring they had. As far as Ulford is concerned, I am the only descendent of Ekkel left alive.

"Gunnar and Leif had been sent to live with my father's brother in your realm. My father and Magnus had the same Elven father, but Magnus's mother was mortal. Magnus was a half-elf, like you. Of all my mother's children, Leif was the most powerful. It is possible he was even more powerful than my mother. He was so young when my mother died, none of us ever truly found out the extent of his capabilities. Gunnar can tell stories, though. Gunnar has no power in the human realm, but he told us of Leif controlling objects and levitating even in your realm. For someone to be able to wield that kind of power in a non-magical realm is…"

Ruth trailed off. She had no words for the magnanimous nature of what she was trying to convey to Kindra. Kindra had managed to scrub herself clean and stepped from the tub and into a towel Ruth held out for her. The women went back to the bedroom, shutting the door to the bathing chamber behind them. Kindra wrapped the towel around her hair and donned a simple pull-over housedress from the bureau. She turned to face Ruth, who had taken a seat on the corner of the bed.

"Why didn't Leif ever return?" asked Kindra. "If he is so powerful, it seems like he would be the answer to all of your troubles with Dredfall.

"Leif feels more kinship with the realm of humans than he ever could with Alfheim. He went to live among your mother's kind when he was only ten years old. In human years, he was the equivalent of about a three-year-old and was treated as such in your realm. Essentially, Leif was raised by humans but possessed supernatural gifts that made it easier for him in many ways. Those same gifts also posed complications which caused him to need to move around. When Leif came of age and Gunnar was sent back to your realm to retrieve him, Leif felt no connection to his people in Alfheim. Leif felt no call to defend what was left of his claim to the throne, nor to protect what was left of his family.

"I know Leif never completely dismissed us, though. He followed the lives of his many children over the years and brought any who showed gifts back through the portals. All of those offspring chose to remain here with us. Though some exhibited power, none matched even Gunnar's strength. You have many brothers and sisters here in Lillerem. I suppose Leif felt he may be providing warriors for us to use in our eternal struggle. All the adult children he brought us make up a powerful force, but it is still no match for Ulford. We have been waiting for centuries for Leif to return and take his place beside his family."

"I don't understand where I fit in to this power struggle." said Kindra. "Are you expecting me to convince Leif to return? Believe me, even if he did return, I do not see him as a capable leader. To me, it seems he has enough trouble taking care of himself."

"You deserve the truth, Kindra. We do not know where you fit in. We were so surprised to find an adult child of Leif's that had not been brought to us, yet held power. We still don't understand why Leif hid you from us. Gunnar told us the sword sang to you. It chose you. It means something; we are simply unaware of what that meaning might be. We do not understand the scope of your power. Most importantly, we do not know the strength of your connection to your Elven ancestors."

"Well, I'm not sure I hold more power than you or Gunnar, but you are lucky, on one count. I feel a strong connection to all of my ancestors. I research them and collect the stories of their lives. I try to perpetuate their memories and allow those family members to survive through me. Though I do not really know you, and I've never met the brothers and sisters I have here, I feel a responsibility to protect you all as family in any way I am able. It is unfortunate that a man as powerful as my father, who might be able to rid this realm of the likes of Ulford, does not feel the same way I do."

Ruth rose from the bed. "I am going to have my own much-needed bath. I'll see you downstairs for dinner in the kitchen. It is a bit too late for a formal meal, but I am sure Einar is already putting something together for us. I suggest you try to find your way on your own. I saw how confused you were following me here earlier. If you plan to stay for a while, you'll need to start learning your way around."

Kindra watched Ruth, smile on her face, stride to the door and let herself out. Kindra had thought she had hid her complete ignorance of the passageway well. Either Ruth was very good at reading people or Kindra spoke with her face more than she had ever realized. Kindra opened the shoe drawer, hoping there was something comfortable to go on her feet. She found a pair of fur-lined slippers with leather soles. They were a bit like moccasins. Kindra was really starting to like the magical chest of clothing. She fully understood why those of her siblings who were brought here, chose to stay here.

Kindred left her room and walked down the hall to the stairway. She knew they had come up several flights to get here from the stables. Were the stables on the same level as the kitchen? Kindra was not sure and was forced to acknowledge that Ruth had been correct. Kindra did need to start to learn her way around Millspar. She headed down the flight of stairs.

At the first landing, which Kindra knew she had never been on, she went through the doorway and entered the servant's' passage. She tried one of the doors and discovered it opened into an office. There was a large, important-looking, desk made of wood. Shelves of books stood behind the desk and there were several maps on the wall to the left. Kindra stepped closer to the maps and saw two were from her own world. One depicted the five boroughs of New York City, and the other showed the southern part of Norway, including the area of Husland Farm. Other than his first ten years, these were the two places Leif had lived between his entire life.

Kindra backed out of the room and shut the door. She picked another door to open. This one opened into a great hall. She was currently at the back of the hall, looking toward ornate double-doors. The ceiling was two floors up and covered in skylights to let in natural light. Kindra imagined grand balls being held here and courtesans form all over the realm attending. The room was beautiful. The marble floor was black with streaks of white stone running naturally within the large tiles. Tapestries green with silver accents hung on the wall depicting scenes of elves in the forest.

Gunnar's voice made Kindra jump out of her own skin. "I see you've discovered the main floor of the castle. Unfortunately, you are still one floor above where your dinner is being served."

"I'm sorry. I thought I only meant to peak my head into a few places and see what was around." Kindra gestured to the tapestry hanging to their right. "Everything is so beautiful and ornate and castle-like!"

"You gesture toward an interesting tapestry. That depicts your great grandfather being crowned King by the Fae of the forest. Long ago, mortals did not choose their own kings, nor could the thrown be claimed. The honor was bestowed upon a deserving sole by the Fae. It is probably why the rulers of old were so successful. One does not question the will of the Forrest Fae, and they likely made sure to aid their choice of ruler in any way they could.

"Now, I'm sure you are starving! Let's go down one more level to the kitchen. Einar has prepared some bore over his fire and I swear I can smell it from here." Gunnar gestured to the door from which Kindra had entered.

Kindra turned and went back into the passage. "What are the parties in there like?" she asked as they made their way back to the stairs and down one more level.

"I've only been to smaller gatherings for the court of Lillerem. They are held in the Dining Hall. Since I've been in Alfheim, there has never been a gathering at Millspare large enough to require the Great Hall." Gunnar answered flatly.

On the kitchen level, Kindra found the passage felt familiar. She knew the kitchen was at the very end and could see the door from where they were. She turned toward the door at a confident pace and only slowed as she realized Gunnar was not beside her. Kindra turned to see what the delay might be.

Gunnar was still standing in the doorway from which they had emerged. With arms crossed before him, and leaning on the door frame, Gunnar was wearing a smile. His golden brown eyes were bright, and he was trying not to laugh. He pointed to the other end of the hall.

Kindra looked at the doors on either end of the hall. They were similar, if not the same. She then felt it. It was colder in the direction she had been heading. There was warmth coming from the far end of the passage.

"I see it in your eyes," Gunnar said. "You remembered to use senses other than sight. Excellent! Follow the heat of the kitchen. You might also wish to note that the end of the hall you did not choose smells absolutely delectable." Gunnar laughed slightly.

Kindra headed off toward the door to the kitchen. As she strode passed Gunnar; she gave him a rude gesture. Her eyes showed her displeasure at having been allowed to make the mistake and waste the effort of walking the wrong direction for the single purpose of amusing Gunnar. Her usefulness as entertainment was not quite over yet, though.

When Kindra opened the door to the kitchen, she found the other princes, Viktor and Ruth, seated at the table and already eating. There were comments about her tardiness and her poor sense of direction shouted good-naturedly from the table. Kindra wanted to be angry, but found she couldn't. It was all the truth. She supposed it was actually a good sign that they would poke a little fun at her in this way. It really was like a family. She had seen friends of hers fight ruthlessly with siblings, only to turn around and defend them when others so much as snickered in their direction.

Kindra smiled sheepishly and took a seat at the table. She really did need to spend some time exploring the castle. She wanted to go back to the main floor especially. Kindra had only seen two rooms and was still digesting the refined adornments and beauty she had witnessed. She assumed the floor also held the dining hall, but there had been several other doors in that passage.

What other stunning rooms might there be?

Kindra had just decided to begin exploring in the morning when she realized Joral had been speaking to her. She made her apologies for having been lost in her thoughts and requested that he repeat his question.

Joral rolled his eyes. "You spend a lot of time locked up in that head of yours. You're going to need to try to keep some part of it open to your environment. I wasn't really asking you a question. I was waiting for you to acknowledge that we would be training tomorrow morning."

"Training?" Kindra scrunched up her face. "Gunnar already showed me how to use my sword. I thought I was to practice those movements several times a day. I didn't realize it would require training with someone."

"Gunnar is the expert with the sword. There is no need for me to help you with that. You and I will be doing your magic training."

Kindra wasn't sure how she felt about this. She was curious to know what her magic was able to do for her, but at the same time she was nervous about it. Ruth had basically told her that they had no knowledge of her magical capabilities. Though Joral had used the phrase "*training*," Kindra couldn't help but feel like it might be more like magical testing. The people here, kind and helpful as they seemed, had a war to fight. They needed to know the extent to which she might be a help or hindrance in that war. That might even be the only interest this family had in Kindra.

Kindra looked at Joral and nodded. She would report to him after breakfast. Knowing Joral, he'd probably be here in the kitchen, tapping his toe as she finished her oatmeal. That was, of course, if she found her way up to her room tonight, and back to the kitchen tomorrow morning.

# CHAPTER 15

Kindra need not have worried about finding her way to the kitchen. She opened her eyes in the morning to find Joral standing at the foot of her bed. He was holding a tray with a bowl and glass balanced on it. Kindra might have found the gesture kind if Joral hadn't shoved the tray into her lap the second she sat up.

"Einar insisted you have a proper meal before we begin magic training," he admitted, as an explanation for the offering of food.

That made more sense. It was not Joral showing kindness. It was Joral reluctantly obeying the command given to him by Einar. Kindra smiled at Joral and did her best to look like she believed the breakfast had been brought up out of kindness and that she was grateful. She ate the oatmeal quickly and rose from bed while sipping the juice from the provided glass.

Kindra placed the glass atop the magic clothing chest and pulled her nightgown over her head and flung it on the bed. She smiled when Joral spun around and started studying the wall as if he had noticed a small crack that needed attention. Kindra was not fully awake, and she hadn't embarrassed him intentionally. She had actually forgotten he was in the room in her push to get herself out of bed and dressed. It was amusing though to see this battle-hardened Elf warrior blush. The color that rose to his face had made his scar stand out even more than usual.

Kindra found pants and a tunic in her wardrobe. Today, there were sturdy boots with laces in the bottom drawer. Who programmed this thing? She was beginning to accept that it somehow knew her exact size and was capable of picking colors to compliment her complexion, but she still couldn't accept that it also knew the type of clothing to provide as a match for her plans for the day.

"It reads the information from your mind," Joral said.

His back was still to her. Had she spoken the question out loud? She was pretty sure she had only been musing about the bureau in her own mind. Did Joral have a similar ability to her clothing chest? *What is Joral's power, anyway?*

"One of them," Joral said, "is the ability to read minds."

"Well," said Kindra slowly, "I appreciate your honesty. That is one bit of trickery that could have cost me some friends. I'll have to be careful what I'm thinking."

"You can try." Joral smiled. "The funny thing about thoughts is that they are notoriously difficult to control. Most of the time, you do not even consciously realize you are thinking.. The good news is that you have pure thoughts. It was what convinced me to trust you so quickly."

Kindra immediately started trying to remember all the things she had thought about Joral. Had she been cruel? *"Oh Jeez, he's reading your thoughts right now, you idiot! Stop. Stop thinking. Make your mind blank."*

Joral started laughed. "You were more kind than most, and I do recall you thinking me handsome in spite of this wicked scar. Besides, it is something I need to think about doing. It is not as if I hear everyone's thoughts persistently throughout the day. That would be incredibly overwhelming and, therefor, useless. It is mostly in times of silence, or when someone is looking at me as if they are sizing me up that I find myself in need of exploring the thoughts of others."

Kindra considered his statement. There were plenty of times in her own life that she had wished she knew what someone was thinking. She could also understand reaching into someone's thoughts during a silence for the same reason. Of course, most people just asked a person what they were thinking about during those times, but if she didn't need to ask, she probably wouldn't either. She quickly finished dressing and made for the door.

Joral turned from the wall to follow Kindra, but made no move to guide her. Instead, he said, "You'll go to the same floor as the kitchen, but you will turn away from that end of the castle when you reach the bottom of the stairs. It will be the second door on your right."

He was helping her to learn about the castle. Breakfast might not have been his idea, but this choice to help her learn on her own was a kindness. Kindra entered the stairway from the hall and went down to the kitchen level. She entered the passage and turned to the right. She opened the second door and stood, taking the room in.

It was a gym; or it was like a gym, anyway. They were standing on a platform above an area about the size of a football field. There were ropes hanging from the ceiling, and she could see a climbing wall off to the left. The floor below them held an obstacle course to which the climbing wall and ropes belonged.

Kindra began descending the stairs to her right. They twisted once and turned her back in the other direction, so she landed on the floor facing the obstacle course. The floor was rubbery, though she didn't know what material it actually was. She turned to look at the far side of the room and saw men training with swords and staffs on the left. On the right, there was an archery range set up to fire from the center of the gym toward the far right side.

Joral walked to their immediate right. The area was completely open except for some racks holding various training swords, staffs, and other weapons she did not know the names for. It was another area for sparring, but this side currently held no occupants. Joral stood about twenty feet away and faced her.

"Ok," he said. "teleport to me."

Kindra closed her eyes. She thought about appearing in front of Joral. Nothing happened. She scrunched her face with effort and tried to think harder about being in front of him. She pictured his face directly in front of hers.

"All you are achieving is making it look as if you are in the process of using the privy," said Joral with slight irritation. "I have an idea."

He started over to the obstacle course. "When you thought you were about to fall in the stream, you teleported yourself to the other side to keep from getting wet. You did not think very hard about it. It was only a quick and definite thought about where you wished to be."

He motioned for Kindra to climb up on a log. It wasn't a difficult feat. There were two small steps so a person could get right up on top of it. She started walking back and forth on it as if it were a round balance beam with a diameter similar to that of her waist. Kindra turned on the log and started back toward Joral in time to see him release a lever. The log began to roll. Kindra had been standing slightly off to the right of center and both of her feet kicked out in that direction. Her head pitched toward the ground.

In a flash, she was standing before Joral, face-to-face and close enough to share breath. It was the same image she had put in her head when she was trying to teleport to him a moment ago. She must have defaulted to that image in her panic and her body had listed.

"Are you crazy?" Kindra yelled into his face. "I could have cracked my skull wide open!"

Joral wiped a bit of spittle from his face. The princess was angrier than he had anticipated. Her green eyes were shining as if they had been replaced with cut emeralds. They were actually emitting their own green light. He had intended to start slowly, but it looked like things were going to pick up more quickly than he had planned.

Kindra made to push Joral hard in the chest. She never touched him, but he went flying backward and onto his rear. Kindra looked toward the rack of weapons and one of the wooden training swords went flying into her hand. She held it above Joral's head and took a deep breath.

Joral shot up and tackled Kindra. They both went down, Joral pinning Kindra beneath his body. He grabbed her in an embrace and held on tight. He bent close to her ear, even as she writhed to get free, and whispered in her ear. "Shhhhhhhhhhh now. I am no threat. You are well. You're actually quite beautiful when you are this angry, but you are well. Shhhhhhhhhhhh now."

As Kindra realized she could not move her arms to get free, she started to calm. She was calm enough that she considered biting Joral on the shoulder to see if it might convince him to free her. Kindra figured, if she were calm enough to be planning her next move, then she was calm enough not to need to make a next move. She relaxed her body in Joral's embrace. He let her go.

Joral propped himself up on his arms. He had one knee on either side of Kindra's hips. He reddened immediately. Now that Kindra's anger was a memory, he found there was no decent reason for him to be mounted above her like this, and he stood quickly.

Joral put several feet between himself and Kindra. He looked down at the ground as he said, "I'm so sorry. I forgot who you... I didn't mean to... It must have looked like..."

Kindra smiled. All anger had left her at the sight of how embarrassed Joral had become. "It really is quite adorable how discombobulated you become at any hint of impropriety. In the future, I'll have you know it would be best to forget who I am and think of me as one of your soldiers. I needed to be shut down. You did it the best way you knew how."

"That being said," Joral still couldn't look Kindra in the face. "It seems you easily have access to your power when you are scared or angry. That's pretty common when children first discover what powers they wield. Only, you are not a child and your powers are very strong. If I am a tad flustered, it is because training a full-grown female is different from training children."

"As I said, think of me as one of your soldiers. That will help with the full-grown female part. I will not take offence to any perceived improprieties, I assure you. As for my power, you say it is strong, but I cannot see how you can discern that. All I've done is catch myself when I fall and push you away because I was mad at you."

"It was in your eyes," said Joral in a low voice. "Most magic wielders have a little twinkle or spark in their eye when using magic. Your eyes actually glowed. That is an indication that you possess a great deal of power."

Kindra moved closer to Joral. She could smell him now. It was an earthy smell that was not off-putting. She had a pretty good idea of how her magic worked at this point. Kindra could control things, including her own body, with her thoughts. She was, indeed, her father's daughter. Kindra put her hand on Joral's shoulder. She looked up at him.

"Thank you for today." She said sincerely. "I learned quite a bit about myself in very little time.

"You can use this space for your sword training as well. You should practice that and magic three times a day when possible. I'll leave you to do so now."

Kindra didn't want him to leave. Joral turned and started up the stairs. She called his name. He turned to look at her but did not make a move to come back down the stairs. Kindra wasn't sure what to say. She knew she wanted him here, but didn't have a reason.

"I could use a sparring partner." Kindra called to him. "Gunnar has me doing those sword dances, but it would be nice to do some fighting with a practice sword."

Joral turned back. "I could use a reminder of what it is like to fight an ordinary person. I usually spar with Bane, and it makes it difficult to remember that it is possible to actually win a sparring match every now and again." He said as he walked back down the few steps he had already mounted.

"I'm choosing to not take that as an insult," said Kindra. "You princes do not get out much and I believe your lack of forethought before speech is a side-effect of that."

Joral reddened slightly, but he just nodded toward the open mat. Kindra took up her position and waited for Joral to mount the offensive. Joral stood with his sword lowered at his side. Kindra dropped her own sword and looked at Joral quizzically.

"I'm sorry Kindra. I'm just not accustomed to attacking someone who doesn't pose a threat."

"Again, I'll choose not to take that as an insult." Kindra said, even though she was feeling the unintentional insults acutely.

"You're just standing there. There is no reason for me to attack you because you are not attacking me."

Kindra understood. Joral, for all his toughness on the exterior, was a protector. He did not fight to hurt people. He fought to defend himself and others. Like lightning, Kindra lifted her wooden practice sword and swung for Joral's head. Joral spun out of the way and brought his sword around to strike at Kindra's back. Kindra, having followed through with the sword dance she had been taught was already standing to face the blow and blocked it with her own sword. Joral smiled. You are better than I thought you would be.

The two continued like this for over thirty minutes. At that point, Kindra was having trouble lifting her arms. Joral did not seem tired at all. Maybe he was breathing a little heavier, but not enough for Kindra to be sure. Kindra placed her sword back on the rack. She gave Joral a little bow and smiled.

"That was quite fun," she said. "I'm going to go wash up and take a stroll around the castle. I'm still trying to learn my way around this maze."

Joral gave a tiny bow back. Kindra had done it in jest, but maybe this was an appropriate way to end a sparring session after all? "Enjoy Kindra. I'll see you for the midday meal."

The fact that he referred to lunch as the midday meal did not throw her as much as the sound of her name coming from Joral's lips. It sent a strange sensation down her spine. She then became a little queasy when she realized it was a twinge of attraction. Kindra's genealogical analysis put Joral as her half-first cousin, once removed. That was even legal in the human realm, but it still creeped her out a bit. Maybe she just had a thing for the warrior look.

Kindra made it back to her room easily. She found herself wishing someone would have witnessed it to congratulate her on the achievement. She used the wash basin for her face and hands and then applied a little lilac scented oil as an afterthought. Had she been home, she would have showed after her workout, but she didn't think the servant girls her would appreciate drawing her bath three times a day. She donned a simple emerald dress from the magic chest of drawers and complimented it with a pair of brown leather slippers. She turned to head out the door, but stopped. If the castle were attacked again, the slippers would be a poor choice. It had been difficult riding in a gown before, and she wanted to be a bit more prepared if it happened again. She opened the bottom drawer and swapped out the slippers for a pair of brown leather boots. They were not what she would have normally thought to compliment her dress with, but they were practical. As she stood before the mirror, she noticed that only her toes stuck out of the dress and no one would even know what she had on her feet. Kindra felt much more confident as she walked into the hall.

She went to the stairway down the hall and descended one flight. She had only opened two of the doors in the hall below her and she was looking forward to seeing what other items of beauty the castle had waiting. Kindra entered the hall and noted the door to the study and the one to the ballroom. There was a third door on the same side of the hall, but much farther down. She supposed that made sense. The ballroom was quite large, so wherever that door led, it would be on the other side of the ballroom. Kindra headed for the door.

As Kindra made her way past the shimmering green orb sconces, and looked down her emerald dress to the emerald carpet at her feet, Kindra couldn't help but feel as if Millspare had been designed to match her eyes. She knew emerald and silver were simply the house colors, but it was nice to think of how well those colors complimented her looks.

There was a little twinkle of anticipation as Kindra gripped the door handle and prepared to open the door. When she opened it, the room was dark and windowless. She felt around for a light switch, and then remembered where she was. She went back out into the main hall and grabbed one of the wall sconces. The glowing orb inside stayed bright. It seemed this was an advantage of magic over electricity. The glowing spheres did not need to be plugged it to work. She was excited as she went back through door number three.

Kindra let out a long sigh. She was in a cloakroom. She smiled and gave a little huff. It would make sense to have a servant's entrance to the cloakroom. It also made sense to have a cloakroom next to the ballroom. Well, now she knew. She closed the door behind her as she went back to the passage. She returned the torch to the wall and looked to the other side of the hall. There were two doors on that side of the passage. To her left was a dead end. To her right and past the stairs she had taken to get here was a bend in the passageway.

She opened the door nearest to her and dazzling bright sunlight blasted the skin on her face and forced Kindra to squint her eyes. Kindra stepped into a courtyard with paved paths and beautiful landscaping. There were stone benches along the pathways. Kindra took one path and began strolling through flowers and shrubs of all colors and sizes. Some, she recognized, but other species were foreign to her. The path wound toward the center of the courtyard, where Kindra was met with a fountain carved from marble. If she were to describe the fountain, it reminded her of a birdbath Jess's grandmother had displayed in her front yard. The bird bath depicted two cherubs facing each other and blowing horns in the air. The fountain before her depicted two elves facing each other and aiming bows, knocked with arrows, toward the sky.

The courtyard was fully enclosed. From the center, Kindra could see there were at least two doors on each of the four sides of the square expanse. Unlike the shape of the area itself, all the paths were curved, and they wound toward the center. There were several benches here, and Kindra took a seat on one of them. She sat and listened to the sound of the water in the fountain and felt a peace that she had not known since she was a child. There were birds singing in the courtyard as they flitted through the trees. They stopped to drink from the fountain and one even landed on the bench opposite her.

Kindra supposed there was no need for social workers and psychologists here. If this garden was any indication of the tranquility that could be achieved by simply sitting on a bench, Kindra would not have a job in Aergroth. Then again, Kindra had not seen many children here. She supposed there was not even a need for a school, let alone a school psychologist.

All at once, the sounds of the birds stopped. The bird on the bench across from her cocked its head to listen. Kindra did the same. She heard shouting. Someone was attempting to gain entry to the castle. *Not again. Not yet.* Kindra didn't want to flee now. *I just returned to the castle and I'm finally starting to feel comfortable here. At least I opted for the boots instead of the slippers.*

Kindra followed the winding path back to the doorway from which she arrived. She ran across the hall and opened the door to the ballroom. She ran through the enormous space and slammed through the imposing doors on the opposite side of the vast room. This let her out into the main hall near the arched entryway to the castle. She looked out through the archway and was stunned by who was attempting to enter Millspare.

# CHAPTER 16

Leif stood outside of the castle, colorfully dressing down the guards. Gunnar joined them, running from somewhere outside the castle. He and Leif embraced and turned to enter Millspare. Before entering the arched entryway, Leif turned and gave the guards one last rude gesture. Kindra stood like a wall before the brothers, denying them true access to the castle unless they recognized her first.

"Daughter!" Leif exclaimed. "Long-time-no-see. How are the glorious people of Aergroth treating you? Have they convinced you to save Lillerem from complete destruction yet? Does Ulford know you're here?"

Kindra stepped closer to Leif. She smiled broadly and lifted her hand. Kindra slapped Leif across his handsome face. Gunnar's mouth fell open in shock, but he looked more amused than anything else. Kindra was somewhat shocked herself. She knew she had been angry at Leif for omitting himself from her life, especially since there were so many secrets to his side of the family. The secrets that were kept from Kindra were only part of the animosity behind the slap. When Kindra had seen him outside the gates of Millspare, she had felt how Leif's presence grated against the peacefulness of the town. It hadn't just been the words he was shouting; it had been the feeling of disdain that emanated from him. Kindra could feel how little Leif respected this place.

Kindra was outraged at the audacity Leif had displayed by coming here. He had stayed away for over a hundred years and had shown little interest in helping his own people. Leif had waltzed through the castle doors and immediately attacked Kindra for taking an interest in their Elven family and the responsibilities he had repeatedly shirked. He had disregarded her, but that was nothing compared to disregarding an entire nation for which he may be the only possible salvation. To ice the cake, he had come through the doors making light of the situation and demonstrating his disinterest in the cause of his people unabashedly.

Leif turned his eyes to Kindra and smirked. "I see the niceties of Court Life have not worn their way into your blood just yet, dear daughter."

Leif turned to his right and started toward the stairs to the kitchen passage. Gunnar looked from the still simmering Kindra to Leif and hurried off to catch his younger brother. He steered the man left instead of letting him take the stairs and down the short hall through a door. Gunnar left the door open for Kindra, who had only paused a moment before following after the males.

From her explorations of the castle, Kindra knew the room on this side of the ballroom would be the study. She found it interesting that Gunnar had not brought his brother, whom he had not seen in a lifetime, to the kitchen for a meal instead of to this formal office. *"Gunnar probably doesn't want Einar to know Leif has returned at last. Once the old man sees Leif, there will be no discussion of any serious matters."* Kindra mused to herself.

Kindra did not enter the room, but remained in the doorway as Leif sprawled in a chair in front of the desk with one leg thrown over the arm of the brown wood and leather. Gunnar had remained standing and had his arms crossed. He was waiting, as Kindra was, for Leif to explain why he had suddenly decided to return to his birth land. Leif did not seem to be in a rush to do any of the expected explaining. He took in the room in much the same way Kindra had when she had found it during her first exploration of the castle.

As Leif took in the maps on the wall, he said, "I see you do take an interest in the human realm."

"I lived there for many years, lest you forget, brother." He maintained a sense of calm, but Gunner was struggling to keep it. He was speaking through his teeth. "It was my task to ensure you were cared for until you came of age."

Leif huffed a laugh. "I came of age, then that age went. I'm an old man now. My brother left me on my own and never even came back to visit."

Gunnar was losing his grip on calm all together. "We were both supposed to leave. We were to return to our home." Gunnar's voice was increasing in volume. "It was you who chose to stay and never return to our home. You chose to ignore your duties and your family!"

"Family? You were my only family," said Leif flatly. I don't remember our father at all, and I have only the faintest memory of our mother's voice. I have a vague notion of aunts and uncles having visited us when I was very young. I do not even know these people you call family. They mean nothing to me."

Sensing that Gunnar was about to draw his sword and remove his own brother's head, Kindra glided into the room.

"Shall we talk about family?" Kindra asked innocently. You claim to have no loyalty or kinship with your blood, but at least you had the choice to be with them. I am 35 years old and have only just learned who my father is. I hunt him down and discover he is a drunk who enjoys wallowing in his own pity. He is rude and unkempt. The real kicker, though, is that he is a magical elf. Given the opportunity to tell me about my ancestors and their struggles, my father chose to tell me how difficult his own life was because the DMV refused to let him have a car. My mother, a woman who had erased you from her life, was more helpful in sharing information about my Elven family than the man from whom I got their blood."

Leif swiveled in his chair to face Kindra, planting both feet on the floor. "Your mother; yes, we should talk about her. Is she aware you're in Alfheim? If I recall, your mom wanted you to have nothing to do with me or my kin. She made me swear to stay away from her and you for the rest of your lives."

"I know," said Kindra. "She also allowed you to name me. She is the one who sent me to Norway. Kristen told me everything I need to know about you. For some reason, she still loves you."

"Kristen loves me because I raised her and was a part of her life. A privilege your mother denied me with you." Leif narrowed his eyes at Kindra.

Kindra answered back, "You only spent time raising her because she showed no magical ability. If I had been raised by you, you would have shipped me off here to Alfheim when I turned eighteen, anyway. You would have denied me my life with you and with my mother."

"Oh, so you think you have magical abilities? You spend a few days in Alfheim in your Elf form and you think the added strength and ability to heal make you writhe with magic?" Leif rolled his eyes.

Gunnar cleared his throat. Leif looked as if he was about to go on. Kindra drew in a breath to speak as well. Gunnar just cleared his throat louder. Both Kindra and Leif looked to Gunnar with little patience.

"Forsvarer sang to her." Gunnar said simply.

Leif snapped his eyes to Kindra. He took her in from her toes to her head. He looked into her eyes questioningly. Kindra shrugged her shoulders.

"The sword called to…to you?" Leif was having a hard time accepting the information. "Its been at Husland for so many years. It never spoke to me. It never spoke to any of the children I sired. I thought it was just folklore."

Kindra didn't let go of her anger, but did confirm Gunnar's revelation. "I didn't even know it meant anything. Kristen and Nils got so excited. They told me I had to take the tunnel here. I didn't know what I was getting into. I only knew I'd have the chance to trace your side of the family."

"I knew it!" Leif exclaimed. "I'm not the one Lillerem needs. All these years of you hounding me to come and take my place with the family; years of you all begging me to come free you from Ulford, and it wasn't even me you wanted. It's her!"

Leif laughed. "Don't worry Kindra. I'll head on back and explain to your mom that you are an Elven princess and the savior of Lillerem. I'm sure she'll be perfectly fine with giving you up so you can defend the people of another realm."

Kindra's power was beginning to burn inside of her. She wanted to tear Leif's limbs from his body, and her magic was getting ready to help her. Leif sniffed at the air.

"My, my, my…you are powerful, aren't you?" Leif was staring at Kindra. "I can taste your power leaching from your skin. I hope someone taught you how to use it, or we all might find ourselves dead without ever facing Ulford. I'm going to go to the kitchen and grab a bite. I think my daughter needs some time to cool down."

Leif strode out of the room. Gunnar put a hand on Kindra's shoulder.

"He is correct about one thing," Gunnar said. "You need to take a few breaths. Maybe you should sit down?"

Kindra plopped, more than sat, in the chair Leif had recently vacated. She concentrated on breathing in through her nose and out through her mouth. Kindra had coached her students in this breathing exercise hundreds of times. When her anger failed to recede, Kindra made a mental note to do the breathing exercise less often with students. Gunnar cocked his head and chuckled.

"It doesn't seem to be working. Maybe a stroll to the gym? A hot bath might be helpful? I could see if one of the servant girls is up for giving you a massage?"

Kindra couldn't help herself. She cracked a smile.

"Well, you succeeded. I'm now more annoyed with you than I am annoyed with him! You're supposed to be the sage and understanding uncle, not an annoying older brother!" Kindra smiled as she yelled at Gunnar a bit.

Kindra did feel better, though. Gunnar pointing out how ridiculous she must look sitting in a chair and fuming had helped tremendously. She had been acting like a teenager throwing a tantrum. Kindra supposed it made some sense. She hadn't known her father when she was a teenager, so she really wasn't prepared for the sheer frustration the man could make her feel with such little effort. Had she had a father when she was growing up, she may have understood those feelings and the speed with which they could overwhelm her.

Kindra stood and said to Gunnar, "I suppose we should head down to the kitchen to grab some food before Einar serves it all to Leif. He's probably fawning all over his lost little boy."

Kindra headed off to the kitchen, with Gunnar trailing behind her. The anger she had felt had disappeared as quickly as it had overtaken her. She went down the steps and entered the passage. Kindra briskly walked toward the sound of Einar's hearty laugh. She heard a woman giggling as well. Though Kindra had let the anger go, but she was not looking forward to watching some Court Lady swoon over her father. Kindra was both relieved and surprised when she pushed through the kitchen door.

The merry little giggles were coming from Mildred. Kindra took a minute to reconcile the sound of the giggles with the sour woman who had been tasked with helping Kindra when she first arrived at Millspare. Einar and Mildred were sitting at the table with Leif as if their first-born son had just returned from college, after being gone for several months.

Kindra and Gunnar took seats at the table and grabbed at some of the provisions before they could be devoured. Einar and Mildred were absolutely beaming. Gunnar and Kindra ate without speaking. They listened to Leif and the elder elves banter among themselves. Kindra was happy for the older couple. Had she known how happy Leif's return would make them, she might have suggested Gunnar just send him downstairs straight away. Since Leif still hadn't explained his reason for returning to Alfheim, the pause in the office hadn't served to do anything but get Kindra riled up.

A voice came from the doorway. "Well, well…the chosen one has returned after all this time."

Bane nearly took up the entire door frame as he stood with his hands on his hips, his chest out and hand on the hilt of his sword. Kindra wasn't sure if Bane meant to attack Leif or if he was ready to defend himself in the event Leif attacked him. Bane probably wasn't much more confident than Kindra of his reason for the battle stance. He needn't have worried about an attack. Leif didn't even get to his feet. He just blinked himself over to Bane and appeared directly in front of him.

"I think," Leif said to Bane, "you'll soon find I am no chosen one. I can't even take care of myself, let alone defend a realm from an evil king."

"I've heard it all." said Bane. "I know you have the power to make a real difference for Lillerem and I also know you choose to stay in the human realm and try in every way you can to shorten your long life. I don't smell any alcohol on you. Have you had an epiphany?"

"Alcohol is pointless in Alfheim. It's one of the reasons I stay away. In the human realm, I need to force my magic to work. Here in Alfheim, my magic works without thought from me. It heals me against my will. If I have a drink, my body has cleansed itself of the drink's lovely effects before I even get to feel a taste of a buzz." Leif explained.

Kindra digested that statement. Here in Alfheim, Leif was forced to face reality. No matter how hard he tried, there was no substance powerful enough to overcome his magic and keep his mind numb. It offered one reason Leif might choose to stay in the human realm. Since Leif wields so much power, he can use it when he desires in the human realm, or he can tuck it away and lose himself in oblivion. Here, there was no choice for Leif. He was alwas present and aware of reality. It dawned on Kindra that it must be much more difficult for Leif to be here right now than he was letting on.

Leif turned to the table. "Now that we have all had a bite, you might want to accompany me upstairs. I'm sure, by now, my sister has heard of my arrival. I assure you, you will not want to miss the show we will undoubtedly put on for you all."

Leif turned back to Bane and waited patiently for the male to move out of the doorway. Bane, who had probably been sent down here to retrieve Leif in the first place, allowed Leif to pass. He followed right behind Leif to make sure they were indeed headed upstairs to see Viktor and Ruth.

Einar and Ruth started clearing off the table. Gunnar looked at Kindra as if to ask if she had any interest in watching the show Leif had promised. Kindra nodded in answer and stood. She waited for Gunnar to stand and start for the door. Kindra nodded her thanks to the two elder elves and followed behind Gunnar.

"Kindra." Mildred's voice had Kindra turning back and waiting. "I saw it in your face. You understand how difficult this really is for him. Don't let Ruth be too hard on him. We really do need all the help we can get. With the two of you here, there is more hope than I ever imagined possible."

Kindra had heard Ruth, but she wasn't sure she would be able to bring herself to take her father's side if Ruth chose to attack him. She didn't want to speak, for fear she might admit this to Ruth. In response, Kindra nodded her head once to acknowledge she had heard Ruth's request, then walked out of the kitchen to catch the big show.

Kindra followed the sound of silence to locate Leif. It was as if the entire castle knew this was a pivotal moment for the future of all elves in Lillerem. Even the servants Kindra passed were walking quietly down the hall. The nearer Kindra got to the ballroom, the quieter everyone seemed to be. She was surprised to find the room was actually being used. It wasn't like there were so many people that they couldn't have just meet in the office. The main doors to the ballroom were closed, so Kindra knew she would be calling all eyes to her when she swung open one of the doors. The desire to see what was happening was too great to avoid the announcement of her presence.

When Kindra opened the door on the left, all eyes did turn to her. The scene was almost comical. Looking at her from throne-like chairs at the far side of the room as she walked through the door, were Ruth and Viktor. Bane and Joral stood on either side of the rulers, and Leif knelt before the four of them. When Leif turned his head to see who came through the door, Kindra was happy to see he looked shameful. At least she knew he did care and understand that he had left his own people to fend for themselves. She had bought into his haughty attitude until this point.

Kindra was grateful to find she was not the only one entering the outlandishly large room. Gunnar had followed her to see the spectacle as well. There were now four princes and two princesses in the room. Kindra allowed herself to wonder if Viktor felt terribly outranked at this moment. There was a possibility he was enjoying his position of power as the leader here in Aergroth, but from what Kindra knew of Viktor, she supposed he probably hadn't even noticed the amount of nobility gathered in the room. When Kindra thought about it, she decided the only thing that mattered was that Leif was on his knees and Viktor was on a throne.

Gunnar headed to take up a position next to Bane, so Kindra headed to stand next to Joral. She really hoped she was not expected to act as some kind of guard, but did like feeling as if she were part of the court and also someone to which Leif should be groveling. This was a momentous event, yet Krish was missing. Maybe this was more of a family matter than a political matter? Bane and Joral might just be here as muscle, and Gunnar and Kindra were probably uninvited guests posing as extra muscle. That seemed like the most likely reason for Krish's absence. He hadn't been asked to be here, and he was polite enough not to invite himself.

Leif spoke. "As I was saying, I am here to serve you both. I have no good reasons for why I did not return when called, but I am here now and wish to offer my help in any way I can."

Kindra was surprised. She glanced at Gunnar and saw that he was having a difficult time keeping the same reaction from his face. Bane and Joral, ever the impassive warriors, showed no reaction at all. Viktor had allowed a small smile to his lips. He was happy to have Leif back in the fold. Ruth, on the other hand, did not look to be convinced as easily.

"My dear brother," Ruth began. "Forgive me if I do not swoon with appreciation at your generous offer. Of course, we will gladly accept your help and are glad you have finally chosen to return to this realm. Do not expect to command respect simply by being in attendance. I expect you to prove your worth, your loyalty, and especially your dependability. Our realm was foolish enough to put our hopes in your return before, and we learned to make do when those hopes were dashed. I am not going to allow myself to have false-hope this time. I will grant you my gratitude as you earn it."

Viktor did not look happy with his wife's response. Mildred had been right to warn Kindra that Ruth might not make this easy on Leif. If the state of Lillerem did actually depend on Leif's return, Ruth might chase him back to the human realm before he did anything to help the cause. Kindra slowly stepped out of the line and went to stand beside Leif. She chastised herself for the entire eight steps it took to reach him. This male had given her no reason to trust him and Kindra had seen only some of his power, but there had been something in the way he followed her here. Kindra knew in her heart that it was not coincidence that Leif had stayed away from his home for over a hundred years and just happened to decide to come back once she had ventured into this realm.

Kindra addressed the court on behalf of her father. "Leif has little to lose and much to offer. He is alone in the human realm. He doesn't even own a dog. If he has not been here before this, his reasons are indeed his own and not because of any human connections."

Leif looked at Kindra as he tried to determine if she thought she was actually helping his situation, but Kindra went on. "I suppose you might consider me his connection to the human realm. He has known about me my entire life, but swore to keep away from me at the bequest of my mother. Though he has not said as much, I suspect his connection to the human realm has been his many children. As each one matured, he would bring those with Elven gifts here to this magnificent place. He was not able to do this for me. Instead, I found my own way here without his guidance. I suspect he is here to offer support for me, more than anything. Since I feel a connection to my Elven family, and fully intend to stand with you against Dredfall, I anticipate that Leif can be trusted to do the same."

Kindra did not know if she should remain next to Leif or returned to her spot next to Joral. It had been much easier to decide where to stand when she thought she was on opposite sides from her father. Now that she had defended his honor in a small way, she wasn't sure if she had switched sides or if she was now on both sides. How did this kind of thing actually work?

Ruth saved Kindra from her indecisiveness. "Thank you for your thoughts, Kindra. They have been noted. I cannot say that I have completely been swayed and I suddenly believe my brother to be a model citizen, but it heartens me to see you have faith in him."

# CHAPTER 17

That evening, there was a formal dinner. It made sense that Leif's return called for one, but Kindra couldn't stop thinking about the last formal dinner. They hadn't even gotten to the end of the dinner before they were evacuating and running off into the forest attired in eveningwear.

The wardrobe read her mind beautifully. The gown, in the same green as Kindra's eyes, was not quite a dress at all. The skirts were actually more like pants; flowing pants with very wide legs. With the outfit on, it looked like a velvet gown, but if Kindra needed to hop on a horse at any point, her skirts would divide to either side of the horse just as pants would have. The whole getup was long enough to cover her lace-up boots so that the shoes that peeked out could pass for a pair of pumps.

Kindra was walking out of her room when she whirled and embraced an afterthought. She pulled down the bodice of her dress and strapped her sword belt around her waist. Kindra carefully slid Forsvarer into the sheath and down under her skirts. She pulled the bodice of the jumpsuit gown back up. The A-line styling of the gown completely hid the fact that she was wearing the sword. Kindra made a mental note that she would always need to think of dresses like this when she went to the wardrobe.

Kindra strode from her room, feeling prepared to flee the castle if needed. Once they stopped to rest, she could belt the sword on the outside of her clothing and everyone could compliment her on how clever she had been to bring the sword to dinner. Kindra hurried down the stairs and through the passage. She entered the dining hall through the rear servants' entrance. She felt much more comfortable using the passageways at this point, than taking the scenic route to the main entrance of the dining hall.

In the dining hall, there was no evidence of Leif's experience with groveling in the ballroom earlier in the day. As at previous dinners, Ruth and Viktor were at the head of the table. Gunnar sat to the left of Ruth and Krish to the right of Viktor. Bane was next to Krish, then Joral was beside him. There was an empty seat to the left of Gunnar, and then Leif was seated to the left of the empty chair. It seemed the princes had decided Kindra would sit between her father and her uncle. Kindra also suspected the seating was symbolic. A person's importance at court could be determined by proximity to the rulers. Kindra had been placed closer to Ruth than her father had. This was a statement. Being that Leif was equidistant from the rulers with Joral, it seemed he was more welcome and respected at court than the events of the afternoon had hinted he might be.

Kindra took her seat and joined the meal. No one looked up to acknowledge her presence and conversations continued as usual. The lesser members of the court, at the far end of the table, were bantering about trivialities as usual. Kindra had not been introduced to any of them and had not deigned to learn any of their names. She couldn't understand the purpose of these haughty individuals here at Millspare. They seemed to enjoy the lavish life the castle provided, but no one in the group seemed to repay the kindness in any way except to be decorations for the halls. Other than the single male that had tried to speak to her at the first formal brunch Kindra had attended, none of the Lords and Ladies of the court had approached her. At that first brunch, Kindra had been dressed as a Lady. Though she was still dressed formally, since she had been using the magic wardrobe herself, Kindra's manner of dress had been more subdued. Maybe the lower court had decided Kindra was not important enough to know.

Leif was speaking, and Kindra brought her attention to him. *Is it wrong of me to be so nervous to hear what might come out of his mouth?* Kindra did not need to know her father well to know he would speak his mind and was, in no way, schooled in the polite traditions of life in the castle.

"So Joral, Gunnar, I hear you have both been training my daughter in magic and swordplay, respectively. How is that going?"

The table fell silent. Kindra knew she should be concerned about Leif, but she had not expected some of the first syllables he spoke to betray her relationship to the families of Lillerem to the castle gossips at the other end of the table. Kindra waved at the owners of the eyes, looking her over again in a new light. It wouldn't take long for everyone she encountered here in Aergroth to know she was daughter to the most powerful elf alive. This was a story that was too good not to gossip about. First, the chosen son of Ekkelle returns to Alfheim, and then he joins his daughter at Millspare. Two mysteries solved at once; the location of the Elven savior and the full identity of the mystery woman at the castle.

Gunnar rolled his eyes and huffed at Leif. Ruth looked at Kindra as if to ask if she still stood behind her earlier defense of her father's dependability. Leif looked around the table and lowered his head slightly. It was Viktor who was the first to smile and become jovial once again.

Viktor looked to Leif and said, "Well, I suppose we no longer need to worry about announcing your arrival or planning a party to welcome Kindra formally. I am grateful to you for having saved me the coin, Leif."

Viktor then looked down the table at the useless members of the court. "Have no fear, it is no secret. You will not be punished for sharing information."

Kindra suspected his seemingly kind remarks were intended to serve an alternate purpose. Viktor was probably hoping that by making it safe for them to discuss what they had heard at this table, the courtiers would be less excited about having a dirty secret to share with anyone who would listen.

Leif gave a slight nod to Viktor in thanks for attempting to cover his faux pas. Though no one had specifically told him not to mention Kindra was his daughter, he had to realize it would be better for Kindra if people remained ignorant of her relationship with him. Leif looked at Kindra and gave her a quick nod of apology as well.

The same Lord who had attempted conversation with Kindra the day the castle was attacked looked at her now. "Is it you we have to thank for the return of our dear Prince Leif? Many assumed he was dead. First, you show up at our door and he followed soon after."

Kindra did not want to give this sniveling Lord an answer, but she put down her fork and addressed him. "I doubt I am the direct reason for his return, but I welcome your praise for a job well done if you care to give me the credit."

Kindra caught the corner of Gunnar's mouth turning up. At least he appreciated how Kindra had noncommittally answered. Ruth, too, was smiling at Kindra. She approved of how Kindra had fielded the question as well. Maybe she was getting the hang of noble double-talk. It should be easy for her. The nobles spoke as her middle school students did. One could speak his or her mind as long as things were said as if in jest. One should say what was expected, but changing the tone of voice could make those usual words have a different meaning. It was one of the things that drove her mad about her students. They could say such hurtful things without using mean words at all. Students never got in trouble for it, because the denotation, when repeated for administrators, seemed harmless on the surface. There was no way to explain how one just felt that the connotation of ordinary words was malicious. Again, Kindra was satisfied with her comparison of the courtiers to middle school students.

Dinner ended with no other conversation of note. She rose to return to her room and was nearly at the servant's exit when she heard harsh words from the passage. The princes had left through the same door before Kindra. She moved into the passage and saw Gunnar with his hand around Leif's throat. Gunnar had him pressed against the wall in a way that made Leif stand on his toes to avoid being choked.

Gunnar sneered. "You likely just brought Dredfall to our door. This time, they won't be here to scout and surveil. They will be here for your daughter!"

Leif couldn't breathe, let alone form words. His eyes were wide and fearful as he tried to draw breath. He silently pleaded with his older sibling to let him go. Gunnar did not seem to notice Leif's frantic state. He was enraged. He was beyond perceiving his surroundings. Gunnar did not even scent Kindra standing behind him. Leif was able to see her stepping closer, though. He turned his pleading eyes to her, since he was getting no reaction from Gunnar.

Kindra's chest tightened. She did not like this male. She did not feel for this male as an individual, but Leif was a person. He did have feelings, even if Kindra could not begin to understand what drove those feelings for Leif. Leif had no forethought. He was not a planner, and probably had never considered anyone's feelings but his own, but that did not mean he was cruel. Kindra raised her hand to tap Gunnar on the shoulder.

Suddenly, Gunnar flew backward into Kindra. She went sprawling onto her rear and Gunnar stumbled into the wall on the opposite side of the passage. Kindra looked at Leif. He was rubbing his neck and staring daggers at Gunnar. It hit Kindra then. Leif had used his magic. Why did Leif stand there for so long, allowing himself to be choked if he could have used magic to shrug Gunnar off at any time?

Kindra stood and dusted herself off. She nodded to the two princes. "I see you two have my best interests in mind and there is no reason for me to be involved..." Kindra's voice oozed sarcasm.

Gunnar had the decency to look a bit ashamed as he said, "Kindra. I didn't mean to overstep, but you must realize that Leif endangers all of us by calling attention to your relationship to the most powerful elf known since the times of King Andril. I would not have him-"

Kindra didn't hear the end of Gunnar's plea. She was already making her way up the stairs to her room. These males were unbelievable. Was it a bad thing that Leif had let her relationship with him be known? Yes, it was possible that this would cause the armies of Dredfall to act. Did it matter, though? They would act regardless. Maybe it was actually better to bring them sooner. At least it would stop the threat of these minor attacks, where people lost their lives a little at a time. Maybe it would be better to just have a war commence?

When Kindra got to her chamber, she dressed to go to the training room. She was angry, but had no single person to direct that anger towards. She supposed she was a little angry at just about everyone around her. This would include herself. She was starting to realize she should not have gotten herself involved in her Elven family problems. She missed her mom. She missed Jess. She could really use some solid advice from someone practical. Maybe Jess would be able to use math to explain all the impossible events Kindra had encountered since she'd seen her father at the cabin.

Kindra was beginning to understand that she was not capable of making her own choices. Back home, she did all the things her mother needed from her. If she was at work, she based her choices on the students' needs. If she was out with Jess, she had ideas, but Jess usually pointed out the flaws or downside to her plans before Kindra had the chance to act. In hind-site, that last part was usually a good thing. Even when Kindra did come up with her own ideas, they were usually not good ones.

Now that Kindra was here in another realm, she had quickly fallen in line and found new people to rely on to make her choices. She felt as if she were making decisions, but the reality was that she was bending to the needs of everyone around her, as usual. Her Lillerem family was expecting her to save them. She had agreed to train her body and to learn to use her magic. It had seemed like she chose those things, and in a way, she had. It had sounded exciting. The reality was that she never would have wanted any of this if other people around her hadn't made it seem so enticing. They were grooming her.

Dressed in a shirt and trousers that allowed her to move freely, Kindra stepped into the training center. She started down the stairs and saw Joral practicing at the archery range. Kindra's heart sank a little. She was looking forward to working alone for a while and trying to make a decision or two for herself, for once. Kindra headed off toward the obstacle course. She stood before the start of the course and began stretching her muscles. It felt good to feel the pull on her hamstrings and calves as she bent at the waist. Through her legs, she could see Joral watching her from the corner of his eye.

Kindra slowly stood up and rotated her body so the next time she bent to stretch, she would not be giving Joral a view of her rear. She bent again and closed her eyes. She could feel the stretch easing the tension in her lower back. Maybe it wasn't practice with magic or swords that she needed. Kindra was wondering if the castle offered a Yoga class when she slowly stood again and was looking directly at Joral. It was unbelievable how quietly these elves could walk.

"You are going to leave, aren't you?" There was no judgement in Joral's voice. "I can see it in your body language. You are not here to get ready to take on an army. You are here to relax. You are contemplative. You…you miss being home where things are simpler."

Kindra stared at him while combing through her feelings. She hadn't been outright thinking about leaving. Kindra had been thinking about her mom, Jess, Yoga classes and her students though. She was defiantly not thinking about Dredfall, King Ulford, singing swords, and Elven fathers. A smile started to creep across Kindra's lips.

"You almost had me. I was just starting to marvel at your people skills. Stay out of my head, Joral." Kindra blinked away.

Standing atop the first obstacle, Kindra called down to Joral, "What if I did leave? Leif is here now. He has full control of his powers. He has also been alive long enough to fully understand the politics and family dynamics here." She disappeared again.

Joral watched her appear at the top of the second obstacle. "You know, the point of the course is to improve strength, balance and speed. You're not supposed to just teleport to the top of each obstacle."

Kindra turned toward the rope bridge to her left. She teleported quickly, three times, touching the bridge once near its start, once in the middle and once toward the end before finally willing herself to appear on the pillar at the far side of the bridge. She turned to Joral far below and gave a little smirk, as if to ask if that was more like what he had meant.

Joral dipped his head a bit. "Better, but still not exactly what I envisioned. I was thinking you would need to use your muscles a bit more. You stretched them out and got them all ready to go, but here you are hopping from station to station without putting them to any use."

Joral mounted the rolling log in one swift motion and moved across it. He climbed the rope net to the pillar that led to the bridge Kindra had just crossed. Kindra watched his muscles move. It did seem like traversing the course without teleporting was trying on the muscles. The notion made her even more comfortable with her choice to teleport through it. Joral began crossing the bridge, using his core to remain upright and balanced. There was no room for him to join Kindra on the pillar once he reached the other side. She teleported back to the ground.

Joral reached the pillar and turned in time to see Kindra walking over to the sparring area. She picked up a sword and began the careful steps she had learned with Gunnar in the forest. Joral wished he could teleport. He stood at the highest point of the course with no way to get down but to go back or go forward through the course. He reached up for the zip line, which would take him half-way to the ground level. From there, he swung from one rope to the next rope to reach another pillar. He walked most of the way down a gently sloping ladder and jumped to the ground before reaching the next obstacle.

Kindra was in the middle of a downward swoop with Forsvarer when she felt resistance and metal sounded off metal. Joral had taken up a sword and blocked her latest swing. The pair danced through the swordplay motions for a few minutes without speaking. It had a similar feeling to the stretching she had done. Though her muscles worked harder than they had before, she found her mind relaxed and her body felt good. She watched Joral and saw he had a look of calm on his face as well. There was an easy silence between them as they both concentrated on their steps.

At the end of a set, Kindra stood and stared at Joral. "You must think I am petty. I complain about my father and feel as if he has betrayed me. Your father is the very man who continues to attack your family here at Millspare. How can I think my father is so evil when I am standing here with you?"

"You mean, you are reminded of how terrible fathers can be each time you look at my face?" Joral asked and looked down at the floor.

"The scar is a reminder, yes. That isn't the sum of it, though. As bad as your father is, you are still here laughing and enjoying your family. True, you are preparing for war, but you don't let it weigh on you personally. Not in a way that would make others notice it, anyway."

Joral gave Kindra half of a smile. "Essentially, you are telling me that I am very good at hiding my self-pity."

Kindra laughed. "Well, if there is self-pity, then yes, you are excellent at hiding it."

Kindra left Joral in the training room and went back to her room for a bath. Mildred was there waiting for her. Kinda's eyes lit up at the sight of the woman returning to her duties. She looked Mildred over and didn't see any remnants of injuries. There was no limping or groans as Mildred went about readying Kindra's bath. Kindra stripped off her sweaty clothing and hungrily entered the warm bathing tub.

As Kindra sunk down into the water, Mildred spoke. "There is a rumor you are thinking of leaving us."

Kindra didn't look up. There hadn't been time for Joral to speak to Mildred, so it must be more evident than she thought that she had been missing home.

"If you leave us, we will all be upset, but there is one admirer in particular who would be heartbroken." Mildred said, with her back to Kindra.

Kindra did not want to acknowledge that she had been thinking of how much she missed home. She really didn't want to admit that she had been considering…even if not seriously, that she wanted to go back to the human realm. Kindra just wanted to soak in the tub and weigh her options between heading back home and doing what she knew was right for all the people here. She also did not want Mildred walking out of this room, thinking there was something between her and Joral.

"If you mean Joral, I should remind you that we are cousins, and though the Fae may find it a good match, I am a bit sickened at the thought."

Mildred laughed. "Oh no, child! Not Joral. He is easy to like and easy to be with. You and he could be the closest of friends, but I haven't seen him looking at you the same way another has."

"Well, Einar is married to you, and Viktor will always belong to Ruth. Every other male here is related to me, unless you mean one of the courtiers and I can assure you I have no interest in any of them. Kindra was wide-eyed at the thought of one of those driveling Lords fawning after her.

"Hmmmmmmm" Mildred hummed. "Related in some way...yes; but not by blood."

With that, the older woman left the chamber. She left Kindra sitting in the tub, feeling like one of her middle school students. It was as if a girl at lunch just came and whispered in her ear that she knew someone who liked Kindra, but she couldn't tell. Kindra wanted to chase after the woman, but she didn't think anyone would appreciate her running through the hall naked. Instead, Kindra sank farther into the water. She closed her eyes and started running through the family tree. *Gunnar is my uncle, Bane? Cousin. Joral? Cousin. Krish? Cousin. Wait...no!* Krish was technically her first cousin, once removed. It was the same relationship as Bane and Joral, but Krish's father Erik had been adopted by King Lars and his male mate! If King Erik was not a blood relative, then neither was Krish.

Krish had to be her admirer. The heir to the throne of Lillerem had barely spoken to her, though. Krish had spent far less time with her than Gunnar or Joral. The only prince she may have interacted with less was Bane. Kindra ran through each conversation she'd had with the beautiful male, but there had been no hint that he saw her as anything other than a nuisance. When she had woken from her fall from the cliff and seen him, she had nearly fell in love with the almost white hair, the face, the ice-blue eyes... Of course, he had then held a sword to her throat and that had been the last she had thought of him in that way.

Krish had been the person to take the lead in introducing her to Lillerem, Millspare, and had even made sure she had gotten to her room that first night. He had been the one to help her onto her horse when they had fled the castle the following evening. It had been Krish that was her primary companion and guide right up until Gunnar had started teaching her to use Forsvarer and Joral had started helping her with her magic. Kindra had assumed he was happy to hand her off so he could handle his other duties. It had seemed he was the leader of the four princes and that he had only taken on her care to meet expectations from the others.

As Kindra toweled herself dry, she was still thinking about Krish. She really didn't know much about him at all. He was absolutely stunning and covered in muscle. He was a leader and the other princes looked to him for direction. Krish had also been the only prince absent from Leif's formal reintroduction to Ruth and Viktor. Kindra wasn't sure if he had not been in the ballroom that day because he was indifferent to Leif's return, or if it was because he cared a great deal. If it was the latter, was Krish unhappy or glad that Leif had returned? Kindra had been so wrapped up in herself and the return of her father that she hadn't given much thought to Krish's absence from the ballroom at all.

Kindra's wardrobe selected a pair of pants and a bright purple tunic for her to wear, along with riding boots. It seemed the wardrobe had felt Kindra needed to go horseback riding. Maybe she did. It would be a nice way to see some of the area beyond Millspare, while not fleeing for her life. She could get some fresh air and, in the process, learn more about Aergroth.

Kindra knew there must be another way to reach the stables, but she took the route she had taken before. She went down to the formal dining room and through the rear servant door. She followed the smell of hay and manure to the end of the passage. Kindra walked down the path between the stalls and marveled at the various breeds and sizes of the horses kept by Millspare. She made her way to the stall that held the brown mare she had been given to ride when they had fled the castle.

The mare was munching from a feed bucket, but looked up as Kindra approached. Kindra looked into the Mare's eyes, mesmerized. The horse's long, dark lashes matched her dark main and tail. Kindra stroked the horse's neck and ran her fingers along her fuzzy face, down to her nose. The horse nuzzled Kindra a touch, as if she knew Kindra was feeling a little lost and lonely.

Kindra spoke to the horse. "I never even asked what your name is. I suppose I am a selfish princess. At first I was only thinking of you as transportation as I ran from danger, but I could have asked. Once we were up in the woods and I was performing sword dances for Gunnar, I should have asked. How could I be so wrapped up in myself that it didn't even occur to me to ask about your name?"

"Her name is Branka. It means magnificent protector, if you ask the Vikings of your world."

Kindra whirled to find Krish tending to his own horse in the stall behind her. "I'll have to take your world for it, considering the Vikings have been gone for thousands of years."

Kindra turned back to the mare. "Well Branka, I suppose it wouldn't be a proper pity party if we were the only guests."

"Branka is a superb listener. If she had thumbs, she could probably save the World on her own with all the information she has overheard and had shared with her in confidence. That horse has more intel than any spy we've ever had in our army. I think it's her eyes. They make you want to tell her your secrets"

"You know an awful lot about her. You must spend quite a bit of time with Branka yourself."

Krish laughed. "Of course I spend time with her. She is my horse."

*His horse? Krish had given her his own horse to ride when they had fled the castle?* There it was again. An important detail she had missed by making assumptions that the brown mare had just been some extra horse for her to ride. Mildred had seen Krish hand his own horse to Kindra that evening. It was probably the thing that had made Mildred realize Krish had taken more than a subtle interest in the newly found princess.

"If Branka is your horse, then what are you doing cheating on her in a different stall?" Kindra pretended to be offended on Branka's behalf.

Krish gave a low chuckle. "I am heir to the throne of Lillerem, but my most important job is as a stable hand. Most of the horses here belong to Viktor and Ruth. I care for them all. I even care for the horses of those who visit here at the castle. It proves to be a handy position when one wishes to know the identities of all visitors to Millspare."

"As long as those visitors arrive by horseback…or, I suppose, a carriage drawn by horses, and as long as the driver didn't intend to leave and pick up the passengers later." Kindra mused aloud.

"Almost all drivers will stop to water the horses before heading off. As a bonus, the drivers are usually prone to useful chatter." Krish chuckled again.

Kindra cocked her head at Krish. "So, what do the other lords and ladies think of a crown prince serving as a lowly stable hand?"

Another voice came from down the aisle of stalls. "Krish is known throughout the realm as an incredible horseman. I'm sure they speak in secret about the oddity of a prince doing a job that could be expected of any local child, but I've never heard a complaint from anyone about the care of a single horse."

Kindra watched Viktor strode closer. She noticed Krish with his head down. For whatever reason, it did not seem that he was looking forward to a conversation with Viktor. Indeed, Krish actually turned his back to Viktor and continued brushing the horse in the stall with him. Kindra waited for Viktor to approach her. Kindra was amused to see Viktor walk over to Krish's stall instead.

"You've been avoiding me, Krish. I'm here to determine why that is. I'm really not sure if it is something I did to you, or something you did that you wish to keep from me."

Krish kept his head down, but his blood started to simmer. He didn't know how to explain what he was feeling, let alone give an explanation of why he was feeling it. The root of the issue was really simple. Krish did not want Viktor to put his faith in Leif. The problem was explaining that to Viktor without offending him or Leif. If Krish upset Viktor, Viktor might not trust Krish implicitly with his armies and scouting parties. It was simply in Viktor's nature to keep trust from those who he did not find to be of like-mind. If Krish upset Leif, Leif might run back to the human realm and refuse to help in the fight ahead. To win the coming war, Krish would need Viktor to trust him and the realm would need Leif's help. At the same time, Krish did not want Viktor to place too much responsibility on an unreliable elf such as Leif. The whole situation just left Krish feeling angry.

Kindra cleared her throat. "This is about my father, isn't it? At first, I thought you backed away when I started training, but that wasn't it at all. You didn't just back away from me. You pulled back from everyone when Leif arrived."

Krish snapped his head to Kindra. She had figured it out. She didn't press Krish, and she hoped Viktor would know well enough to do the same. Kindra couldn't tell which expression was winning on Krish's face. *Was he more angry or hurt? Was that confusion?* It was killing her to stay quiet and not press for information. He'd have to speak, eventually. The silence was getting heavier by the second.

In the end, it was Viktor who couldn't handle the wait. "Do you not agree with my allowing him to stay?"

"No, that I agree with."

"So then, what is it that you disagree with, if not that?"

"I'm afraid, Viktor. I'm afraid that we will ride off into battle with the sense that the war is all but won. We will turn around at some crucial point, and our savior will have vanished."

Viktor tilted his head quizzically. "Do you think I am foolish enough to believe Leif will handle Ulford alone? Do you think I expect Leif to take over the war room and layout plans that we all shall blindly follow? I am no fool, Krish. I put more faith in Kindra's role in the war ahead than I do Leif's participation."

Had Kindra heard him correctly? Was Viktor still speaking of her role in the war as if it had not changed? Leif was here now. The most powerful Elf in hundreds of years was among them, and Viktor was still banking on the role a middle school psychologist was going to play. Maybe she should go home. That would teach these Elven rulers to make assumptions about her.

Krish replied to Viktor. "I wouldn't count on either of them saving the world. Leif has proven to be selfish and unpredictable. Kindra has her own life in her own realm. She has only begun to master her magic and has very little skill with a sword."

Kindra's mouth fell open. She had just started to appreciate this horse-loving male and now he had gone and insulted her! Well, she supposed it wasn't really an insult. Krish had basically stated that she was a poor fighter who couldn't use her magic well, but it was true. She couldn't believe he had written her off as returning home to her own life, though. Then again, hadn't she just spent most of the day trying to decide if she should do just that?

Viktor stepped toward Krish. "I would not presume that either of them would carry the torch into battle. They are of the same blood. Both are prone to being stubborn, both can be selfish, and neither has a true connection to our people here in Alfheim. We would carry out our original plans, as intended. The difference now is hope. We can hope to have one or both of them by our side."

Viktor was now standing between Krish and Kindra. His back was to Kindra while Krish faced her across the aisle. As Viktor went on attempting to convince Krish that nothing and everything had changed since the arrival of Kindra and then Leif, Krish watched Kindra. She was no longer listening. She was somewhere deep in her own mind. Her eyes refocused, and she opened the latch of the stall. Kindra turned to Branka. She climbed the wooden posts at the side of the stall and then hauled herself onto Branka's back. There was no saddle. Kindra took hold of Branka's mane and gave her a little kick. The horse left the stall and headed out of the stable with Kindra bareback upon her.

Krish looked back at Viktor. "Half of your hope for a better kingdom just rode bareback out of the stable on my horse."

Kindra didn't need to ride fast. This was a good thing, considering she didn't feel all that confident riding without a saddle. Kindra felt better just being away from the males in the stable. She had thought it was difficult to have her mother poke her nose into her life, and now she was experiencing a similar controlling sensation from a court in a completely different realm. On a positive note, it did make Kindra feel better about her relationship with her mother. Her mother had raised her and could at least claim some right to trying to influence Kindra's life choices. The people here, though mostly related by blood, had basically met her and made the assumption she would do as they wished. There was still that gnawing feeling that even though she had felt as if she wanted to help the people of this realm, it may have actually been her natural predisposition to following others' wishes that made it easy to make that choice. Maybe she really didn't want to help anyone, but just wanted to please those around her.

Kindra was lost in her thoughts and the clopping of Branka's hooves. She did not see the male step out of the trees into her path. Branka pulled up short and nearly dumped Kindra into the dirt. If she'd been driving a car, the male would be among the bug guts of the windshield. Thankfully, this mode of transportation offered another sentient being to make split-second decisions. Kindra slowed her breaths and dulled the roar of her own blood in her ears while Branka clopped around a bit to shake out her own jitters.

# CHAPTER 18

Leif was standing in the middle of the path Kindra had been traveling. He waited calmly as both female and beast calmed their nerves enough to acknowledge him. The male didn't look at Kindra. Leif gave her space to compose herself..

Kindra was not nearly as kind. "What the fuck was that? You scared the shit out of me!"

Clearly, she had not had sufficient time to calm her nerves. Leif waited and watched as Kindra took a deep breath, then another. Her face returned to its usual color and her eyes started to lose the panic they had in them just a moment earlier. After a third breath, Kindra apologized for her outburst and gestured for Leif to state his purpose in interrupting her peaceful trek through the outskirts of Aergroth.

Leif did not say much. "Go back home."

Kindra stared at him for a moment. "I'm going to head back soon. I wasn't planning to stay out all day. I just needed some time to think."

"That's not what I meant. Go back home to New York. This is not your fight."

Kindra sat straighter in the saddle. *Who does this male think he is? Yet another person trying to control my actions. Is there not a single person, in any realm, who will let me decide for myself what I want to do?* Kindra drew in breath to spew venom at Leif and all the other controlling family she had here in Lillerem.

Leif gently raised a hand before she could speak. "I'm not here to tell you what I think you should do. I am here to tell you it is ok to do what is in your heart. I figure everyone here has been telling you it is your duty to defend the people of Lillerem. Some may even expect you to give your life for a country of which you have barely seen a sliver. I wanted to tell you it is ok to go home."

"Go home? Why would you want me to do that? Are you so desperate to have someone to share the burden of being the one who abandoned his people to live in the human realm?"

"Kindra, we are more alike than you would care to think. There are many reasons I stayed away from Alfheim. It's hard to put any of those reasons into words, but there was always conflict in my heart over them. I often wondered if I was letting my family down, then the next moment I decided I would stay away just to defy them. I wondered if I really was destined to save an entire realm, then the fear of failing to do that would keep me rooted to the spot where I was. Ultimately, it was easier to be a disappointment, but feel like I was making my own choices and living my own life."

"Based on how you were living that life when Jess and I found you at your cabin, I'm not feeling as if we have much in common at all." Even as Kindra spoke the words, she was marveling over how similar his internal battle sounded to her own.

"Maybe so," Leif said. "You are the only reason I am standing in this realm now. I have no intention of saving these people. The only one I really even know is Gunnar, and I have not truly known him in decades. The other people here only know me as a child and a man who has forsaken his own kind. There is no reason for me to lose my life for them."

"What are you suggesting?" Kindra asked. "Do we go back to Norway and live happily ever after with Kristen and Nils while the people here live under Ulford's tyranny?"

"If that is what you desire, then it sounds like the perfect life to me." Leif said the words, but the look on her face told Kindra he wasn't hopeful. He knew that wasn't what she wanted.

"You know I'd never leave my mother. I could not live in Norway."

"Fine." Leif laughed. "You can live in New York near your mother, and I'll live in Norway with Kristen. You can come for vacations in Norway as often as you like."

Kindra smiled. "Would you be willing to pay for airfare? This is starting to sound like the kind of life I can deal with."

Leif's green eyes sparkled. "Airfare is not something we elves worry about; not even in the human realm."

Leif gestured for Kindra to follow him off into the trees. Kindra followed him to an area covered with thick flowing bushes growing up against a rock face. She dismounted and left Branka to munch some grass from the forest floor. As she neared Leif, he reached out toward the purple flowers on the bush nearest to him. Kindra waited for him to pluck a flower or two, but he pulled back the branches of the bush instead. Covered by the beautiful mask of the purple flowers was the mouth of a cave. Go ahead, Kindra. It's less than a mile walk and you'll be home.

Kindra's mouth fell open. It was another portal. She presumed this one would take her to New York. From this spot, she could literally walk straight home. She looked over her shoulder at Branka. The horse looked up at Kindra as if to tell her she was on her own with this decision.

"Don't worry Kindra. I'll get her back to the stable safely. I may not know Krish well, but I know enough that he would follow you to the human realm to get his beloved horse back home." Leif cupped Kindra's face in his hands. "It does not matter to me what you decide to do. I am grateful to have seen the adult you have become and to know your mother raised you well. It was torture to know nothing about you, and I am surprised and proud that you have inherited so many of my traits."

Kindra smiled sadly. "I think that might be the only nice thing I've ever heard you say. I appreciate you offering to take Krish's horse back. It makes this choice even easier."

Without another word, or even a look back at Branka, Kindra entered the mouth of the cave. She found the torch she knew would be hanging on the inside wall. It was already burning with firelight. Kindra lifted the torch from its sconce and headed off into the darkness. Just as the light from the mouth of the cave began to fade, she felt dull pain throughout her body. She became queasy, but remained calm. Kindra knew her body was returning to its human form. She touched her teeth with her tongue and found that her canines were no longer elongated. She didn't need to reach up to know the slight points of her ears were gone as well.

Kindra was within a few steps of a rock wall at the end of the tunnel when it slid open for her and revealed a basement. She left the torch in the sconce at the end of the tunnel. There was a book of matches on the ground. That matchbook was all the evidence she needed to know she had, indeed, re-entered the human realm. She stepped into the dim basement. Light filtered through one filthy window. She could see well enough to know there was a staircase in front of her. The cave wall behind her slid shut.

Kindra made her way up the dim staircase. At the top, Kindra opened the door to reveal a small cabin. The familiarity swept over Kindra as she took in the living room at the end of the short hall. Same couch, same coffee table, same rocking chair, and same table with the same video game console...she was in Leif's cabin. The man had his daughter guarding the gate in Norway and he guarded the gate here in New York. Leif hadn't quite abandoned his people. He was protecting them from another realm.

Kindra reached for her cell phone, hoping there was service here. Her hand met flowing material where her back pocket should be. She shook her head. Her cell phone was on a kitchen table in Norway. At least that was where it was the last time Kindra had seen it. She supposed Kristen would have at least moved it to the counter at this point. Aware that she would be faced with a fairly long walk, Kindra was glad for the boots she had taken to wearing, regardless of her chosen attire.

She trudged off to Leif's bedroom and threw open his closet. She really should not have bothered. The closet was nearly empty. It seemed most of the clothes were piled about around the room. Kindra discovered a flannel shirt that didn't smell too badly protruding from under the bed and ripped the only pair of jeans on a hanger from the sparse selection in the closet. Kindra pulled off her own clothes and tossed them on the unmade bed. Kindra pulled on Leif's clothes and sat on the edge of the bed to lace up her boots.

Kindra turned back to the clothes she had discarded in a pile on the bed. She wrapped them around Forsvarer, still in its scabbard and attached to her belt, then put the entire bundle at the bottom of Leif's closet and shut the door. Kindra studied her reflection in the hall mirror. She looked as if she had just stepped out of paper country in the deep woods of Maine, or maybe as if she were headed to a 90s grunge concert. The jeans were a little baggy, but her hips held them up. *Jess is never going to let me live this outfit down.* Kindra banged out of the front door and hopped down the steps. She began her long walk to the location the locals referred to as a town.

When Kindra reached a small corner deli, she felt tears of relief begin to invade her eyes. She had walked over five miles in her human form. She may have been working out while at Millspare, and she had built her endurance and muscle mass, but there was no way to prepare for the toll the walk had taken on her while in her human form. Kindra might not be longing for the slight points at her ears, but there were other benefits to her Elven form that would have made this journey less of a burden.

Kindra walked into the deli and asked the twenty-something at the counter where the payphone was located. He snapped a grin to his face and pointed to the back corner of the store. Kindra wove through the aisles and was not pleased to find the shell of a payphone hanging on the wall next to an ATM. There was no phone, just the old silver and blue box with some wires protruding from the back, where a phone had once been. Kindra went back to the clerk at the counter. She did not need to speak. The look on her face conveyed her impatience.

"You asked where the phone was, not if I had a phone that actually worked." This guy thought he was smart alright.

"May I borrow your cell to make a quick call?" Kindra asked. She did her best to keep the annoyance from her voice.

"Sorry lady. I've got personal shit on my phone. Use this instead." The clerk pulled a cordless phone from under the counter and held it out for Kindra.

Kindra took the phone and dialed Jess's number. Her voice was cheery on the other end of the line. "Hello, Jess Bennett speaking."

"Jess! It's so good to hear your voice! It's Kindra."

"I knew it! I kept answering my phone for all numbers at all hours. I even answered the ones from Iowa that were obviously solicitations or scams. I knew you'd call eventually, from somewhere!"

"Well, I'm calling from a deli out by Leif's cabin. It's on the corner before you make the last turn onto his road." The clerk pointed to a large sign over his head. "The place is called 'Hawk's Deli and Convenience.'"

"I'll look it up online. I can be there in an hour and a half."

Kindra looked at the clock on the wall. School had let out about five minutes earlier. *At least I have decent timing.* Kindra returned the phone to the clerk. He was watching her as he stroked his scrawny goatee. She had no money, and it seemed the clerk was beginning to suspect that very thing. Kindra turned and walked outside. She went around to the side of the building and took a seat on one of the yellow concrete humps that designated each parking spot. If anything, the wait would afford Kindra time to think about how she was going to explain all that had happened since she had left New York to Jess and her mother.

Her mother knew what Leif was. She had known there was something to see in Norway. Beyond that, Kindra was not sure what her mother knew or believed to be the truth about Alfheim. Jess, on the other hand, would be more likely to believe the fantastic tale Kindra had to tell. Despite her love of math and logic, she loved a good fairy tale.

Kindra began replaying the entire story in her own mind. Part of it was to reassure herself that it had really happened. Sitting here, in a backwoods part of New York, it was easy to begin to tell herself the last week had never happened. Had it only been a week? It seemed to Kindra she had over a year's worth of experiences in that time. She was fairly confident her story would not be boring. There was a lingering concern that neither Jess nor her mother would fully believe all she had to tell.

Kindra was thinking about Krish when Jess pulled into the lot almost two hours later. It was the look in his eyes when he had realized how offended she had been by his and Viktor's conversation this morning. The look had been one of genuine regret. As she opened the door to Jess's car, Kindra was wondering if Krish had realized she had left

Alfheim by now. Her thoughts were interrupted when Jess threw herself across the console to wrap her arms around Kindra's neck. Jess planted a loud kiss on Kindra's cheek and all thoughts of Krish were gone. Jess sat back in the driver's seat and eyed Kindra's choice of attire. She wrinkled her nose, but said nothing as she pulled the car out of the lot.

Jess peppered Kindra with questions for the first twenty minutes of the trip back home. She didn't even pause long enough to realize that Kindra wasn't answering any of them. Kindra didn't mind. She had been wondering how she was going to manage holding off on the details until she could sit down with both Jess and her mother so she wouldn't need to tell the story twice.

Jess finally took a breath and glanced over at Kindra, sitting quietly in the passenger seat. "You're not planning on answering any of these questions, are you?"

Kindra gave Jess a slight smile and tilted her head. "Which questions do you mean?"

Jess spluttered some unintelligible words. There was something in them about best friends and secret keeping, but Jess was frustrated beyond the point of full sentences that were coherent.

Kindra put a stop to Jess's attempts at speech. "I planned to wait until we were with my mother, anyway. Don't take it personally."

Jess pressed her foot down on the accelerated a bit harder. "To your mother's house, it is. Did you plan to call her to let her know you were coming?"

Kindra plucked Jess's cell from the holder on the dash and dialed her mother. The phone range three times before her mother answered. She started speaking before Kindra had a chance to announce who she was.

"Jessie! Have you heard from Kindra? I spoke to Kristen again this morning, and she still hasn't heard from her. I know I keep asking you, but I just know she'd reach out to you before she thought to call me."

Kindra smiled at Jess in apology. It seemed her mother had been calling her friend quite a bit since she'd disappeared to Alfheim. Kindra suspected that the same was true for her sister at Husland Farm as well. It was also not lost on Kindra that her mother fully expected that Jess would be Kindra's first contact. She felt a little tug in her chest, having proved her mother correct. Kindra had not even considered calling her mother to pick her up. Logically, though, Jess had been the one to accompany Kindra to Leif's cabin and would know the way. Kindra failed to convince herself, knowing all her mother would have needed was the address of the deli and the GPS would have guided her there.

"Hi Mom! It's Kindra here!"

"Kindra! Is Jess in Norway? Why aren't you just using your own phone? Kristen said she was keeping it charged for you. Are you coming back to New York? Should I fly-"

"Mom! Jess and I will be at your door in fifteen minutes. Put the coffee on. I have an incredible story for you both."

# CHAPTER 19

It was almost midnight when Kindra had finished her tale. The trio had switched from tea to coffee after the first hour. The questions shooting from both Jess and Gretchen had made the time required for the story extensive. They had demanded so many details that were irrelevant in Kindra's eyes. Jess had wanted each of the Elven princes described in unnecessary detail. Gretchen had wanted to know about Leif's long-dead parents. None of the information she shared had any bearing on the story itself.

The three of them sat quietly at Gretchen's kitchen table. Jess and Gretchen were out of questions. Kindra had relayed every minute of her journey from the time she had landed in Norway to the time Jess had picked her up at the corner deli upstate. No one spoke. It was not a relaxed silence. Kindra was drained. Jess and Gretchen sat tensely, as if there might still be more to come. Gretchen slowly wheeled over to the counter to refill her coffee cup. Still, no one spoke.

The silence was broken when Gretchen threw her coffee mug into the sink with enough force to break it. She didn't turn her chair toward Kindra before she began speaking. She did not yell. Her voice was eerily steady.

"All your life, you've done everything in your power to help those in need. You even chose a career where you were destined to work with a population of students who couldn't fend for themselves and would always need support. I don't understand how you walked through that portal and came back home, knowing you could help all those people."

Kindra stared at her mother as Gretchen turned her chair to face Kindra. Kindra's lips were parted slightly as if she were going to speak, but she could not think of what to say. It was only hours ago that her mother had been so happy to see her, and now Gretchen was upset that she had come home.

It was Jess who spoke next. "Your mom has a point. It's rather surprising that you turned and ran."

Kindra could feel her body heating up. The anger strained to boil out of her mouth. She took a breath, then another. These women would not listen to her if she couldn't hold it together.

"I was hoping you would have understood from my story that I was feeling as if I were being controlled; like I didn't have a choice in the matter. It was simply expected that I would hoist up my skirts and run off to save the world."

"So you left for spite?" Gretchen was flabbergasted. "You came back home to prove to those royals that you could leave if you wished to and didn't have to do what they wanted?"

Kindra narrowed her eyes at her mother. "No. I was simply tired of being steered in a direction other than one I would have chosen for myself." Kindra was speaking through her teeth. "Ruth and Viktor took one look at me and began to make plans which they expected to come to fruition. No one even bothered to ask me if I was interested in helping the cause!"

Even as she spoke, Kindra was trying to remember how she had been roped into the grand plan. She remembered discovering her magic and being put-off by the idea that there might be plans and events to follow in which she was expected to partake. She remembered killing that male in the woods and retching afterward. Then it came to her. The moment things had changed. She had been shown to her room by Ruth. Ruth had spoken about Leif being so powerful, but unwilling to return to Alfheim and fight. Kindra's exact words to Ruth replayed in her head, *"I feel a responsibility to protect you all as family, in any way I am able."*

Kindra had agreed to help. She had said she would help in any way she could. That was before she had really started to be able to wield her magic or wield a sword. Had her words been only that? When she had thought there was nothing she could do for them, Kindra had offered Ruth everything. Even during her speech defending Leif's intentions to Viktor and Ruth, Kindra had said she felt a connection to her Elven family, and fully intended to stand with them against Dredfall, Once Kindra had actually started to find some skill and thought she might actually be helpful, she had turned and ran.

Kindra returned her attention to the two women watching her. She knew they had seen the change in her face. She knew they had witnessed the moment where she realized she had made the choice to help. Kindra had not been convinced or cajoled. She had said she would help in any way she could, then threw up her hands and cried that she had been manipulated when she realized how real this fight would be and how difficult it would be to prepare for it. This was not renting a U-Haul and helping a friend move. Kindra had promised to help save an entire kingdom.

Kindra let her head hang a bit. "I can see what you're both thinking, and you are correct. I ran. I realized that the entirety of Lillerem might depend on my choices, and I found it easier to believe those choices had been made for me. It was unbearable to think I had chosen incorrectly, or that I might fail. It was so much easier to turn around and leave."

Gretchen's face had softened. She could see the conflict within Kindra. She understood that her daughter wanted to help but had been farther from her comfort zone than any person should ever find themselves. Jess, on the other hand, had not softened one bit.

"You lied to them, didn't you?" Jess accused. "I can see it written on your face. You told them you would help them and then changed your mind. That is not you! I have never known you to back down from a fight, nor to make a promise and fail to follow through. This was Leif, wasn't it? This was that drunken fool convincing you it was better to be selfish. I can't believe you listened to that ass."

Kindra fired back at Jess. "He went to Alfheim for me. He made me realize it was ok to go home because he had arrived to do the job. He was going to handle it, so I didn't have to be involved."

Jess was not backing down. "You can laud him for finally taking responsibility for his own fight if you want to, but it doesn't change the fact that you made a promise. It doesn't change the fact that having both you and Leif there would make the battle easier and presumably prevent the unnecessary loss of many lives. You left a man to do a job he never wanted to do. How do you know he hasn't already left them all to fend for themselves now that he has succeeded in sending you home and removing you from danger?"

"Male." Kindra said quietly.

"What?" Jess was confused.

"You called him a man. He is a male, but not a man. He is not human."

The women sat in silence once again. It was now far past a normal bedtime for Jess. Kindra knew the women liked to be asleep sometime around 9:30 on school nights. She was still here, though. Kindra couldn't understand why. Kindra had told the story, including the details about the handsome Elven princes. That should have satisfied Jess, yet she was still here.

"You should head home, Jess," Kindra said to her friend. "I'll stay here tonight. Pick me up on your way to school tomorrow morning. I'd like to check in and get back to the kids. I'm sure some of them are having complete meltdowns at the disruption in their routines at this point."

"I'm not going to school tomorrow, Kindra, and neither are you."

Jess didn't mention that she had decided to take the day off as soon as her friend had phoned her for a ride. She had figured her friend would have so much to tell and they would be up late discussing some dreamy man, or men, that Kindra had trounced around with on her vacation. Jess had certainly not anticipated that her friend would be asked to save an entire realm while on that same vacation. She was glad she had taken the day, though. There was no way she would be functional early tomorrow morning.

"I'll call home. I'm going to let Sean know not to expect me. It seems we're all going to be spending the night here."

Jess stood and went to the hall closet. She pulled out two blankets and dropped them onto the sectional. It had been many years since Jess had crashed on Gretchen's couch, but it was time to revive the tradition. Her friend, who dealt with crisis daily, was having a crisis of her own and was not even fully aware of it.

Gretchen started rolling herself down the hall. She called back, "I'm going to get some sleep. I will see you both in the morning."

Gretchen stopped in the bathroom to get ready for bed. The water ran, the toilet flushed. Gretchen wheeled back into the hall and down to her bedroom. Kindra and Jess did not speak to each other the entire time. As Gretchen's door closed for the night, Kindra stood and placed all the dirty mugs into the sink. She made her way to the couch. Kindra sat and pulled off her boots and Leif's old jeans. She left the oversized lumberjack shirt on. It did make a good nightshirt. Kindra pulled one of the blankets over herself and closed her eyes.

Jess's voice came from the kitchen table. "I know you aren't going to be able to sleep. That's a good thing. I think you should use the time to really think about the choices you are making."

Kindra had not answered her. She did feel anger toward her friend right now, but that wasn't what had kept her quiet. Kindra hadn't spoken because Jess was only stating the truth. As Jess walked into the room and took her own spot on the couch, fully clothed except for her shoes, Kindra realized the anger she felt for Jess was minuscule. Right now, most of the anger inside Kindra was directed at herself. She had been so concerned about being controlled and convinced to do Ruth's bidding that she had not seen how easily Leif had manipulated her into returning to the human realm. Kindra was going to need to pay much more careful attention to how she interpreted the direction of others if she truly wanted to avoid feeling manipulated. What was she going to do? Could she possibly go through the rest of her life ignoring every bit of advice offered to her? It just seemed like the more people said they cared about her, the more they were hiding their own agendas.

Kindra lay coiled in her blanket, staring at the wall. She was truly trying to dig deep and discover what it was she wanted to do. It was impossible not to consider the needs and desires of others. Kindra sat up and blew out a breath. She conceded to the realization that she had no idea how to do what was best for her. There simply was no such thing in her world. Every choice she made, even if it was one that made her happy, was measured by how productive it was, or the benefits the decision had for others. Even if she tried to weigh her choice based on how happy each path would make her, she had to accept that she would be happy because she had made others happy and helped someone else out of a bad situation.

Kindra stood and went to the kitchen. She grabbed a bottle of water and sat down at the table. With her new personal discovery, that her own happiness depended on her ability to make others happy and help people, Kindra mulled the choice she faced over. Which course of action would help the most people and make the most people happy? She considered her students at school. Kindra knew she was good at her job. She knew the kids were able to confide in her and felt safe in her office. She did need to admit, though, that there were other people that were qualified to do her job. It was entirely possible that the person who had been sitting at her desk for the last week was doing a better job than she ever had. Kindra concluded that though she was helping many students, it was help that could be provided by someone else.

Kindra next considered the effect her decision would have on her mother. Gretchen had only one child. Kindra was, much of the time, Gretchen's sole connection to the world. Kindra provided the entertainment, as well as news updates, and simply companionship for Gretchen. Though it wouldn't be the same as seeing her daughter, Jess might be able to provide some of that for Gretchen. It might even help out with the next person Kindra needed to factor in to her pending choice. Her choice would effect Jess as well. Jess was married and could never be truly lonely. She had a built in companion, even when she occasionally wished she could simply be alone. What Jess would not have, if Kindra were not around, was a female to confide in. As the years stretched on, Gretchen's ideals had seemed to align more with Kindra's. Since Jess and Kindra had many of the same convictions, she expected the age gap between Jess and Gretchen would not be an issue, and friendship between the two women did not seem as preposterous as it had when the girls were younger. It was possible that Jess and Gretchen could lean on each other in Kindra's absence.

Kindra screwed the cap back onto her water bottle and carried it into the living room. She put the water on the coffee table and returned to her little nest on the couch. She got under her blanket, proceeded to flip around and shuffle her pillow until her head was in the perfect spot to keep her neck from being stiff in the morning.

"So." Jess's voice came from the other side of the sectional. "Have you figured it out? Solved your other worldly problems?"

"Possibly." was all Kindra said before pulling the blanket to her chin and closing her eyes.

In the morning, Kindra woke to find Jess and her mother quietly sipping coffee in the kitchen. It was rare that Kindra could sleep through the sounds of coffee being made. It was either a testament to how tired she had been, or to how relaxed her brain had become once she had accepted her personal fault of only being happy if others were happy as well. Kindra pulled a mug from the cabinet and made her own cup of coffee.

"I'm going back," Kindra said, as she pulled out a chair and joined her mother and Jess.

"We know," chorused Jess and Gretchen simultaneously.

Kindra smiled and shook her head. Is this what the morning's conversation topic had been? It probably was, but it needn't have been. It was more likely that Jess and Gretchen were simply discussing the length of time it would take before Kindra made her decision to return to Alfheim. The best part of the process had been, despite Jess and Gretchen both being upset that she had abandoned the people of Lillerem, neither woman had pressured or tried to persuade Kindra to return. Other than the displays of initial shock at the choice Kindra had made to leave Alfheim, they had let Kindra draw the natural conclusion that returning was the right thing to do. Kindra had decided on her own that Lillerem was where she could do the most good for the most people. It was a bonus that Kindra might be the only person who was able to provide that help.

"I don't know how long I'll be gone, or if I'll even be able to come back." Kindra did not mention the possibility she could die. It didn't seem necessary.

Jess told Kinda she would go straight to the Human Resource Department at school that afternoon. She came up with a story about Kindra having traveled to Norway and been in an accident while hiking in the mountains along the fjord near the house where she was staying.

To Kindra, it seemed just outlandish enough for the school to accept it as truth for the time being. Who would ever make up such a crazy story? The truly made-up stories always involved a requisite dead grandmother. The story also allowed for Kindra to return to work and clear up any misunderstandings. Upon her return, she would be able to provide a true version of the story, once she had worked out what the true version would actually be.

Once Jess had reminded Kindra that she was a math teacher and no one believed a math teacher capable of anything but relaying boring facts, Kindra agreed that it did sound like a good plan. With Kindra's approval, Jess had gathered her things and left for her home. Jess would shower and put on fresh clothes before flying to school to report the tragic news that her friend had taken a fall and was in a medically induced coma.

Gretchen swiveled her chair in Kindra's direction. "Do you really think that outlandish story will work? I'm not even going to mention that what you two girls are doing is just asking for Karma to come for you."

"Compared to saving an entire realm, losing my job for not calling in appropriately does not seem that important. Jess can't get in any trouble because she was only relaying the information she was given by my sister Kristen from Norway." Kindra was completely calm and kept a straight face as she said this.

Gretchen raised an eyebrow. "I'm concerned you might actually believe your own story is true."

"You must admit. The crazy story Jess came up with is more likely to be believed than the truth." Kindra said ruefully.

Gretchen sighed. "Good luck to you both. Now, would you please pass the sugar?"

Taking in a little breath, Kindra raised her hand off the table and pointed it in her mother's direction. Instantaneously, the sugar bowl glided over to sit beside Gretchen's coffee cup. Gretchen dipped her spoon in the bowl and was about to tip the sugar into her mug when she froze.

"You're not supposed to be able to do that here," Gretchen whispered.

Kindra remained calm. "Why not? Leif could fly here in the human realm. It doesn't seem like a very big deal to move a sugar bowl."

"As I understand it…" Gretchen tried again. "Leif told me only the most powerful magic wielders can use magic in the human realm. That was how he was able to identify which of his children he should direct toward Alfheim."

"See, you just said it yourself. Plenty of Leif's other children were able to wield magic here. Why shouldn't I?"

"I went with Leif a few times to look in on those children. The magic they displayed was almost imperceptible. The color of their eyes might change slightly with a change in emotion, or the room might change a degree or two in temperature. It was nothing anyone would notice unless one knew to look for small changes. Objects floating through the air were never part of the equation."

"That's nothing," said Kindra as she suddenly materialized in front of the sink.

Kindra cocked an eyebrow and fixed a little smirk on her face. Her mother looked at the chair where Kindra had just been sitting and then back at Kindra. Gretchen checked the chair one more time and started to shake her head slowly.

"Have you been hiding this from me the whole time? Were you using tricks like this to sneak in and out of the house as a teenager?"

Kindra raised a single eyebrow again. "That is where your mind went? You assume I spent my life using magical powers to trick my mother and keep from being grounded?"

Though Kindra was laughing, Gretchen did not even crack a smile. She was having a very hard time believing her daughter had been hiding this talent from her. Gretchen had spent the first five years of Kindra's life watching for a hint of any magic and had been relieved to find none. She had started watching Kindra more closely again when Kindra had hit puberty, thinking it might be the kind of thing that manifested as one hit adulthood. Gretchen had been happy to see absolutely nothing.

Kindra seemed to be following Gretchen's thoughts. "Relax mom. It is not a failure of your observational skills. It was more of a failure in my own self-confidence. For my magic to work, I have to desire something to happen, and then it does. Since I never thought to do anything other than by applying old-fashioned manual labor and grit, I didn't even know I was capable of doing many things without lifting more than a finger. Even when I was in Alfheim, it took me falling backward into a river and desperately desiring to be dry and safe on the other side to believe I carried any magic within me."

Kindra thought about how ridiculous her classmates had sounded discussing attempts to use "The Force" after seeing Star Wars. She had rolled her eyes and bit back the urge to explain that it was only a movie. She had commended herself at the time for being polite and not pointing out how stupid each of them sounded, recounting attempts to move candy bars from high shelves or make the mean lunch monitor trip and fall. It was quite possible that if Kindra had tried it, the woman would have ended up on her face in the middle of the cafeteria with her tweed skirt hiked up to her waist. It was probably a very good thing that Kindra had never imagined herself to be anything other than normal.

"Kindra!" Gretchen said loudly. "I don't usually interrupt your mental musings, but this is important. Please focus!"

"Sorry. I was just thinking about how amazing it is that I really had no idea I had magic all this time." Kindra confessed.

"I suppose that answers my question. I was still trying to determine if you had hidden it from me. Have you told Jess?"

"No mom. You are the only one I've shared with."

Kindra did not miss the little smile from Gretchen at hearing that she was the only one Kindra had trusted. Gretchen was also a little pleased that she had learned something before Jess, though Gretchen would never admit that to anyone.

"Are you afraid of how Jess would react? Do you think she would try to take advantage?"

Kindra let out a puff of air that was not quite a laugh. "Only in the way Jess would take advantage. She'd have me do practical things like changing her lightbulbs without needing to go get a stepladder."

Gretchen smiled. "I suppose you're right. Jess really isn't the bank robbing or murderous type. It's probably safe to let her in on the secret."

"Actually, I think this one might just be for the two of us. At least, for right now."

Gretchen couldn't help herself. She flung open her arms. Kindra bent and allowed herself to be wrapped up and pulled close. She hadn't meant to make her mother this happy with her comment, but that had been the result. When Kindra pulled back, Gretchen had tears in her eyes.

"I really am so proud of you. I will miss you terribly, but I couldn't imagine you not following through with this. You are a true champion of those who cannot defend themselves. It doesn't matter what realm you are in. When you are true to yourself, the surrounding people reap the benefits." Gretchen beamed up at her daughter.

Kindra took her mother in. She memorized her long brown curls and soulful brown eyes. Her mother's useless, thin legs wrapped in a pair of flared jeans reminded Jess of how much this woman had fought through to be sitting here now. Gretchen was the picture of strength, and Kindra could only hope she had inherited a fraction of that strength.

# CHAPTER 20

It was evening when Jess pulled her Rav-4 to a halt in front of the porch at Leif's cabin. Kindra had changed her clothes. She went with black stretch pants and a plain black oversized t-shirt. She figured the pants could be worn under any dress, with no one needing to know. It would be an addition to the precaution of perpetually wearing her boots. The black t-shirt made an awesome nightshirt. No one would need to see it, but she could use it at night instead of the nightgowns that practically went up to her chin. She was planning to find a way to get this back to Millspare with her as well. As intuitive as her magic wardrobe could be, it didn't seem able to produce items for which it had no reference. Maybe once it saw the t-shirt, it would spread the news to all the wardrobes in the land and start a trend. The night gowns were very pretty, but nothing beat a big t-shirt for sleeping.

"I keep expecting Leif to stumble out onto the porch and piss on the hood of my car," Jess said.

Kindra broke from her magic wardrobe thoughts and conceded a nod to her friend. Kindra had not really thought about what she would say to Leif when she saw him again. She wasn't angry that he had convinced her to leave. Kindra felt he had truly done it to keep her safe. She was sure he believed this was one small thing he could do for her, since he had been able to do nothing when she was a child.

Gretchen drew breath through her teeth. "That does sound like something Leif would do. The worst part is, I can picture him looking surprised at your anger when you saw him do it. He never really believed anything he did had an effect on other people. I never worked out if he was actually oblivious, or if he just couldn't fathom that other people's feelings should matter."

Kindra exited the car and went to the trunk to retrieve her mother's chair. Gretchen banged on the rear window to get Kindra's attention, then beckoned her back.

"There are too many stairs. Even if you girls get me into the house, there are still the basement steps to worry about. After that, Jess will be on her own, trying to get me back to the car. I'm going to wait here."

Kindra crawled into the backseat and wrapped her arms around her mother. Neither woman said a word. They just clung to each other. Finally, Gretchen pushed Kindra back and quickly swiped the area under her eyes. Kindra leaned in for one last squeeze and kissed her mother on the cheek.

"I'll see you soon, mom. I love you." Kindra ducked out of the car.

Jess and Kindra mounted the steps and stepped into the cabin. Jess immediately started poking through magazines and mail piled on various surfaces. She had pulled open a draw before Kindra finally gave her a raised eyebrow. Kindra went to Leif's bedroom, and Jess followed. Kindra went straight for Leif's closet, but Jess stepped into the hall bathroom to snoop in the medicine cabinet. Kindra tossed her t-shirt on the bed, but left her leggings on as she pulled her dress over her head. Thankfully, Kindra had not skipped out on Alfheim in the middle of a formal dinner. No dress was practical, but this one was at least simple. It was almost the color of light denim, though made from something less sturdy. There were no ruffles or lace, but the stitching was elegant and decorative.

Kindra was strapping her belt on over her dress, Forsvarer's hilt shining from its sheath, when Jess drew in a loud breath from the doorway. Kindra turned to find her friend standing with her hand over her mouth. Her eyes were wide. Kindra spun in a little circle and finished with a curtsey. When Jess didn't react, Kindra sat on the corner of the bed and mocked sipping tea like any lady of the court. She had her pinky held high and all. Jess had started shaking her head.

"It's not the dress," Jess started. "The dress is quite beautiful. It's the whole package. The dress, the boots, the belt, the sword; you look like you could save an entire realm. I was having a hard time visualizing my sweet school psychologist friend slicing through necks and spraying blood on her sweaters. Looking at you now, though, you have the look of a warrior."

"You do realize I am wearing a gown, right? Most days, I don't even wear dresses to work!"

"It's the whole look," Jess said. You look badass with your sword strapped over your dress. I don't know how to explain it, but you look tougher in a gown than you do in regular clothes. It must be the sword."

Kindra shook her head and beckoned for Jess to follow her. Kindra headed down into the dark basement area. It was lighter down here today. Kindra noticed it had a dirt floor, and the foundation was actually made from individual rocks. It was quite damp, to the point where the walls actually looked like they may be dripping in some places. Kindra strode to the wall across from the base of the steps. This wall was dry. She placed both hands on the wall and part of the wall pulled back from the rest of the foundation.

"Magic," Jess said under her breath.

"That's nothing. I know the door doesn't open for just anyone, but I'm not sure if it's actually magic." Kindra explained.

Jess went to peer into the tunnel, but she jumped back a little the moment she was too close.

"There is some kind of shield, or membrane, that feels like prickles." Jess was a little frustrated.

"Yes. The more energy you put into trying to enter the tunnel, the more force the tunnel will use to repel you," Kindra warned. "The tunnel can only be used by those with high quantities of Elven blood."

Jess mumbled something about an equal and opposite reaction. Kindra wrapped her arms around her friend, the sword digging into Jess's side sharply. Jess pulled back and flicked the hilt with her fingers.

She shook her head and pulled Kindra back in. When the girls pulled apart again, Jess's eyes were moist.

"I really can't get over you. The sword is just crazy and from what you've told me, you even know how to use it! You're all full of elf genes and about to save another realm."

Kindra couldn't imagine what her friend would have said if she had seen the magic Kindra possessed in concert with her new sword skills. Even Kindra wasn't sure she fully accepted how competent she had become with both in a short amount of time. If not for the magic, Kindra knew her sword skills would be nothing but subpar. With the magic, she could make up for her lack of skill with surprise and mobility.

"I'm really going to miss you, Jess. Please take care of mom."

"You know I will. We became best friends for a moment there while you were gone. I'm sure we'll jump back into that soon enough." Jess said with a sigh of resignation.

Kindra gave Jess a knowing smile, then turned her back and stepped into the passageway. Jess watched a torch flare in the darkness, and the opening was bathed in firelight for a moment before the door slid shut. Jess stayed there for a moment. She waited for the wall to reopen and for Kindra to reappear. This couldn't be the end. That had possibly been the last time she would ever see her friend, and it was over already. It felt like there should have been more.

Jess accepted that the door would remain closed and turned to go back up the stairs. She had mixed emotions. Jess was proud of her friend and happy Kindra had found a meaningful purpose. She was also jealous and slightly bitter that Kindra had put this quest of hers before the friendship she and Jess had enjoyed for years. Maybe that was the key. She and Kindra had been friends for years. They had been able to enjoy a lot of time together, and Jess was glad for every minute of it. She decided she was being petty and depriving the people in Alfheim similar enjoyable years with friends and family by expecting Kindra to stay here in the human realm.

Jess went straight to the front door when she crested the basement stairs and trudged down the porch steps to her car. She climbed into the driver's seat and stared out the windshield. Gretchen did not interrupt Jess's silence. Jess turned the key in the ignition and turned the car around. She bumped the car down the driveway to the main road. As she pointed the car toward home, she glanced at Gretchen in the rear-view mirror. There were tears dripping down her cheeks to match the ones just beginning to spill from Jess's eyes.

"She'll be fine." Gretchen said. "That girl is sweet and helpful, but also tough as nails. She'll help destroy the enemies of Lillerem and then return to us. She has to come back. I don't know what to do without her here."

The tears were running down Jess's face now. She knew exactly how Gretchen felt. If Kindra didn't make it back, Jess would be lost. She had her husband, but it was not the same. There was no way to replace a friendship that had spanned as many years as hers and Kindra's friendship had. Her dogs made her almost as happy, but sometimes you needed to talk to someone who could talk back. Besides, a dog's life wasn't nearly long enough to form a relationship that spanned decades.

"What are we doing?" Gretchen asked suddenly. "It's as if we are holding a funeral for someone who has only been gone ten minutes. On top of that, she isn't even dead!"

Jess noticed that Gretchen hadn't ended her statement with the word "*yet*." Jess appreciated that. Omitting the word made everything sound more hopeful. She smiled at Gretchen and forced herself to give a little laugh.

"You're right. She'll be back before we know it. It just stinks that we can't even expect a postcard or some other kind of update." Jess conceded.

"Well Jess, we have each other until Kindra comes back."

Jess wiped the tears from her cheeks and raised her head up. Her new best friend could be a bit demanding at times, but it was also a comfort to share the feeling of emptiness Kindra's absence caused. When she dropped Gretchen off at her home, Jess would suggest they meet twice a week for tea. It would be nice to talk together and speculate about Kindra's adventures, and it might also keep Gretchen from feeling the need to call constantly. The ride home was quiet. Each woman stayed lost in her own thoughts.

When Jess pulled the car up in front of Gretchen's house, she popped the trunk and pulled Gretchen's chair from the trunk. She already felt Kindra's absence as she struggled to lift and unfold the unwieldy thing. Jess rolled the chair to the back door, where Gretchen had already swung her legs out of the car. Gretchen hoisted herself into her seat. Jess bent down to give Gretchen a hug, and Gretchen held her for a few seconds longer than a traditional hug goodbye. Jess knew the woman was barely holding herself together. She knew she would fall apart too as soon as she was out of Gretchen's sight. Gretchen gave Jess an extra squeeze, as if she were reading Jess's thoughts.

Gretchen waved to Jess from her open front door a moment later and Jess gave a little honk before pulling away from the curb. She entered her home and closed the door behind her. She slumped in her chair. Gretchen was very proud of her daughter, but she was also so afraid she was going to lose her forever.

The phone rang. Gretchen's head shot up. The ring sounded almost offensive. Gretchen just wanted to sit in silence and wait for Kindra to come home. The caller ID barked out a long, unfamiliar number. Gretchen rolled over to the hall stand and picked up the phone.

"Hello?"

A heavily accented female voice answered from the other end of the line. "Gretchen? This is Kristin calling from Norway. I wanted to call and check in with you. Is this a good time?"

Gretchen smiled. Leif's family might not have appreciated Gretchen when she and Leif were together, but Kristen was a good person. She had called Gretchen a couple of times while Kindra had been off in Alfheim the first time, and on days Kristen hadn't called, Gretchen had phoned Kristen. Gretchen could tell the woman had grown fond of Kindra in a short time.

"Hi Kristen. It's good to hear from you. It's actually a really good time. I needed to hear the voice of someone who understands."

Kristen's voice grew clipped. "Is everything alright? Should I be concerned?"

Gretchen sighed. "The honest answer is, I don't know. Kindra came home, and she was fine, but now she has gone back and I'm afraid she has left for good."

Kristen asked Gretchen to tell the story. After checking that Kristen had a robust long-distance plan with her cell service, Gretchen launched into the tale. It took over an hour. She explained how Kindra had returned and recounted Kindra's entire adventure in Alfheim. When Gretchen retold the part of the story where Leif had convinced Kindra to return home, Kristen was appalled.

"I can't believe he did that! How could he be so selfish? Does it make someone selfish if they do something that hurts so many, but they do it to save someone they love? Can a person be selfish on behalf of another?"

Gretchen let out a sound that was part laugh and part yelp. "I do believe you've summed up so many of my thoughts. I feel as if I don't know what to be thinking. You haven't let me finish, though. Leif did convince Kindra to come home, but she decided to go back. We dropped her off at the gate thingy a few hours ago."

"She's going to save them, isn't she? I fear Dad is going to be terribly disappointed that his little plan to keep Kindra safe has failed."

"It has failed, hasn't it?" Gretchen whispered. "My baby is in serious danger."

"Oh, no!" Kristen backpedaled. "I didn't mean that Kindra was in danger, well…she probably is in danger…I just meant…I didn't mean to worry you. I was only referring to Dad's plan failing. I wasn't trying to point out…"

Gretchen saved the woman from herself. "It's ok Kristen. There is no way around the truth. Kindra made a choice. That choice has put her in danger, but it is more important to her that she does all she can to help as many people as possible. I am not happy that I may lose her over this, but I am so proud that she chose this for herself and that she is so brave and selfless. It's also marginally satisfying for me to know she is returning against Leif's wishes."

Kristen offered a little laugh. "I love my father, but he has always put himself before anything and anyone. Anyone but Kindra. She is the only child of his that he has simply left to live his or her own life. I don't really understand it."

"That might have something to do with me," Gretchen conceded. "I made Leif promise to stay away from both of us."

"That would explain it. He never got over you, Gretchen. If there were anyone on Earth Dad would listen to, it would be you."

"Understand, Kristen, I will always have a place for your dad in my heart. I loved him deeply. Had it not been for his inability to love, I would have stayed with him. He is incapable of love for anything, including himself. He understands devotion to another, and he often treated me like I hung the moon. It was when he perceived himself as having been wronged, or when he felt as if too much was being asked of him…"

Gretchen trailed off, but Kristen summarized. "He was perfect until things became difficult. At that point, he'd place blame or simply run away. I always knew it was really his own behavior he was disappointed with, but he had an angry way of making me feel like it was my fault."

"You've got it," said Gretchen. "Please know that you were never alone in that feeling, Kristen. It was very hard not to drown with him when he fell down into that dark place."

There was silence on the line for a moment. Gretchen was trying to find a way to hang up the phone on a more positive note when Kristen blurted, "Why don't you come stay with me in Norway?"

Gretchen immediately began making excuses. She cited the difficulties of traveling while in a wheelchair, the costs, and the fact that Kindra might return to find her mother gone. Even as Gretchen spoke, she knew all of her reasons sounded weak. Jess was here if Kindra came back. Jess had a husband to support her when she was missing Kindra. She had co-workers and students to keep her busy. What did Gretchen have? Gretchen was fully prepared to sit at her kitchen table and wait for her daughter to return, but when would that be? It was possible that Kindra would never return.

Kristen must have heard the uncertainty creeping into Gretchen's voice as she had rambled off her excuses. She told Gretchen to book a flight and come for a visit. Kindra couldn't possibly save the world in under a week. Gretchen would miss nothing and time would go faster if she had something to do. She knew Kristen was right. Gretchen also knew Norway was beautiful and loved the idea of having a place to stay with only the flight to worry about. Kristen threw in a few comments about making krumkaker or even kransekake before Gretchen finally agreed to the trip.

Gretchen hung up the phone and texted Jess, "Off to Norway. I know you'll be ok, but I need to keep busy."

The phone rang seconds later. "

"I know exactly where Kindra gets her phone etiquette from! When dropping news about leaving the country, pick up the phone and call. That is not text-level news!"

Gretchen grinned as she pictured Jess tearing into Kindra in a similar fashion, likely with some regularity. She apologized for the indiscretion, offering the excuse of not wanting to disturb Jess so late at night.

"Disturb me? The content of your text disturbed me! Have you lost your mind? Seriously though, are you ok?"

"It's ok Jess. I have not lost mind. I do think I need to do this in order to stay ok until Kindra gets back though. I'm going to stay with Kristen, so you need not worry about me being alone."

"I suppose it makes sense. I like the idea of you not having to be alone. I give you permission to go."

Gretchen laughed. It was a genuine laugh. It felt good to feel something other than emptiness. It would definitely be better not to be alone. As soon as she said goodbye to Jess, she opened her laptop and booked a flight to Norway. She smiled to herself as she noted that it would be the same journey she had sent Kindra off on, just over a week ago.

# CHAPTER 21

Kindra had been much more aware of her entrance into Alfheim on this trip. She could feel her ears stretching into points. She had been completely aware of her canine teeth elongating until they grazed her lower lip. Kindra felt her muscles gain strength and her magic barreled through her insides. It had still been uncomfortable, but she had welcomed it.

Kindra reached the end of the passage and extinguished her torch. It would be night as she exited the passage, and she didn't want the light to draw attention if anyone was around. Kindra pressed the wall, and it gave way to a warm, clear night on the other side. Kindra took a deep breath of the clean air that rushed in to greet her. She stepped into the night and headed toward Millspare. She did not get far.

Kindra heard low voices after taking only a few steps. She moved into the tall grass on the side of the path. As Kindra's eyes adjusted to the dark, she could make out several figures in black leather armor. These men were not any she recognized, and they were not wearing Millspare's green. Kindra could not hear what the men were saying. They were not whispering, but their voices were low enough that she would need to get within feet of them to attempt to discover who the men were.

Kindra stepped slowly and lightly. It took time to move this way. She was not sure if just blinking herself closer would be heard. Kindra might find herself landing on a twig or some dry leaves. She was about 3 feet from the men when she started to understand some of the conversation.

"…soon Ulford…go to the next checkpoint…after the fall…be here to kill Ruth…"

It was only parts of sentences, but it was enough. These men were here as part of a planned attack. If there were men stationed here, this was not a small force designed to test Millspare's defenses. This was more. *Was the castle already under attack? Did the court even know these men were here?* Kindra needed to know more. She'd have to learn what she could on the way to the castle.

Kindra left space between herself and the men as she made her way around them. She moved as quickly as she could without making a sound. She saw several more small groups of men, then came upon a larger group standing around a large mechanical device made of wood. In the dark, it didn't hit her right away. Kindra squatted in the reeds, watching the men walk around the equipment. Her stomach flipped as it occurred to her what she was seeing. The men were a catapult battalion. The wooden machinery would be used to launch large boulders toward Millspare. There were buckets. There was an oily, sulfur-like smell. Kindra couldn't breathe.

It was the farthest distance she'd ever teleported. Kindra manifested herself in the office of Millspare. She had been right to assume everyone would be gathered there. Viktor, Ruth and the Princes looked surprised, but Leif looked ashen. Einar was in the corner, pulling the strings tight on Mildred's worn leathers. The emerald green die had darkened over time, giving it a more menacing hue. It was well oiled and cared for. Most noticeable, though, was how terrifying Mildred looked with those leathers on.

Einar was still dressed for the kitchen. He was no longer a warrior. He was an excellent cook, and he loved his wife dearly, but he would not be going into battle. Kindra could see the fear and love in his eyes as he helped his wife suit up. Einar, and all those elves like him, were reason enough for Kindra to be in this fight. Elves live a long time. Kindra would like as few as possible to live those lives without their mates.

Leif was the first to speak. "What are you doing here?"

Kindra cocked her head. "I would think that question would have an obvious answer, and it seems I have perfect timing."

"I know you plan to fight. We had agreed you would go home!"

"I did go home," Kindra replied, flippantly.

Leif spoke through his teeth. "Why didn't you stay home?"

Kinda took in the faces of the people gathered in the room. The princes looked at Kindra, waiting for an answer. Leif must have told them she had left Alfheim. Ruth, Viktor, Einar, and Mildred looked at Leif quizzically. It seemed Leif had not informed the latter four of Kindra's departure.

Kindra shrugged. "Where else would I be? If I intend to save the world, I probably should be at the site of the battle, right?"

Leif realized Kindra was not planning to explain herself. He was also not inclined to explain to the non-princes in the room why Kindra's presence was a surprise in the first place. He let the conversation drop. Instead, he took a position where everyone could see him and addressed the room.

"The enemy has come to Millspare. We are likely surrounded. It is imperative that we hold the gates and do not allow the vermin entrance. We will set up-"

Ruth did not allow her little brother to finish. She strode towards Leif and placed herself directly in front of him to block him from the view of the others. Her voice was strong as she took up the speech.

"The battalions have already taken positions at the four corners. The gates are each guarded with a double-strength band of soldiers to prevent entry through those points. We are well practiced with keeping the forces of Dredfall at bay and will depend on our time-honored formations to hold off this attack as well. Bane and Joral take posts at the front and rear gate, respectively. Gunnar, you will control the archers. Krish, coordinate the battalions and take the lead…"

Kindra's head spun as Ruth gave orders. None of the military jargon made any sense to her. She didn't even have a strong enough command of the castle layout to know what the locations of the battle stations were in relation to the parts of the castle and grounds she had explored. Kindra was beginning to wonder why she had thought she could be of any help. These people have been defending this home for hundreds of years and they had precise plans of which she knew nothing.

On her way back to Alfheaim, Kindra had conjured images of herself leading thousands of troops to battle and slicing through the enemy lines with little effort. As she considered this, Kindra realized her manifestations had not included blood or sweat. She had convinced herself that she would be the hero of this saga and had ignored the required bloodshed and effort that would be required to survive, let alone to win even a small battle. The battle that was forming around them was no small skirmish. It seemed likely that Ulford had sent the entirety of Dredfall to Millspare's gates. A loud crash came from outside. It had not been close, but it pulled Kindra from her thoughts.

Ruth ceased giving orders. Einar, nearest to the door, ran out of the room to see what the commotion had been about. He returned seconds later, puffing from the exertion of moving so quickly. Ruth motioned for him to take her position and address the room with his update. Einar took her spot in front of the royals.

"They've landed at least two additional bridges to cross the ravine. The bridges are each of a size to hold ten men across. They will be able to march in, any moment and they will come quickly," the older male reported.

There was screaming outside. Kindra looked toward the door as if she would be able to see the source. She did not need to see to know the cause of the screaming, though. Between the troops streaming across the bridges and the castle were people…a whole city full of people. Kindra was out the door of the office and into the main hall before anyone could stop her. She stopped in front of the huge entrance door and spun in a circle. She really wasn't sure where to go. Heading straight out the main entrance did not seem prudent when there was a contingent of soldiers on the other side for the specific purpose of keeping anyone from opening the door and getting inside.

Kindra changed direction. She whirled and sprinted down the steps and into the servant corridor. She ran through the passage, through the kitchen doors, and pushed her way through the rear door. Kindra headed up that flight of stairs to the passage that led to the formal dining room. Instead of entering the dining area, she went in the opposite direction and took the route on which she had been led the night they had all fled the castle into the woods. Kindra easily found her way to the stables and hurried past all the stalls to the end.

Branka stood pawing at the ground. It was as if she had been waiting for Kindra and was getting impatient with the delay. Kindra hoisted the saddle onto Branka without incident. She gave herself a little mental pat on the back for her success as she adjusted the stirrups and synched Branka up tightly. Kindra stuck her foot in the stirrup and pushed herself up. She swung her leg over Branka's back and leaned over to grab the reins. As she did so, Kindra whispered to the horse.

"We're going to need to go fast, girl. We're going to need to head straight for the scary sounds. When we get there, I'm going to jump off and you can run right back here to stay safe."

Kindra knew the horse didn't understand what she said. It seemed like a good idea to go over what little she had in the way of a plan out loud, though. Branka sprung from her stall and headed toward the commotion. There was a possibility Branka understood, after all. If that was the case, then Branka either liked the plan or was placing a lot of trust in Kindra to come up with something better in the next few minutes.

The horse sped around the castle wall. Kindra could see the soldiers stationed in front of the castle. There was no fighting yet. Dredfall's troops had not made it through the town yet. Kindra's head lifted. She was going to be in time to save the people. Branka twisted through the streets. The screams were closer now. Kindra started to see people running toward her. Parents carried children as they ran toward the castle. *Did they expect to be granted entry? Was that a thing?* She knew it happened in the time of serfdom. All the people who worked at an estate would huddle up behind the walls of a castle to stay safe. These people weren't farmers, though. None of the people outside of the castle worked for Viktor and Mildred. None of these people would be hiding behind the walls.

As the number of people fleeing from the Dredfall army grew, Branka started to struggle to push forward without trampling anyone. Kindra dismounted and gave the horse a slap to send her back to the stable. Branka turned and looked at Kindra, then joined the throng of people headed toward Milspare. Kindra threaded her way through the crowd until she was no longer making forward progress. She ducked into an alley and climbed an outside staircase to the second floor of a building and found herself on a covered porch. The columns were wrapped in thick, flowering vines. Kindra used the vines to climb up to the roof. Now that Kindra could see where she was going, she began teleporting herself from one rooftop to the next.

With every jump, Kindra saw Dredfall's army more clearly. The trebuchets and catapults became more imposing; the troop numbers seemed to grow continuously. *What, exactly, did she expect to do against that army on her own? Should she just stand right in front of the entire force and tell them to go home?* She'd be dead before she even had time to hear the soldiers laugh!

At last, Kindra was out of rooftops. She crouched at the edge of town, taking in the enormity of the enemy force before her. Kindra had the element of surprise, but that was all she had. She might have powerful magic, but there were bound to be elves in those ranks nearly as powerful as her. They would have more experience and there were a lot more of them. The various launchers Dredfall had towed into battle posed the biggest problem. Kindra watched as oil-laden boulders were loaded into baskets and slings by teams of four to six men and readied to be fired into the town. There would be nothing left of Aergroth before a single troop was required in combat. Kindra had her plan. She was going to disable as many of those launch crews as possible.

With a blink, Kindra was at the nearest catapult. No boulder had been loaded. She grabbed a bucket of oil and dowsed the entire wooden structure. Kindra set the oil ablaze with a torch grabbed from a nearby holder and was off to the next launch station. She looked the trebuchet over and couldn't even figure out exactly how the thing fired. This time, she didn't even take the time to drench the thing in oil. Kindra kicked over all the buckets and threw the torch toward the nearest puddle. It caught, and she was off.

It took the enemy longer than it should have to discover what was happening. They didn't seem able to believe they had been infiltrated and a lone soul was running around torching all of their munitions. Kindra had not thought through her trajectory from machine to machine. She was simply hitting each one she came to as she made her way down the enemy lines. This made Kindra an easy target. She teleported herself to the next launch site. When she went for the first bucket, a net came down over her.

"Really? A net?" Kindra was incredulous.

She half-closed her eyes and summoned her power to skip to the next station. Nothing happened. For the first time since Kindra had begun her pyrotechnic spree, she was scared. Why weren't her powers working? Why was she glued to this spot? Why was a simple net holding her in place? What training she had started to kick in when her initial shock passed. She grabbed for her boot knife and began sawing at the net. She felt her hand slowing. Her hand then stopped. Kindra let the knife fall to the floor, but she had not commanded her limbs to do any of this. It was as if someone had control of Kindra's body.

A tall male stepped into her view. He held his hand in front of him as if he were holding her at bay. Wait. He wasn't keeping her away; he was keeping her in place. This was the person controlling her body. A smile curled on the side of his mouth when he saw the moment Kindra connected the dots.

"I suppose you thought you were untouchable? It didn't occur to you that in this army of thousands, there would be at least one soldier capable of mitigating teleportation?"

Kindra did not like the look of self-satisfaction on the male's face. It was especially annoying because, though she had known there would be soldiers with powers, she hadn't had the forethought to conclude they would dispatch soldiers with powers designed to battle a specific magic. Kindra's feeling of foolishness dissolved as she realized that perceived strength was actually a weakness. Teleportation was not Kindra's only power. After all, she had been told she was the most powerful elf alive. Well, half-elf…and maybe it wasn't the most powerful, but it had been something close to that. What Kindra desired became reality. She took a deep breath and decided that the male holding her body hostage was about to have heart trouble.

As Kindra formed the thought; as she pictured the male clutching at his own chest in agony and disbelief, the scene played out in real time before her. First, he went to one knee, then he was lying on his side. Kindra tried to blink herself to safety, but she still couldn't teleport. The male holding her in place was near death, yet Kindra was still frozen in place.

A voice came from behind Kindra. "It seemed you also made the assumption that only one soldier would be sent to deal with you."

How many of them were there holding her in place? Kindra supposed it didn't matter. She was still stuck. At least she had managed to take out more than half of the artillery the enemy had brought to the battle. Maybe it was enough to create a little favor for those preparing to enter the battle from Millspare? She might not be written into the history books for saving the world, but surely her efforts would have some effect. Kindra found she could live with that. She had done her part.

The wind picked up suddenly. This was not a gentle breeze. This was like the wind in your face when cruising across a lake in a speedboat. The fires Kindra had started spread fast. The clothing of the soldiers trying to dowse the flames caught. Those soldiers panicked and ran into other soldiers. Soon Kindra was watching bodies burn.

Someone grabbed her around the waist. Kindra was lifted about ten feet in the air, the net still over her body. She was being carried back toward the town. Kindra registered the smell of burning flesh more than she heard the screams of the soldiers below. It made her stomach turn. Death by fire was near the bottom of Kindra's list of preferred ways to die.

Kindra and her captor touched down lightly on the roof of a single-story building, away from the outskirts of town. There was yanking and cutting and then Kindra way free of the net. She whirled and found Leif standing behind her, wild-eyed, with his knife in one hand and the remnants of the net in the other. Kindra was surprised to see genuine relief flood his face when she looked at him.

"You're ok! You're perfect! You don't even have a scratch." Leif quickly began to recover from his elation and brought his voice under control as he said the words.

When it fully hit him that Kindra was not injured in any way, he screamed. "What the fuck were you thinking?"

Kindra shrunk back. As odd as the look of relief had been on Leif's face moments ago, it had been much easier to deal with than the screaming. It reminded Kindra far too much of the drunkard she had first seen at the cabin in the woods. Kindra inhaled deeply. This was Leif's fear dissipating. He had just saved her life; he didn't intend to hurt her.

Leif picked up on her reaction and was now taking deep breaths, trying to pull himself together. Kindra saw surprise on his face, as if he couldn't believe he was the one acting this way. He covered it quickly and put on a stern exterior. Leif looked as if he was about to begin a reprimand when his face softened. He reached out and pulled Kindra into a hug.

Kindra stood stiffly, with her hands pinned to her sides by Leif's unexpected embrace. He was shaking. Was he angry? Scared? No….he was most certainly laughing! Leif held Kindra out at arm's length. He started shaking his head slowly. Tears caused by his laughter welled in the corners of his eyes.

"I don't know why I'm upset. I shouldn't be surprised. You are of my blood, but you are also of your mother. Your mother would never leave someone to suffer if she thought she could help just a little. I sent you away, hoping you would return to your realm and remain safe. I never should have expected you would have stayed there just because that is what I would have done. You are so much more than I ever was, Kindra. Since sending you home did not work to keep you safe, I need to accept that I will need to do what I can to keep you safe here."

Kindra opened her mouth to tell Leif his protection wasn't needed. It never came out. He had just swept her from death and carried her away to the rooftops. Had it not been for that, she would now be part of the burning chaos on the outskirts of the city. She turned to Leif; to her father.

"Thank you" was her simple statement. She followed it with a question. "What do we do next?"

The corner of Leif's mouth turned up. "I suppose suggesting you return to the human realm is not an option?"

Kindra did not even offer a hint of a smile. "No. The people of the human realm are safe, wrapped in ignorance. My family in this realm is in immediate danger, and I intend to do whatever I can for them. I'm willing, though you never were. If protecting me is what finally gets you to help your family's cause, I'll take it. What do we do next?"

Leif looked back toward Millspare. The streets of the city were empty. The people had all retreated to the castle or locked themselves in their homes. There was no movement below.

"Right," Kindra said. "We go back to Millspare. The burned remnants of Dredfall on this side of the city are no longer a threat. We don't know how Millspare is faring against the other half of Dredfall's forces."

Leif wrapped an arm around Kindra's waist and began to lift into the air. Kindra put her hand on his shoulder and squeezed. Leif returned them to the ground.

"I don't think we should just fly in there for the entire army to see." Leif waited for Kindra to continue. "Let's go separately. I'll blink myself back in to the office. You work your way in from the outside. We'll take up positions where we are needed."

"So.... the plan is that we really don't have a plan? We're just going to get inside and figure out what we can do to help?" Leif had his crooked smile pinned back on his face.

"That sounds about right." With her last comment, Kindra blinked herself half-way across the city.

# CHAPTER 22

Kindra sat on the roof of a blacksmith shop just outside of Dredfall's main force. Dredfall had breached the ravine on the side of the town and soldiers were swarming Millspare. There were men flying Dredfall's banners surrounding the entire castle. Ladders were going up against the castle walls and being pushed back over by men with forked pikes. The ladders tumbled down into the enemy soldiers below, only to be erected again. Men immediately began to climb and archers from the castle walls began shooting those men off the ladders. The ladders would then be pushed off the wall and into the soldiers waiting below. The same scene played on repeat all around the walls of the castle. It did not seem that any enemy soldiers had been able to get up on to the wall.

Kindra knew this could not go on forever. It would only take one Dredfall soldier to mount the wall and spur his comrades to give a bit more of a push. One man over the wall would become a torrent in minutes. Once those soldiers started pouring over the walls, it would be over for Millspare. As Dredfall's men attempted to mount the walls, there was a small contingent of enemy soldiers working a battering ram at the front gate. A tree trunk had been mounted on a cart. Men held handles on either side of the wheeled contraption. They would run the cart at the main gate as fast as they could and ram the tree trunk into the large doors at the archway. The crew would then roll the cart backward again to push into the door another time. Archers from the walls of

Millspare picked soldiers off the cart, but just as many of Millspare's archers were being hit by archers from Dredfall's army below.

As Kindra watched two archers fall from Millspare's wall into the throng of Dredfall soldiers crashing the carted log into the gate, Kindra blinked herself to the other side of those doors. As she appeared inside the castle walls, she whirled around in time to see the doors buckle a few inches and heard the sound of the enormous iron bar pulling out from its mooring on the sides of the archway. It would only take one or two more shots from that battering ram before the main gate doors collapsed in on themselves and Dredfall soldiers could come right in through the front door.

There were no Millspare defenders here in the hall. They were all up on the castle wall. Soldiers needed to make their way down here or Dredfall would be unimpeded once they brought the doors down. Kindra blinked into the office. She expected to find the rudimentary command she had left behind barely an hour earlier, but the office was empty. All those who had been in attendance had made their way to posts elsewhere. Kindra had fled the chamber to help the people of the city. Though Kindra had heard Ruth sound off the defensive plans, none of it had made sense to Kindra and she found she was not quite sure where anyone with the power to move a regiment of soldiers was stationed.

Too late, Kindra realized she had been living in a movie again. She had assumed, like in the movies, some commander would stay here in the office to coordinate the battle. She thought she'd blink in, warn that person about the breach of the gate, and runners would be sent to call soldiers to the main hall. There were no runners. There was no commander in charge.

Kindra ran through the door and out into the hall. She ran up the stairs to the top of the wall. As she ran, Kindra screamed.

"The gate is about to be breached! Men are needed at the gate!"

All around Kindra, men fought. She ducked and dodged through archers firing down at the enemy. She jumped over the bodies of the fallen. Kindra screamed her warning the entire time. No one stopped her. No one even seemed to notice her. These men were all involved in their own conflict. There were no soldiers to spare to send down to the gate. Kindra collapsed against the wall and put her head between her legs. She pictured Dredfall's soldiers manning the battering cart for the last push it would take to bring down the gate. She could see a soldier pierced by an arrow, only to be replaced by another before the first man had even hit the ground. The ram was about to make contact. *Oh, if I could just freeze that ram in place while I found some soldiers to meet them head-on!.* Of course, it was too late. Kindra would hear the gate smash below any second.

The crash did not come. Instead, the surrounding soldiers began to cheer. Kindra pulled her head from between her legs and looked to her left as boiling oil was poured over the side of the castle walls. No screams came from below. She watched as soldiers continued to fire arrows down into the Dredfall forces, but the Millspare soldiers were smiling. Kindra turned and risked a peek over the wall. Thousands of Dredfall soldiers were frozen below the wall. The only movement came when an arrow pierced the armor of a frozen soldier and that soldier fell to the ground. She had desired to freeze the soldiers below and it had become truth. A flaming arrow from Millspare's wall hit the battering ram, stuck on its final approach, and the ram went up in flames.

With the boiling oil that had been sent over the walls from Millspare, the fire began to spread. The soldiers below did not move. They did not scream. The fire slowly consumed each of them and bodies began to drop to the ground. The smell of burning flesh, the cheers from the soldiers upon the wall, the silence from the soldiers below, made Kindra's stomach flip. Kindra was horrified by the thought of what it would be like to be the men of Dredfall now, as they watched flames approach and were unable to move. The enemy didn't have a chance. It was unthinkably cruel, and Kindra had caused it.

Kindra stood and made her way, dazed and numb, through the soldiers on the wall. She was trying. She really wanted to convince herself the men deserved to die, but she was struggling. They may have come to kill her family, but Kindra had not even given them the option to flee. She had sentenced every Dredfall soldier at the wall to death and given them no choice but to watch that death come for them.

Kindra was dimly aware that there were fewer soldiers around her now. She knew Millspare's army would be riding out to meet what little remained of Dredfall's forces. Those soldiers would have the option to fight or run. They would not be forced to watch death come for them. If those soldiers stayed to fight, they would deserve death. Those soldiers could choose. The soldiers she froze had not had that choice. Kindra had not given those soldiers a choice.

A hand on her shoulder spun Kindra around. She found herself looking at an ugly scar, cut through an otherwise beautiful face. There was black dirt and blood on his face, hands, and clothes. He pulled Kindra in close and spoke into her hair.

"I know it was you. You did this. Thank you."

Kindra mouth was pressed into Joral's filthy chest. She wasn't sure he could hear her, but she said, "They couldn't even run" before her legs gave out and Joral was forced to keep her from falling to the ground.

Kindra woke in her Millspare bedchamber. She cracked one eye and saw she was far from alone. On her right, leaning against her magic bureau, stood Joral. He was picking dirt from under his absolutely filthy finger nails. It did not look as if any of the dirt or blood had been washed off after the battle. Leif had pulled a chair up next to her bed and was lounging with one leg swung over the chair's arm as casually as one could at someone's bedside. He was putting on a good show of looking as if he did not care about the well-being of the bed's occupant. Krish sat on the foot of Kindra's bed. He was not doing as good a job as Leif in his attempts to look unconcerned. He had been staring at Kindra when she had cracked an eye open and was now waiting to see what she would do next.

Kindra debated. She could close her eye and pretend she had never opened it. Krish would say nothing. She could go on sleeping and avoid all the uncomfortable questions and answers that awaited the waking world. Also, she could open her eyes and meet these men head-on. If she did that, she should probably have a quip ready to lighten the mood.

It was Mildred that saved Kindra from having to decide how to approach the men waiting around her bed. The woman came bustling into the room and told them all to get out. She even swatted Krish on the head as she shooed him off of Kindra's bed.

"Why don't you males go have a bath? This whole chamber smells of blood and sweat." Mildred pointed to the door and waited.

The males made their way from the room. None of them seemed willing to argue with Mildred. Krish was the last out of the room and he shut the door as he went. Kindra fully opened her eyes and smiled at Mildred. Mildred looked at Kindra with a satisfied smile of her own.

"I know, I know!" she said. "How can you ever thank me for getting rid of the lot of them so you can have a little peace? I shall tell you how. You can go take a bath of your own. It wasn't just those overgrown males causing the stench in this room!"

Mildred was dressed in her maid's clothes. The battle leathers were gone and her skin and hair were clean. Kindra could not help but think that she had imagined the battle-hardened woman Einar had laced into leather. Kindra supposed a warrior this clean had every right to command others to go take a bath.

Kindra pulled back her covers to find she was not wearing clothes. At that moment, she was even more grateful Mildred had removed the males from the room. Kindra quickly made her way to the tub of warm water Mildred had waiting in the bathing chamber. She slipped, happily, into the suds. A warm bath was a very good way to start. Kindra had just closed her eyes and started to relax into the tub when a chair scraped across the floor and Mildred set herself beside the tub.

"Silly girl! You were thinking I chased the males out so you could relax? You must know me better than that at this point in our relationship. I'll scrub your back and plait your hair for you, but you best start telling me the story of how the Dredfall army came to be frozen in time."

Kindra slid down into the tub until her head was under the water. Seconds later, Mildred was pulling her back up and taking a bar of soap to her hair and shoulders. "You don't get to go drowning yourself just yet. Spill the story first. Joral seems to think you were the cause of it, and I believe him."

"I killed them all, Mildred. All I had to do was think about how much easier the battle would be if time would freeze and I could warn someone the gate was about to give way. I just pictured it happening, and they were all frozen in place. They didn't even have a chance to turn and run."

"Child, the way you are sending those words from your mouth, you're making it sound as if what you did was a bad thing. Have you considered how many people's lives you saved? Even those who would have survived would have become slaves of Dredfall. There would be no more Millspare. There would be no more Aergroth. Lillerem would be a bit smaller and Dredfall would have grown. You might say your actions arrested the fall of an entire kingdom to Ulford."

We don't know that," said Kindra. She starred into nothing. "All we know is those men watched death come for them and they had no choice but to burn."

"They didn't all burn," said Mildred. "Many of them took an arrow before the fire ever reached them."

"I can't believe you're making light of this." Kindra buried her head in her hands as Mildred began pouring water onto her scalp from a pitcher to wash the soap from her hair.

"I'm not making light. Burning is a bad way to go. I'm just pointing out that not all of them had to face that. I'm sorry you feel causing that pain wasn't worth the lives you saved."

"Oh, it was worth it. I just didn't think that saving the world would feel this ugly." Kindra looked up at Mildred.

Mildred stared back into Kindra's eyes. "This is no Fairy Tale girl. This is real. I suppose magic wardrobes, teleportation, elves, and kingdoms are what the Fairy Tales of your realm are made from, but those things are real. It is quite possible your mind hadn't accepted that until you felt the pain of taking life. That was real for you. It's hitting you now. This is no book. This is your life. This is your family. Leif kept you sheltered in the human realm. Here in Alfheim, death and war are life for all of us."

Kindra thought about home. She thought about the news each day. Death, war, famine and power struggles were daily life in the human realm as well. It simply did not seem real when she watched it on TV. It was someone else's life. She was far removed from those struggles. There was no television in Alfheim. There was only life. Each moment was lived by the people of the realm and the stories were all real. They happened to your friends and family. They did not happen on TV, where one also watched fictional stories of war and death. It was easy to confuse the news and the Fairy Tales on a television screen. It was easy to pretend none of it was real.

Mildred was snapping her fingers in front of Kindra's face. "Are you in there?"

"Yes. Sorry! I'm here. You're right. I guess it all just became very real to me. I'm just glad it's over."

"I don't want to disappoint you, girl, but it's never over. Dredfall has been a threat for decades. It isn't going to go away because we defeated an army. Before King Andril united the realm, there were regularly wars and power struggles between the peoples of Elfheim. Under King Andril's unified reign, the people of Lillerem engaged in battle with the Svartålfar repeatedly to keep hold of the Kingdom."

Under the fractured rule of King Blaith's children, the Kingdom has seen infighting as well as border incursions from the Svartålfar. All elves are raised to fight. Even the children of cobblers and farmers can wield a sword. When the townspeople fled for Milspare as Dredfal attacked, they did not simply enter the gates and cower. Those were the soldiers manning the walls. They are the archers; they are the swordsmen. Milspare keeps a very small guard. The army of Aergroth is its people. Millspare is simply the town's defensive position."

When Kindra had swept out of the office to save the people of the town, she had thought of them as defenseless villagers. She had seen the people as fleeing the army, but had not realized they were falling back to a defensive position, not looking to be sheltered. Kindra felt foolish. Those people hadn't needed saving, and she had been willing to die to protect them.

"Stop thinking, girl. I see you replaying your actions. Focus on reality. You saved a town from destruction. You gave the people time to man the walls of Millspare. You kept the people of Aergroth alive by allowing the army of Dredfall to be killed. That is all. Keep it simple. Do not analyze your actions. You cannot change them."

Mildred held up a towel. "Go tell your wardrobe you need riding clothes. I imagine there is someone waiting for you down in the stable."

"Is Branka alright? Was she injured?" Kindra couldn't believe she hadn't thought about the brave horse before now.

"The horse is fine, girl. I'm sure she'll be happy to see you."

Kindra dressed in the riding clothes offered by her wardrobe and headed toward the chamber door. She paused. Kindra returned to the bed and grabbed Forsvarer from its place, leaning on the nightstand. Though she had never even drawn the sword during battle, she felt better having it sheathed on her hip. She turned and headed into the hall, where she promptly collided with Joral.

"Are you alright? I recognized your magic last night. I knew it was you."

"I am not ok. I am working on it though. Mildred has me trying to focus on the good I did instead of…" Kindra didn't finish her sentence.

"I can understand that," said Joral. It's a lot. Having that kind of power, knowing what little effort it takes…All I'm saying is I understand."

Kindra forced a tiny smile, for Joral's sake. "Thank you, cousin. It means a lot to me to know you understand. I will not dishonor you by telling you I am fine with this responsibility. I don't know if I will ever accept these new abilities. I am, on the other hand, grateful to you for helping me to discover these powers."

Kindra knew she had come off far too formally. Joral's face fell. He looked disappointed. Kindra was about to turn. Instead, she pulled Joral into a hug. Tears began to stream down her face. She wanted to explain so much to this male. She wanted to thank him for making her feel capable. She wanted to thank him for his guidance. Kindra wanted him to know he was not the ugly, scared and discarded son of an evil king that she knew he saw himself to be. She had no words for this. Instead, she stood crying in his arms for several minutes before she pulled back and wiped her tears. He looked into Kindra's eyes and Kindra knew he understood. He knew he was important to her, and that was what Kindra wanted him to know. Kindra gave Joral's hand a squeeze and turned to go to the stables.

Kindra entered the stables and went directly to Branka's stall. The horse had her head in a feed bag and was happily munching away. Kindra picked up a brush and climbed into the stall. Kindra started brushing the horse down, pouring her relief that the animal was unhurt into her strokes.

"You're such a brave little lady! You took such good care of me last night. I'm so happy you're ok."

The horse went on munching from the feed bag. "You know Branka, Mildred gave me the impression you would be much happier to see me. She made sure to send me right down here."

"I don't think it was Branka that Mildred was sending you to meet." The voice came from behind Kindra.

Kindra suddenly felt foolish. She had thought she was here alone as she poured her heart out to the horse. She was grateful the animal had carried her through the streets of the town, but she knew she'd been simply singing the praises of the horse as a general thanks for having made it through the night alive. It was simply easier for Kindra to give credit for that to the horse instead of fully accepting her own role in the destruction and loss of life from the prior night.. Kindra turned slowly and found Krish looking a bit sheepish.

"I figured I could save you the embarrassment and walk away, or at the very least, stop you before you gave the horse credit for saving the world. I like that you came down to check on her, though."

"She deserves the credit. She's a really brave horse." Kindra said, as she turned her gaze to the ground.

Krish cupped his hand under Kindra's chin. "She is a brave horse indeed. She played a big part in saving a lot of lives last night and she deserves all the praise she gets."

Kindra was pretty sure they were no longer talking about Branka, but she played along. "I'm guessing she'll get whatever she wants for a while. I see a lot of extra feed bags and hay in her future."

"I should hope not!" Krish mocked being appalled. "We wouldn't want it all to go to her head. It's best to keep treating her the same as we always did."

"I think she'd appreciate that," said Kindra.

Krish lifted Kindra's chin a little higher, so she was forced to look into his eyes. His eyes were green. Had she known that? She must have noticed before. How could they not be green? How could any male have a right to be this beautiful? When the princes had found her in the woods that day, hadn't that been her thought? Hadn't she wondered how she could be surrounded by such beautiful males?

Kindra waited, but the kiss that was supposed to come next wasn't coming. She stood on her toes and she kissed him. He pulled her into his arms and returned the kiss. Krish pulled back a little and spoke into Kindra's forehead. "I was wondering if you would ever do that."

Kindra pushed back to stare at Krish, incredulous. "You wondered when I would kiss you? You're the prince! What right do I have to even think about kissing you?"

"Forgive me, your highness. You seem to be forgetting that you are a princess. You have every right to plant a kiss on the lips of any prince you wish." Krish chuckled.

"Oh, yeah…" murmured Kindra. "One more thing I had been trying to forget. And, you're wrong; there are very few princes I'd feel comfortable kissing. Most of the princes I've met are my family. One of them is even my father!"

"This is Alfheim. I'm not sure about your father, but your uncle and your cousins are probably acceptable for kissing." Krish said with a straight face.

"I'm going to choose to pretend I never heard that," Kindra said as she placed her lips on Krish's, keeping him from saying more.

Branka let out an annoyed snuffle to let them know she did not appreciate having her meal interrupted. Krish backed up into the next stall, pulling Kindra along. He never let his lips leave hers. As he backed into the empty stall, he tripped on the gate and went over backward. He landed in a pile of hay with Kindra on top of him. She pulled back and smiled at him slyly.

"You did that on purpose."

"I was just trying to give Branka the peace and respect she deserves," said Krish as he pulled her back down into the hay with him.

JENNIFER ABRAHAMSEN

# EPILOGUE

Kindra enjoyed several weeks of carefree living in the hands of Millspare. She trained daily with Gunnar on her swordsmanship and worked with Joral to hone her magic skills. She also spent a lot of time down in the stables. After all, Branka really was a brave horse, and she did deserve a lot of praise and attention.

The entire court was sitting at a formal dinner when Ruth pulled a piece of straw from Kindra's hair and asked when the wedding would be. Kindra turned bright red, her eyes grew wide, and she worked hard not to choke on her mouthful of pheasant.

"Wedding!" she exclaimed. "What wedding?"

Krish wiggled his eyebrows at her. She looked to Leif, who was nodding to himself as if he hadn't really thought about it before, but now that Ruth brought it up, it seemed like the right course of action. Joral stared down at his plate with resignation. Gunnar was looking at Krish with a question in his eyes. Bane continued to tear into the bird on his plate as if Ruth had never spoken.

Kindra looked from one prince to the next, waiting for one of them to speak. It was Viktor who ended the silence. "It makes perfect sense. Krish, as the future king of Lillerem, would need to marry a princess. It is quite possible that Kindra is one of the few remaining princesses in the Kingdom. She is certainly a princess with great power and would make a formidable queen someday."

"Queen!" Kindra yelped. "Have you all lost your heads?"

Kindra had been much louder than she had intended. All the courtiers at the table were now looking at her. Even Bane had stopped chewing to see what the commotion was about. Kindra was at a loss for words. It had not even occurred to her that marriage would be an expectation. She had been very happy these past weeks, living her little fairy tale life. It was a vacation of sorts. It had all gone back to feeling like a story she was part of instead of real life.

Kindra leveled her gaze at Ruth. "You can't expect me to simply leave my entire human life behind. I have friends and my mother. I've already been away from them for too long. They probably think they have lost me forever. It would not surprise me if they have even held a service for me and said their goodbyes."

As Kindra spoke, Ruth simply stared back at her. Ruth waited for Kindra to make the connections. Kindra had left the human realm thinking she was leaving to face her own death. Jess and her mother had accepted that. At this point, they probably had already accepted that Kindra was lost to them. It might actually be very painful for Kindra to return to the human realm and have her mother discover Kindra had survived and not bothered to let Gretchen or Jess know. Kindra had simply stayed here in Alfheim as if the rest of the world was suspended in time. Kindra had been away from her mother for nearly a month. Her mother and Jess had probably already mourned Kindra. Hell, Jess and Gretchen had been acting as if Kindra were dead before Kindra had even stepped through the portal to return to Alfheim.

Kindra was being selfish, thinking she could just walk back into her old life and pick up where she left off when she was done playing princess in Fairy Land. Kindra pushed her plate away. She slowly shoved her chair back from the table. She stood and made her way to the servants' passage. Kindra stumbled her way toward the stables. She was vaguely away of Krish calling after her and of Ruth advising him to let her go.

Kindra mounted Branka when she reached her stall and allowed the horse to walk off in the direction of the animal's choice. Bareback and losing her thoughts to the sound of Branka's hooves on the ground, Kindra recalled the last time she had found herself in this place. It was the day Leif had shown Kindra the portal home. It was the day Kindra had run from a family who needed her and into the arms of the family Kindra thought she needed more. It was that same family, back in the human realm, which tugged at Kindra now.

She could go back. She could duck through the portal and check in on her mom. She didn't even need to let her mom or Jess know she was there. Kindra could go through the portal, walk from Leif's cabin to town, hitch a ride to her mom's place, and just look in on her. She could make sure her mom and Jess were doing well and had each other. Jess had her husband, so she would be fine. Maybe Kindra would only need to check in on her mom. It would only take a day or so. She could decide then. Kindra could come back to Alfheim and marry Krish and one day be a queen if she wanted. After, of course, making sure her mother was going to be ok.

Kindra was nearing the portal to Leif's cabin. She had made up her mind. She was going to go check in on her mom before making any permanent decisions. Something was up ahead on the path. It was a body. Laying half on the path and half in the bushes right before the entrance to the portal. Kindra slowed Branka. It was a female. Kindra rode the horse right up to the form on the ground. Kindra was confused. The female was wearing jeans. Those were clothes from the human realm. She was pretty sure those were Adidas on the female's feet. Kindra dismounted and moved closer. The female was face down. Kindra did not want to touch a dead person. She turned to get back on her horse and bring Krish down here when the woman on the ground let out a low moan. *Not a body! The female is alive.*

This made a huge difference. This meant time was still valuable. Kindra went to the person's side and rolled her onto her back. The face that came into view belonged to Jess!

"Oh my God, Jess! What are you doing here?"

Jess didn't respond. Jess did not even open her eyes. Jess was barely breathing. Kindra started to lift her friend. Another example of the number of movies Kindra had watched. Was she actually thinking she was going to lift her friend from the ground and carry her back to the castle? Even if she could get Jess off the ground, would she be able to lift her onto Branka without injuring Jess further? Even her elf strength wasn't going to allow her to carry Jess back to the castle quickly.

It took a moment for Kindra to calm down enough to remember her own reality. Kindra wasn't fully human. Kindra was in Alfheim. Elven strength was pretty amazing, but also still unpredictable for Kindra. There was an even chance Kindra could lift Jess up off the ground, or drop Jess on her head and kill her. She sat with Jess's head in her lap and took a breath. She blinked herself and Jess back to the stables. Branka would find her own way home. She had done it before. Krish came running from one of the stalls when the two women appeared on the floor in the middle aisle.

All dinner conversation from an hour earlier forgotten, Kindra looked up at Krish, eyes wide. "I found her lying in the path outside the portal. It's Jess. I don't know if she's still breathing."

Krish scooped Jess from the floor and started into the castle. He didn't exactly run, but he was moving very quickly up the stairs and calling for a healer as he went. Kindra scrambled to keep up. She took up the chant for a healer to be called. Krish slammed through one of the doors to a bedchamber adjoining Kindra's room. He placed Jess on the bed as a troop of people came through the doorway behind Kindra. Mildred went straight to the bed, followed by one of the castle healers. Gunnar and Joral held back in the hall, but Leif came up beside Kindra.

"Is that who I think it is? Is that your friend from the woods? How did she get here?"

Kindra had no answers for Leif. She was still asking herself the same questions, so there would be no answers for her father. The two of them watched as the healer began checking Jess over. A second came through the door and took up a position near the bed. Mildred began to peel off Jess's clothes, and Kindra grabbed Leif's arm to steer him into the hall.

Once in the hall with the other princes, the questions started to be thrown from several directions at once. "I have no answers," said Kindra. "All I can tell you is I was riding the path near the portal entrance and I found her lying half in the road. She was face-down, and I thought she was dead. When I saw she wasn't, I tuned her over, and it was Jess. I blinked us back to the stables."

Kindra sat down against the wall of the hall as Leif explained to the other princes that Jess was Kindra's friend from the human world. Bane was the one to make the obvious statement that the portal should not have let a human through. He explained, to no one in particular that Jess was not supposed to be able to enter Alfheim. He must have known he was only speaking out loud because he did not look to anyone for conformation.

It was Gunnar who calmly spoke next. "We must assume Jess has at least a small amount of Elven blood if she survived the portal. We don't know if she is in her current state because of the portal, or if something happened to her before or after she came through the gate. It could be that she simply followed Jess's path because she wanted to see her friend, or there may be a more nefarious reason for her to have wanted to attempt traveling down the tunnel."

A sharp look from Kindra had Gunnar back peddling a bit, "Not nefarious on Jess's part, but it is possible someone else's actions caused her to feel coming after you was her only choice. Either way, I don't think we will know the answer unless Jess wakes."

Again, Kindra's eyes burned through Gunnar like hot knives. Again, Gunnar found kinder words. "...when Jess wakes up."

"I'm going back." Kindra's head was in her hands so the words were not loud, but everyone heard them.

"That would be foolish!" The immediate and sharp reply from Joral whipped Kindra's head up. "We know nothing of what sent your friend here. You have no understanding of what awaits you in the human realm."

Leif held a hand up to Joral. "If anyone is going to the human realm, it will be me. I'm well equipped to handle that realm and I have practiced using my magic there."

"So you can disappear and not return for another few hundred years?" Krish's lip curled at the corner. "I think not; certainly not alone, at any rate."

Leif's temper flared. "How long have you been waiting to get that one in? Have you forgotten who you have to thank for pulling dear Kindra from a net outside the city? The entire castle would have fallen if no one had gone after her! You remind me why I stayed away from this place so long!"

The sound of a clearing throat came from the doorway of the chamber in which Jess was being tended. Mildred stood with her arms crossed. She stared hard at each of the princes. Her eyes met Kindra's next. They did not soften for her.

"Listen to the lot of you. You're acting like children. I can't tell which of you is trying to impress the other more. You're like peacocks strutting around feeling as if each of you has all the answers. The last I checked, none of you is king yet." Mildred leveled her eyes on Kindra. "You may be worse than the others combined. You have a friend in that room that was close to death. Instead of staying here because she will undoubtedly need you, all you can think about is running off to get yourself killed."

Kindra ignored the chastisement and focused on a single word Mildred had used. "Was? Jess was close to death? You said will as well. You said she will undoubtedly need me. Is Jess ok?"

"She will be." Mildred's voice softened at last. "She is weak, but I came into the hall to tell you she is awake. You should go show her a face she knows."

Kindra stood quickly and went to the door. She stuck her head into the room. Jess was on the bed with piles of pillows propping her up. Not for the first time, Jess wondered how many pillows were actually in this castle. Was there a huge linen closet somewhere off the servants' passages, the size of one of the bedrooms? There probably was. It was probably so full of extra pillows that they would all tumble out if the door were opened.

Jess's voice ripped Kindra from her thoughts of Millspare's excessive number of pillows. "Are you planning on coming in?"

Kindra let go of the doorframe and ran to the bed. She wrapped her arms around her friend. She didn't let go until her back started to cramp from leaning over the bed. Even then, she held on for an extra half a minute.

"I can't believe you're here! When I left, I was thinking I'd never see you again and if I did, it would be because I had gone home, not because you came to Alfheim." Kindra paused for a moment. "Actually, why did you come to Alfheim? The trip could have killed you."

"The tingling was bad when I went near the tunnel. As I entered, it became more like shocks. I had to get here, though. I had to find you if you were alive. They're gone, Kindra. I'm so sorry. I had to tell you. They're both gone."

Kindra let sat on the bed next to her friend. She was not following Jess's words. She couldn't think of who "they" would be. "They who? Who is gone?"

"I'm so sorry, Kindra." Jess was crying now. "Your mom and Kristen. The house was a mess. They're gone."

The princes had come in from the hall. Sensing the heart-felt reunion was over and more trouble had just walked into Millspare, they all approached the bed.

Jess looked from one face to another. She already knew who Leif was, but Jess must have sensed the others were people of importance, because she did not wait for introductions before speaking again.

"Your mom went to Norway to go stay with Kristen for a while. I spoke to her a few times while she was there, and it seemed to be good for her to have Kristen as a distraction and a new place to explore. She was originally going to stay for a week, and then it was two weeks. I called her on Tuesday of the third week and I didn't get an answer.

"My phone rang about an hour later from your mom's cell. When I answered, it was a man. He said Dredfall had come to the human realm and I should prepare to be the next to my grave. I knew what Dredfall was from what you had told us. At first, I thought it might be a joke, since Dredfall was in an entirely different realm. I had basically convinced myself that it was the only explanation, but then I got a call.

"It took some time because Gretchen and Kristen are not relatives. The police had used information from the website where Gretchen had bought the plane ticket to find me. Gretchen had listed me as an emergency contact. The police told me there had been a home invasion and Gretchen was found dead, along with the owner of the home. The mail carrier had noticed the front door cracked open for two days in a row and called the police."

Kindra let out her breath. She had not realized she had been holding it until Jess had stopped speaking. Kindra had been holding Jess's hand, but she had dropped it at some point during Jess's story. Kindra stared into her friend's blue eyes. She looked at the freckles dotting the bridge of her nose. Anger and pain crawled from the pit of her stomach and up her throat. Kindra ran for the bathing chamber and retched into the water basin. Bile dripped from her lips and her head spun. Kindra shrank to the floor and put her head in her hands.

She raised her voice so Jess could hear. "My mom is dead. Kristen is dead. You got a call from a man who told you Dredfall is coming? You went to Leif's cabin, and you nearly killed yourself by pushing through the portal. Do I have it all correct?"

Kindra sat there for several minutes in silence, and then she spoke again. "What about Sean? Does he know you are here? Jess, what if you can't go back?"

"Kindra! Are you hearing me? Dredfall told me they were coming. I can't imagine the Kingdom of an evil elf would be coming to the human realm just for me. I am not here to save myself. I am here because I think Dredfall is coming for us all! Ulford has sent assasins to the human realm!"

# AUTHOR'S NOTE REGARDING GENEALOGICAL INFORMATION

Dear Reader,

Kindra and I share a love of family history. The names and birthplaces of many of Kindra's ancestors are actually those of my ancestors or my husband's ancestors. I took the liberty of mixing up the family relationships, birth years and marital statuses of Kindra's ancestors to differentiate them from our actual ancestors.

A reader with an interest in Genealogy from Germany or Norway may be able to identify one or more of Kindra's ancestors in actual historical documents, but will find that the person's children have the wrong names or that the person was recorded as living in the wrong location for that time, when mentioned in this novel. Regardless of your interest in family history and genealogy, please do not use any of the data from the "historical documents" mentioned in this novel as sources for your own genealogical research.

"The Fjære Bygdebok: Moy krets" mentioned in the novel is an actual book. It was written by Anne Tone Aanby and was instrumental in helping me trace my husband's family tree. If you have an interest in genealogy from that area, I recommend you purchase a copy. My copy was purchased in Norway, but you might find a copy online. If you have an interest, I should warn you the book is written in Norwegian. The farm names used in this novel and many of the surnames from the farms were inspired by The Fjære Bygdebok. Again though, I have changed most dates, names and relationships for this novel, so much of Kindra's "research" will not match the accurate history contained within Aanby's amazing work.

The website Kindra uses in the novel, "Digitalarkivet", is also a genuine source for Norwegian genealogical information. The meticulous curation of vital records contained in this website cannot be described. Those interested in Norwegian ancestry should check out this free resource for themselves.

None of the characters in this novel are named for, or created in the image of the once living people represented in the U.S. Census Records, Norway Church Records or The Fjære Bygdebok. The names of those documents are used in the novel solely to provide believability to Kindra's character and the fictional cultures from which she descended. The sources Kindra uses for her research are the common sources one would use to research Norwegian ancestors. Leif, Gunnar and Kristen do not appear in the actual research material mentioned in this novel. Their characters are completely fictional.

With hope, I may have inspired you to research your own ancestry,

Jennifer Abrahamsen

# ACKNOWLEDGMENTS

Considering this may be the only book I publish, I apologize in advance for the length of this list. Firstly, I need to thank my husband, Phil. He gave up hours of time with me as I wrote this book. I wrote while we watched TV, which prevented snuggling…even during the sweetest parts of many movies. I wrote while we could have been hiking, or walking the dogs, or doing home improvements together. He did complain, but he kept his fuss to a minimum; for that, I am forever grateful.

Secondly, I must thank my parents. My father, Bob, was instrumental in reminding me that not everyone is interested in books about elves. As in life, he kept me grounded when I spoke about the wonderful book I was writing. My mother, Lenore, encouraged me to write. She is even less enthralled with the genre of fantasy, but she is a book lover. She let me tell her about my book and even read it once I felt it was finally finished.

My cousin Darren needs an enormous amount of thanks. It took some arm twisting to get him to acquiesce to sharing his amazing artistic talent by breathing life into Kindra's character and creating the artwork for the cover of this book. He has been drawing since I can remember and he has always been awesome. As with many artists, he is not a huge fan of drawing to another's specifications so I really want him to know how much I appreciate his work here. I tried to give him a very long leash, but a leash is still a leash, and I am grateful he was able to work around its confines.

I need to thank my colleague, Carol, for her excitement when I told her I planned to write a book over summer break. It was a tremendous motivation for me to finish my story because I really didn't want to disappoint her. When I walked into her classroom almost six months later with a printed manuscript in a binder, her excitement once again pushed me to make sure I got through the final steps to publication.

Another colleague, Patricia, nurtured the idea of a book. It started years ago when she published her own book, (Chiffonade by P.A. LaFraise….yes, you should read it) and solidified the fact that teachers did, indeed, have time to write a book. Patricia was also helpful at the end of the process with regard to publishing.

My middle school students from the high school class of 2029 need to be thanked as well. The better one knows her students, the easier it is to read their minds. Special thanks to Violet and Maya. These two girls are writers, as well as wonderful students and a joy to have in the classroom. Violet shared her writing with me throughout the year and helped remind me what a young adult wanted to see in a story. Both she and Maya were honest in their opinions and unashamed when sharing ideas about writing, the writing process, and thoughts about my manuscript for this book.

Lastly, I want to thank my readers. If you have purchased this book, then my pockets are a few dollars heavier and I appreciate you for it. I hope you enjoyed the story in the pages of "Finding the Past", and encourage you to write an honest review of the book. Your opinion will help guide me as a writer and let me know if more came from this book than simply allowing me to pass some time.

Made in the USA
Columbia, SC
15 May 2024

e9e44fe9-215e-4de7-a280-59069f22e506R01